THE BOOK OF

ELIZABETH

THE BOOK OF
ELIZABETH

A NOVEL

DARBY HARN

All is in endless flux. Each wandering shape a Pilgrim passing by and time itself glides on in ceaseless flow. A rolling stream and streams can never stay. As wave is driven by wave and each perceived pursues the wave ahead. So time flies on and follows, flies and follows, always forever new. What was before is left behind. What never was is now.

—Ovid

For my uncles

Jon Kitchen
1949-2005

and

John Rochholz
1958-2009

I

Alice arrives naked, born again — nothing lost in translation, not even, to her disappointment, the apple belly — to a world skinned in ice. She expected - what did she expect? St. Peter? Pearly gates? Snow of feathers. Sky of angels. Not this blue hell. *Did I die? How did I get here?*

One moment she's walking out to her car, keys in her hand and the next — how to even describe it; the air caught fire. It sparked. Strands of prismatic shimmer thin as cigarette smoke ignited to curtains of auroral light and the back porch drifted like snow into the kitchen. Her clothes smoked away, right off her skin. Her ear rings. The rosary she had blessed by the Pope when he came to Des Moines, and she always wore, like some protection against not going to church, not knowing any of the Bible, her varied sins. The world disintegrated into this arctic wasteland, and in her head she heard the Wicked Witch, *I'm melting, I'm melting.*

The only explanation that makes sense of what she saw is that they finally did it; they finally pressed the button, though she doubts the sense in her living long enough after the blast to witness the disintegration of Carpenter, and the sense in the Russians wasting a perfectly good bomb on it. Carpenter sits on the bend of a closed river more or less in the middle of Iowa. Her dad used to say: God closed the river, Henry Ford closed the railroad and Carpenter closed its doors. She has spent most of her life dreaming of leaving. Most of the girls she went to North High with, they dreamed of their wedding dress, their inevitable children; Alice dreamed about what type of space suit she would wear on Mars.

Alice had it all worked out:

She didn't have the right stuff necessarily, so she would get her teaching certificate and after three or four years of above-average molding of young minds, NASA would naturally see her as a perfect fit to their growing roster of astro-teachers. Then, having so impressed them on that first flight, they would ask her to become a full-fledged, full time astronaut. She of course would accept and move to the Cape, or Houston, maybe; she would get a nice house in the suburbs near the other astro-nauts. They would have astronaut barbeques and eventually she would have astronaut babies. And then after five years — okay, maybe ten - they would choose her to be the first woman — the first person — on Mars.

She had it all worked out. When it became obvious to her that bitter winter of 1986, as it did to everyone eventually, that Carpenter's gravity was no more breakable than the sun's on the earth, she contented herself to dream of other worlds.

None like this.

The wind erodes her to a human stump; the skin of her knees locks lips with the ice. She stands up, red sludge freezing to her leg and she just wanted to get some groceries. She didn't even want to do that. They go every couple of days. Never any food around. Why is that? When Alice was a girl her mother got all the groceries at the beginning of the month: ten frozen pizzas for five dollars, four frozen turkey pot pies for a dollar, two for three dollars bags of generic potato chips, the same things again and again, every month. Now she and Brian buy only enough to keep them until the next time they go, in a few days, and it agitates them both but only half as much as the idea of not going. Why?

She thought, I could wait; go tomorrow. I'm just going to go back in a few days anyway, and every few days after that. I'll be there every day if we have kids. Are we going to have kids? Maybe I won't even have to go in. Maybe they'll just have it ready for me because I go every day, I buy the exact same things and I sit there in the parking lot, watching the automatic doors open and close, the people going in and out. They go in and out of the grocery, the post office, the schools, in and out of one another and they circuit the places they know looking for something different, a new flavor, a bargain, a way to escape the anniversaries, the graduations, the weddings and the deaths. The waiting.

Am I dead? What's happening to me?

It was seven or eight, after dark; she sat at the kitchen table to make out her list. She put a kettle on — did she leave without turning the stove off? Brian was on the couch, a beer between his legs, watching some game show. She looked out the back door on to the wane cornfields, illuminated by a giant, hideous orange light hanging on the front of the garage, fluttering with the giant shadows of millers. Some nights she stood out on the back porch, looking up at the sky, and thought about taking a scrap of gravel from the driveway and breaking out that light. She couldn't see a damn thing with it. Here, the stars don't even twinkle. This can't be Heaven; she can't be dead. She feels the cold, for the moment at least; *I'm alive. Something's wrong. I'm somewhere else.*

The fuzzy glower of a searchlight flares to life in the sky. "I'm here," she says, splitting her lips and she tries to stand up, but she falls back to the ground. The beam prowls across the tundra, slow, steady, certain of its target, until finally it settles on her. She reaches up into the light, warm, engulfing, and there is this hum, this magnetic hum that fills the air. A line of rope uncurls from the sky. It trails across the ground, over a hummock of ice and past. Another line drops, and another; men slide down them, landing in their heavy boots with a crash of ice. Belts and bandoliers web together grafts of ragged clothing on all of them, their faces lost in head wraps and cumulus hoods.

They throw a blanket over Alice and scoop her off the ground in one move; in the next, she is rising into the air, into that light in a basket suspended from ropes. *Where? Who?* She ascends out of the light, not knowing what to expect again, and sees even more bundled men clustered in the prow of a gondola, nestled on the belly of a massive — blimp? She only knows the Goodyear, and that's only from TV; this is nothing like she's ever seen, not even on TV. Rusted armor plates the long and squat hull, layered in armadillo scutes. Long, wide and squat, the ship appears less like a cigar than a sardine as the men — a dozen — pull her in her basket into the gondola, into warmth and into an even greater insanity.

They all barely fit into the main room of the gondola, crates and ammo boxes and junk everywhere. They lay Alice on a flimsy cot and loom over her in steep, spine-destroying angles. All of them carry guns, but none of them do more than emphasize them; a woman, in a droopy white hood and frayed, old wool coat kneels next to her. She rubs Alice's hands, a smile on her face that warms more than anything else she does. The woman looks Asian to Alice, Arabic, something in between; she speaks a language Alice has never heard, but then she's spent her entire life within about 20 miles of where she was born.

"Look... I'm lost," Alice says. "I think I'm really lost..."

The clutch of mismatched men gasps at the sound of her voice. The woman nods affirmatively to the others, like she's saying, *I told you so.* Some wear expressions of surprise, some of quiet disdain at being proven wrong. This entire mission has been a dangerous risk, and few supported it. Their doubt, well placed as it was before, is even harder to support now. She speaks the language. What more proof do they need? The woman reaches into one of her many pockets and produces a small device — it looks like a transistor radio to Alice — and switches it on. It crackles with static.

"What is it?"

"Radiometer," the woman says, in a heavy accent.

"What, like a fucking Geiger-counter?"

The woman puts it away, even more satisfaction in her eyes now, and grabs Alice's hands. She squeezes them tight.

"Who are you people? What's happening?"

"Madel," she says. "My name. What is yours?"

"Was there a bomb? What are you, Russians or something?"

"Name," Madel says. "Your name."

"Alice."

"What year you think this is?"

"What do you mean what year I think it is?"

"What is your year?"

"This is 1986... why?"

More gasps. Madel stands, a smug look of vindication on her face. "She is one of them."

"One of who?" Alice says. "What year is this?"

"1347," Madel says.

"What... but there weren't any blimps in 1347."

Madel knows this from the book; its 'almanack' for 'XIX' years — what kind of years are those supposed to be she wonders, special no doubt, a new age to follow the arrival of the book — begins with the year 1552, and nowhere in any of its pages does it reference any technology comparable to the present day. The discrepancy — the existence of futures yet unlived, 1552, 1986, absent of air ships but present with so much promise — fills her with equal fear and hope. Alice and the author of the book both seem to be from the future, but one in which Madel's past never existed. Why? How? That is what they must find out; that is what will lead them to the author of the book, and their most sacred hopes.

"No," Madel says. "Not in yours."

"I have to get out of here," Alice says, and even knowing there's nowhere to go, runs for it nonetheless.

Alice runs the short length of the gondola to the fore of the ship and finds the crew cabin, standing room only. She runs back through the gondola and then out to the treacherously thin deck that wraps around the circumference of the gondola, clutching railing flimsy as Reynolds Wrap. The rudder creaks like an old screen door opening on a humid summer day as the air ship banks to the east; she looks down and sees a tail turret nestled between twin ducted fans. The tail gunner waves at her. She runs back in — to where? — and a sound stops her, like someone dragging a metal chair across concrete. The others stand back, to give it its room.

The machine lurches forward into the cabin, dragging its knuckles across the deck, a goliath molded together from disparate metal and steel pieces that grind against each other with each heavy step. It looms over Alice, cheek guards curling into wan tusks, a volcanic orange churning inside him, the whole gondola smelling like burnt oil.

"What the hell are you?"

Madel's harried words make no sense, save for one, repeated over and over again, franticly:

"Elizabeth," she says. "Elizabeth."

"Who?"

She drags Alice back to the cot and the others curse in their nonsensical language as the gondola rocks with the machine's every move. They scold him for his clumsy disposition, for the noise he makes; patrol ships lurk in the clouds, their spotlights like moons, descending to earth. Like a shamed dog the machine retreats to a corner, remains still, and silent; the men nervously stroke their beards, all long, dark as their hair, some twisted into braids at their ends. Madel reaches into another pocket.

This time it's not the radiometer she returns, but a small chapbook, a simple brown cover that looks like thin cardboard bound to a wedge of short, square pages.

"You know this?"

Alice opens the cover. On the first page — smooth, the copy smudged and shrunk to fit - she strains to read the title: *Booke of Common Prayer and Administration of the Sacraments and Other Rites and Ceremonies of the Churche of Englande.* She flips through the pages and though the author added an 'e' to the end of many words ('the body of our Lorde Jesus Christe'), and used an f in place of an s in some, she understands exactly what this book is supposed to be.

"It's the Bible..."

"You know book?"

"Well, yeah," Alice says. "But..."

"But?"

Alice flips back to the title page — the books of the Bible following a long preamble of prayers and ceremonies and essays, it seems, written in frustrating English (*'There was never anye thynge by the wytte of man so wel devised'*) - to the elaborate, ornate signature that fills the bottom half.

"There was no Elizabeth that wrote any of this," Alice says, though she can't be sure; her family has always been Christmas Catholics, only ever attending midnight mass.

"You from England."

"I'm from Iowa."

"Iowa is in England?"

"It's in America..." They all greet her with puzzlement. "You've never heard of America?"

"England," Madel says, touching the book. "England is nation of God. Promised land. Elizabeth is from England. To bring God. All Echoes. Sent by God. You, Alice."

"Echoes?"

"Alice. You know England. You know book."

"Everyone does," Alice says.

"No. No one," Madel says. "No things in book happen here. No places exist. Jerusalem. England. Not here."

She touches the book. "Iowa."

"What do you mean they're not here? Where am I?"

"You know Elizabeth."

"I don't know what any of this is! This is all fucked. I don't know who you are or what the hell that thing over there is. I just want to go home. How do I get home?"

"We look. For her. You help us."

"This is all a trick. You're trying to get me to do or say something," Alice says, grasping now, knowing Russians — not that these look like the Russians she's seen in movies — don't usually kidnap Iowans from their driveways.

"You tell us."

"Fuck you, commie."

"Fuck you!" the machine blurts out.

"Shh!" one of the men hisses. He waves his hand dismissively at Alice. "Forget her. She nothing."

Madel refreshes her fading smile with another. "Alice," she says. "Please. Help us."

"Help *you*?"

"We need to find Elizabeth. You help us."

Alice trembles in the frigid air seeping through the porous gondola of the air ship. She quakes with sobs.

"How?" Alice says. "How am I supposed to help you?"

"You are come to show us. God send you," Madel says, on the verge of weeping. "To lead us to promised land."

"God... God, help me..."

Madel smiles again — it would be goofy if it weren't so sincere - and looks up into Alice's eyes with wonder. She caresses Alice's unkempt hair behind her ears, holds her cold, calloused hands to Alice's cheeks.

"You help us."

"The only Elizabeth I know is Elizabeth Murphy. And she's too dumb to be able to do anything like this."

"You lead us to her. I know. I believe."

"Somebody please... somebody please help me..."

A cloud of black smoke erupts outside the slatted windows of the compartment, and the ship shudders. All of the men grip their guns and rush out onto the deck. More sounds of thunder, and more smoke; Alice thinks they must be passing into a thunder storm. Above, it sounds like hail bouncing off the roof of the house. The house disappeared. Madel grabs Alice by the arm, leads her to a small aft compartment.

Madel pushes her to the bunk. "Stay."

She closes the door behind her. Alice runs to it, but Madel locked it; Alice pounds on the door, rickety and loose enough she thinks she could jar it loose but she can't. A hoarse, fatigued cry of fear leaves her mouth, ricochets around the room. She climbs up on the bunk, puts her nose to the tiny, circular window in the wall behind her.

Another blimp — much larger, given how big it seems from how far away it must be — pursues them out of the clouds. A flash of orange — like the momentary lick of flame from beneath the grate of a grill - erupts from its forward chin guns. The puff of black smoke follows a moment later, showering the hull with shrapnel. Alice pounds on the window.

"Help! Help me!"

A pair of smaller craft race away from the other ship, headlong into the stream of machine gun fire spitting from the tail gun. One explodes under the barrage; the other negotiates it so skillfully it closes on the ship and disappears within seconds. Alice hears a terrible crash and the entire ship shudders like the cars of a train coming to a stop. Shouts from outside. *"Eyes! Eyes!"* Gunfire.

Alice pounds dents into the door. "I'm in here!"

The chaos outside escalates; the explosions are inside the ship now, and screams. The sanity of what is happening evaporates like her house back in Carpenter. Alice backs away from the door, and slides underneath the bunk.

The door bursts open. Madel stumbles in, a puffy backpack laced with straps in her hands.

"Put on," she says, dragging Alice out from under the bunk. *"Yalla.* Put on, put on. They coming."

"What are you doing?"

"They kill us!"

"Help!" Alice screams. "Someone help me!"

She guns for the door. Madel grabs her, pulls her back. She forces the parachute pack on Alice, and then once she's secured her own, grabs Alice by the hog collar of the pack and pulls her out on to the deck, to the edge of the railing.

"You first. Count ten, and pull-"

"What? I'm not doing this!"

Two people — one very clearly a man, the other a boy or a girl, adolescent — emerge out of the smoke, clad in black army-like fatigues and face-disguising breath masks.

Madel reaches for her rifle. The man shoots, hits Madel in the throat; she spits blood and tumbles over the railing.

Alice watches Madel reduce to one of many specks of black, spotting an otherwise perfect white.

"Jesus..."

The girl — she removes her helmet, and rust-colored boy cut besides, she is a girl — relaxes her tense posture and approaches Alice. Alice puts her hands out in thanks.

"Help me," Alice says. "Please. My name is Alice, I'm from Iowa... I don't know what's happening. What's happening?"

The girl sweeps a radiometer over Alice. It crackles like Madel's did. She exchanges the device for her gun.

"This is happening," the little girl says, and puts the muzzle to Alice's chest and pulls the trigger.

II

Miranda steps to the sagged deck railing, watches Alice spin a thread of blood away from the air ship. A chute blossoms from her back. Miranda fires off the rest of the clip but hits nothing; Alice vanishes into the cloud cover.

"Now we'll have to go after her," Miranda says.

"A few of them have gone up into the superstructure," Joshua says, as he removes his helmet. "That's who we need to go after. Do the job. Don't pull whiskers off cats."

"Well. There's only so many ways you can skin one."

Joshua kneels down and picks up the little book Madel dropped as she fell over. "What's this?"

"Hurry," Miranda says. "We'll get too far down range."

"Hold on."

Joshua flips through the book, finds his own name.

And it was after the death of Moses the servant of the Lorde, that the Lorde said to Joshua the son of Nun, Moses' mynyster, saying:

Moses My servant hath died and now arise, cross this Jordan, you and all this nation, that lande whiche I give you, thy children of Israell.

"This again."

The only thing about the literature of the Kuzar that interests Miranda is how they managed to string enough words together to get a book in the first place; she lingers anxiously at the railing, counting the miles in her head every passing second the air ship puts between her and the target.

"Just bring it with you," she says.

"The target is dead."

"We have to be sure."

"What is this?"

Joshua has found two copies of this same book on acolytes in Kuzar sleeper cells in the last year, and that icon on the cover — a simple cross — repeated in graffiti on the walls of shacks in the Kuzar ghettos of Clockwork. He thought nothing of it then, burnt it like he did everything else.

"Who cares?" Miranda says.

"What did they want with her?"

Did they find Alice by accident? If so, then why would they be this far south into the contested territories? What does this book have to do with Echoes? What does the book even mean; something about it seems familiar, and not just his name. Something more. He rubs his eyes. They hurt, like some is twisting a screw into the back of each them, always.

His world has a leak in it. That's how Miranda describes it, and why not; a trickle of souls seeps into this earth from some other, drip, drip, drip, at least one a day, somewhere in the world. They come with such solitary force, like the mer-

est drop of moisture in a cloud that will never produce heavy
rain, that in the beginning Joshua sometimes wondered why his
superiors took so much frustration in them. But with experience he knows: the leak is steady. Distracting. Annoying like
the drip, drip, drip of a faucet all night long and there's no
end. Plug one hole, another opens right after. The Echoes have
been coming from before man discovered fire.

The place they arrive is random. So is the hour. These
women — it's always women, with him at least - come in different shapes and sizes, different colors, the oldest ever found in
her eighties, with a considerable story to tell and the youngest
just a newborn, with no story at all but every one of them arrive
inevitably, like the debris of some wreck out to sea the waves
bring in even years after. If not found immediately, their fan-
tastic story — the corruptive, corrosive details of their former
world — will spread like wildfire. It's his job, Miranda's, the
hundreds of others like him and the thousands before, to put
those fires out.

"We have to find her," he says, and pockets the book.

"This is what I'm saying."

"Radio back to the ship. Get a satellite fix. Tell them
we're landside after the target. They need to get in here and do
a sweep of this thing, see what else they can find."

Miranda opens a bulky pouch hitched to her utility belt,
and draws out the receiver of her field telephone.

"Radio One, Radio One, this is Blue Room, over."

Static comes back over the line. No signal at all; there is
only one thing the Kuzar have in their arsenal that causes this
kind of electro-magnetic interference.

Miranda looks back into the gondola and the boulder-
sized hands of the machine vault out of the smoke around
their legs.

The machine throws them into the bulkhead. It howls in anger, swings its fists - hanging off its long, droopy arms like heavy fruit from burdened branches — wildly and Joshua scrambles on his knees across the deck out of the way. Less than a hundred Alephmen are thought to remain in existence, but that they do at all says more than their meager number. The Alephman is a remnant of the world before Canon, a world of anarchy, plague, hunger and war, all but forgotten now.

Miranda appreciates history about as much as she does Kuzar literature. All she cares about is that at last she has the opportunity to go head to head with the legendary champion of the Kuzar rebels that have complicated Canon's millennial peace for centuries; to prove to Joshua that she can. Of all the disparate groups that existed before the integration of the republic, the Kuzar have proven the most stubborn. The Kuzar - a mutt, rootless people Joshua once told her — began nowhere, linger nowhere, drifting from country to country out of Europe into Asia, eventually across the Ice Garden into reclusion in the polar hinterlands of Canon.

She reloads her gun and opens fire. The bullets flatten to nickels. Miranda trades the gun for her short sword.

"Miranda, no!"

She hacks at its long arms, the wrists, the elbows, as Joshua trained her to do; rule #1 when it comes to the machines is that you can't kill them. So don't try. She lands a fatal blow in the machine's neck, but the sword lodges in the armor, too thick; it grabs the sword at the hilt and snaps it in two. The hunched Alephman looms over Miranda, deciding on where best to depress the broken shard of sword in her small, soft body. Her neck, it thinks; their eyes bulge when their throats empty. It loves their big, soft eyes.

Joshua rams an ammo crate into the back of the Alephman's legs. The old machine twists out of the way, swipes at him with the broken sword it collected from Miranda; Joshua climbs up its arm, on to its back. The Alephman veers around the devastated cabin, wailing with fear, with panic and persecution; Joshua shouldn't care that it screams, that it suffers, but he does. If he were doing his duty correctly, if he were smart, he would just get Miranda and run. He is not smart. *I am a gravedigger. I have a gravedigger's hands. My work is never done and it will continue after me. Will they hear me? After? Will they hear me screaming from my coffin.*

Joshua crams a pair of grenades into the seam between the Alephman's neck and shoulder armor, not to destroy it, not to defeat it, but to stop its mad, terrified screams.

Joshua leaps off the machine's back, takes cover behind an overturned table. The explosion accomplishes what Joshua set out to do; if it destroyed the Alephman, he'll never know. The gondola splits in two, spilling the myriad crates, Joshua and Miranda all out into the open sky. Half of the gondola remains attached to the main hull of the air ship, but the other corkscrews away, and enters a ferocious tail spin that tears it to shreds. The air ship lists starboard, and drifts off into the clouds, ablaze. Joshua and Miranda free-fall a mile or more and then together pull their ripcords. Parachutes rocket out of their backpacks and their meteoric descent becomes the soft, slow flutter of a feather to earth.

The ground gleams horizon to horizon. Joshua curses under his breath; they're much further north than he thought. He hates the cold. It holds too much of the world. They ease down to a gargoyle-style perch atop a crag-like berg frozen in place within the ice pack, their chutes winding back into their packs like tape measures; the fragmenting shards of the Kuzar air ship blaze down from the sky in the distance, impacting onto the surface of the ice cap and creating fires that Joshua lusts for. They're entirely in the wrong direction. He detaches a radiometer from his utility belt.

A faint signal, due west; fifteen miles away.

"Let's get moving," he says.

"Waiting for you, slow coach."

"Miranda."

"What?"

"We're completely exposed out here. We're outside Canon boundaries with no support. Keep your head on."

"How is this different from any other assignment?"

"You shouldn't have taken that thing on."

"Are you ever going to just let me-"

"There's a reason they send two of us."

"Someone has to be there to save your ass," she says.

"Watch your mouth."

"What are you going to do?"

He says nothing as he slides down the side of the berg on to the pack.

"That's what I thought."

"Just keep talking."

"What are you going to do?"

"Watch."

"Yeah, right," Miranda says, and drifts into Joshua, nudges him off his path. He nudges back with his hip, almost knocks her to the ground. She laughs, and there's the echo of a smile there in his eyes, all she can see. She folds her arms against the cold, and they walk, elbow to elbow.

"We find the target, we mitigate it and whoever else she's come into contact with. Then we leave. Understand?"

"You're the one who wasted ten minutes gawking over some little book when we could have had her and been done by now."

"We could have had her and been done if you had just done your job right in the first place."

"You make it so boring," Miranda says.

"What about this is fun?"

"Grow up already."

The temperature plunges below zero. Their suits, their training and conditioning, only insulate so much; Joshua realizes after an hour or so that Alice is further away than the dawn. Wounded — probably fatally — even more exposed on the ice than either of them, Alice won't be going too far. The peaks of bergs pierce the cap everywhere, the serrated wind wearing them down to stumps, carving holes into them and through; Joshua finds an eroded cave that burrows half the way into a large berg, and decides to take shelter there for the night. He cracks open the emergency flares intended to signal for their retrieval, and ignites a long-burning powder every agent carries among their thirty some pounds of equipment.

Miranda keeps her pout on her lips, so he knows she'd rather keep going than hole up, but it's hard for him to take seriously as she leans back against the rounded wall of the tiny cave, and settles in with the old-fashioned paper comic book she's been buried in since they left Clockwork.

"You should probably get rid of that, buddy."

"I will."

"Don't get too attached to it," he says.

She nods, absent-mindedly, already back to her book. He thought she might have grown out of them by now, thirteen going on thirty; he's known of her more than procedural interest in the Samaire series for a long time now, but he lets it go without comment, it hurts no one; he just never understood her interest in them to begin with. Comics are boys' things — reportedly - but then Miranda leads something of a boys' life.

Boys explore strange woods, challenge each other in demon-
strations of strength or loyalty, do battle in mock wars to defend the borders of their backyards — so he understands — boys
pretend to do all the things she has done from the time she
turned ten, when she began her formal field training with him.
He has five more years with her, just five short years, and then
she will confirm and be reposted, to wherever Division I needs
a new agent the most.

"Here I thought you didn't like it," he says, trying to sit
up out of the position the tiny cave leaves him with — reclined
nearly all the way on his back - to get a better eye on the narrow
tunnel leading back out to the ice cap.

"It's just..." The paper is yellow, brittle, powdery to the
touch. The colors faded, simple. "I don't know."

They found the copy of the *Collected Adventures of Samaire* at
the town bazaar in Clockwork. Miranda had never seen a paper
version of the comic serial; she confiscated the book as contra-
band, intending to destroy it, until she discovered the stories
in the book - while similar to the ones she read late into the
night in the digital archives at Division headquarters — varied
greatly. Samaire grew up as the ward of a city scientist in those
strips, an unintended casualty of his dangerous experiments,
and not in the wild beyond the Threshold where the same scientist accidentally discovers her in these pages; before, Samaire resolutely defended the city against the monster attacks
from beyond the Threshold. Here, she feels torn between both
worlds, equally hers, and ends up a villain in each. She has a
different color of hair than before (black, not blonde) and her
attitude towards most things, especially boys, seems less quaint.

Text boxes label myriad panels throughout the book,
each of them squeezed tight with tiny letters advising the reader
of footnotes such as *Time enslaves only the foolish — Ed.*

"Who's this Ed?"

"Editor. I think."

"I don't know what he's referring to."

"I doubt any one does at this point."

The Samaire character — a folk hero of sorts among an-
ti-Canon sects in Clockwork — has existed in one form or another for more than a century. It's not the erasure of Samaire's
history that leaves Miranda sullen; it's that now she finally understands how irrelevant that history, all history, truly is. At
some point, someone will rewrite Samaire again, reinterpret
her for a new generation of rebels and the atmosphere of Miranda's youth that once would have frozen into the ice of memory in old age will instead evaporate. This book only proves to
her what she has long suspected: nothing they do, nothing any
one does, really matters. It makes no difference where she was
born, who her parents were; once the Long House selected her,
those things became irrelevant.

Just the same it makes no difference where these people they spend nearly all their waking hours in search of come
from. Everything they know expired in whatever calamity continuously deposits them here; the last trace of their world vanishes utterly — eternally - when Miranda executes her duty.

"It's all different," she says.

"Name's the same."

"That's about it."

"A name is all any of us have got."

Miranda looks up out of the book. "What made you decide on Miranda?"

"I don't know. I just thought it sounded pretty."

"What does it mean?"

"It means go to sleep."

"Who picked your name?"

"My teacher. Michael."

"I like Joshua," she says, a smile creeping onto her face. "It sounds pretty."

Joshua hates his name. Always has. It sounds odd, out of synch with more common names in Canon. It sounds old, Jewish almost, though he can't be sure; the words and names of that people vanished with them in the haze of early history. Some might enjoy its unique quality — Miranda takes personal pride in hers, which is why she returns, casually she would have it seem, regularly to the subject of its origin — but unique isn't something Joshua prides himself in being. If he could get by without a name — why he needs one at all, considering no one knows who he is anyway — he would, but every child officer of the agency receives a name upon his or her induction. Whoever he had been then, whoever he might have been after, ended with his invocation into the order.

Joshua turns over. He can never sleep. He was asleep — he thinks — when he heard the dull, soul rattling ring from his field phone. Never more than a day without it, without the drip, drip, drip of Echoes into the world, through a leaky ceiling over every bed he finds. They pulled up out of Clockwork in a flash and got on the next transport back. He felt light, warm, warmer the brighter the sun got out the window, at least until Alice led them out here onto the ice. Miranda doesn't share his joy in coming home. She liked Mars. She found the smell of burning wood sweet, the dust laden streets, impassable at times, not apocalyptic like Joshua did but something else, something she couldn't quite place; not fun. New. She liked the acting, the pretending to be someone else, an enemy agent, gathering intelligence in the most bitterly divided city on both worlds.

He opens the Book of Common Prayer. The ink they used rubs off on his fingers. He strains to read the small type, the familiar but oddly spelled words; he flips through the pages, stops on one that catches his attention:

"He wil not suffre thy fote to be moved: and he that kepeth thee wil not slepe.
Beholde, he that kepeth Israel: shall neither slumber nor slepe."

He continues strumming through the pages, through the chapters and verses of the Old and New Testaments, to the back page, and the signature of the book's author: Elizabeth. Its deliverer, more likely; some books have individual authors. This Elizabeth appears to have collected all of these narratives into a single whole; he tries to imagine who she is, what she looks like, how she sounds. Voices compel Joshua the most. It's all he remembers in the end of any of the girls — their tiny, frightened and inexplicable voices.

"You should probably get rid of that," Miranda says.

"Yeah."

"Don't get too attached to it."

"Yeah."

The book is a history of the tribes of Israel — a history that never happened. Why do the Kuzar have such an interest in it? Where did they get it? Who — where — is Elizabeth? Those answers have to wait. One mission at a time.

Joshua places the book under his arm, closes his eyes again, in hope. "Get some rest, buddy."

Paper slides against paper, crinkles under fingers.

"Yeah."

Eventually, her fingers get too stiff to turn the pages and she puts the book away. Miranda rubs her hands, blows on them, holds them over the fire melting through the ice toward the ground buried below; finally she burrows into the nook between his arm and his body. The blood Alice threaded as she left the air ship webs Miranda's thoughts; it angers her that the cold will get her before they do. An animal may find her. Maybe she came down in a crevice or gorge; maybe Alice becomes part of the architecture of the north, a nameless statue, never to be seen again. The fire melts beneath the ice. Only a trace of warmth left, if any at all. Miranda closes her eyes and hopes that if someone ever rewrites her life, she will get to keep the name that he gave her as a baby.

III

The world shudders. Ice webs her eyelashes. The little hairs inside her nose, frozen in blood and dew, snap as she exhales. Her breath clouds in the air around her, onto her skin, where it freezes instantly. She goes to rub it away, massage warmth into her cheeks bitten with frost and she slams her knuckles against solid metal. Alice cries out, alarmed and awake. The burning air ship shed wreckage for miles across the ice pack, twisting back to where Alice fell; a plate of its hull armor, bent crooked and nearly torn in half, landed right on top of her, forming a porous steel tent.

She clutches her shoulder, the wound still oozing. *I'm shot. That little bitch shot me.*

She closes her eyes. *Don't close your eyes.* So cold. She left the kettle on back at the house. She thinks about the tea set. She lost it, somewhere, she can't remember when, or how. You put things away, thinking they're small. Every time she went to the store, old man Jane leaned over the front counter with his shit-eating grin and said with dramatic pause: "Ms. Little Lady." He never let her forget it: when she was six, she ditched her mom while she did the shopping and headed straight to the section near the school supplies where they kept the toys, bins of little rubber footballs and green army guys that hung in plastic sleeves from the hooks.

The Little Lady tea set sat there, the same one, for two years; ninety-nine cents for two small plastic plates, two tiny white plastic teacups with little red roses painted around the rim. Just one teaspoon. All of it glued to a simple, cheap cardboard back, but it was all done up on the front in beautiful royal blues, with frilly, elegant Victorian lettering in bright pink. A rose-cheeked girl, prim and proper, blonde and beautiful sat a table in the top left hand corner. She looked right at Alice. *Join me for tea?*

She grew up ten years behind Danny, a decade he spent at the center of his parents' universe as the only child, the first son in a family where that meant everything. Alice idolized him in the same unbridled way as her father and mother, but he never let her off the hook for crashing his party; her father shared his indifference and her mother, by the time Alice came into their lives, her mother couldn't be bothered with anybody. Mostly Alice liked boy things, Danny's things — sci-fi magazines, comic books — but she thought if she had the tea set, she could have friends. Girlfriends. She kept asking her mom for the set, each time they went to Jane's. Alice begged and pleaded for it for months, pulling on her mother's arm, producing tears at precisely the moment old man Jane rang up their groceries and asked, "Is that all?"

It wasn't so much that her mom didn't have an extra dollar for a stupid plastic tea set — she didn't, not always — but it was that she didn't want to give Jane any more than she had to. Alice's father came down from Shell Rock first in '53, and got a job at the old meat packing plant. He saved enough money for the down payment on the house, and then brought his wife and son down a couple months later. They pulled up to the house for the first time, and Laura Vale *screamed*. She hated it. Alice never knew why — no one ever talked about it, except for Danny, just the once on his birthday. This first house, over on the corner of Cunningham and Powell, stood three stories tall; she rode past it on her bike sometimes and Alice wondered what their lives would have been like if they had lived there. Maybe her father would have kept the job at the plant. Maybe she would have had money for college. Maybe Danny wouldn't have been drafted.

Her father had signed the lease already with the landlord — old man Jane — and Jane wouldn't let him out of it. He paid rent on that house for a year, on top of the rent they paid for the house they did get, over on Doyle. They didn't have a dime that first year and when they went to the store, Jane acted like they stole something from him. Her father paid him on time, in cash, never missed a single month's due. They bought their groceries from him. It was never enough somehow. He snickered sometimes when her mother came to the counter.

"See anything you like? Want to take another look?"

She hated him. He wasn't going to get one more nickel out of them than he got coming but Alice had to have the tea set. Finally she couldn't wait anymore and she ran out of the store sobbing, cradling it in her arms, hiding on the floor in the back seat of the car. Laura paid for it, without a word. They never talked about it, except for when Alice, table set and tears dry asked her mother if she wanted to have some tea.

Open your eyes, girl.

Alice does. *Stay awake. Don't fall asleep, whatever you do.* Her body aches from hours of unnatural contortion; she tries to stretch her arms and legs, but every time she moves she hits something cold and metal and it's like she's back under the old International, under the car port in the backyard with Danny. It sat there from before she could even remember — it was still sitting there when she and Brian went over dinner last Thursday - the fire engine red becoming a flaky, sick brown and Danny wasted his good summers, his only summers, in some vain effort to breathe life back into it.

The International seemed so heavy, so gargantuan in its presence, like some ancient, extinct beast found only in the sediment of dry lakes and rivers, in out-of-fashion, rotting car ports off the side of garages. It scarred them all, its underbelly armored with the sharp fins of rusted metal, the thick axel, heavy and blunt; Danny spent hours under there, working his wrenches to nothing and on days she exhausted her passions, her books, her music, on days she felt lonely, she crawled underneath the truck with him. *I'm busy,* he'd say.

Why do you keep bothering with that old thing, Alice asked him, the summer before he left for basic training. The truck had gone a few years without any attention from father or son, after Danny's primary interest transitioned to Jackie Sullivan, but one day in late July Alice found him out there under the hood, tinkering with it again. Danny and her father stood over it on one of the same wood blocks they used to prop her up, her tires long gone, the wheel wells rusting into the upper reaches of the cab. Both of them smoked cigarettes. Beer bottles sat on top of the radiator. They didn't seem to be working that hard; they were both laughing, at something one of them had said.

Supper's almost ready, she said. *Why do you bother?*

Danny shrugged, gave a look to his father, and they both laughed again. *I think she's had it.*

Yep, her father said, and drank from his beer.

You should just junk it. It's an eyesore.

Both men reacted as if she had uttered blasphemy. *Go on, get,* her father said. *We'll be there in a minute.* It took them fifteen more minutes to finally come back into the house, another five to scrub up and join Alice and her mother at the dinner table. *Your food's getting cold,* her mother said, eating already and her father took his cap off, rubbed his hair into a mess. He yawned and she said, *Tired?*

I'll do with my time what I want, he told her.

Just don't go wasting mine.

Maybe I want the boy to have something of mine.

You can leave him ten dollars to junk it.

Maybe we can leave something of yours, then. One of your world famous recipes, maybe — oh, that's right -

The truck — like the house they paid for but didn't live in that first year in Carpenter — formed the foundation of nearly every argument her parents ever had; her father resented her mother for turning her nose up at a perfectly good house and she resented him, it seemed, for holding on to a piece of junk truck that did them no good. Growing up, that's all that mattered to her parents; houses and cars they had no use for. Alice misses the truck now, like she misses her parents, their cold war, its periodic skirmishes that threatened to escalate into something nuclear.

You should just junk the damn thing, her mother said, lighting up another cigarette. *It's an eyesore.*

A moment passed in awkward silence — the debate over what to do with the International turned personal at times - and then Danny broke out laughing. Her father did, too. Alice held her smile in check, careful not to show too much enthusiasm — fidelity — with the men in front of her mother, who went on eating, as if she heard nothing at all. They talked some about Danny going to college. His father wanted him to avoid the draft; he'd fought in the war and didn't want his son to ever see what he saw, do what he did but he never vocalized this. He stressed the importance of education, something he never did. Danny had vague ideas about law school, maybe, but mostly he liked cars, and Jackie Sullivan. He liked Cream and Superman and Alice thinks he would be more apt, more successful — deserving - in this world than she is.

Alice wonders if the same fate that's befallen her befell him, and he was given a second chance at life, as a seventeen year-old on the verge of his limitlessness, or as a boy innocent of his future; or if Danny exists nowhere at all now.

She tries to move inside the wreckage, but she feels like she's been rolled through a steam press, like someone rolled the weight of the entire world over her and she feels dead, buried inside this claustrophobic tomb that smells of ozone, of metal; she's trapped. No one knows where she is. That girl. She shot her. *Why.* No one is coming to help her. There is no help. Alice Vale doesn't exist. She never did.

She fears the people she thought that were coming to her rescue will come again, finish the job. Another shot, to the heart, or the head; maybe they leave her to the elements, or bury her, as all the untidy remnants of her world are buried, in a nameless, shallow grave among the debris of the air ship. A heavy thud vibrates through the wreckage, through the fillings in her teeth; then another. And another. *They're burying me. They're throwing the dirt over me* and Alice pounds her fists numb with cold and pain against the jagged heap and she screams her ragged, shredded scream for help.

I'm not dead. Don't bury me, I'm not dead yet.

A violent tremor, and then daylight; Alice inches up through the gap in the heap. "God," she says. "Thank God."

The cold inside the unlikely shelter the wreckage created pales in comparison to that outside, withering; boreal. Alice came to rest in a frozen marsh south of a glacial ridge towering high as a mountain range far in the distance. The long, uniform line of the icy plateau cleaves the yellow apple rays of the low sun, weak and masked already behind high, periwinkle clouds. The propeller of one of the ship's duct fans lies across the top of the heap at a steep angle. The propeller blade flutters, whines in the frigid, punishing wind and Alice crawls back to the wreckage, out of the wind.

The very earth beneath her moves; the broken propeller rattles off its meek perch, scrapes a long gash in the fuselage of the ship on its way to the ground. A cloud of dust and ice erupts into the air; the wind dashes it away. Alice eases out of the human ball she's made, relaxes the shield of her arms. The propeller is gone, but the wan, blue shadow it cast over the wreckage remains. She hears the ice groaning, crunching, cracking; something scrapes it away, back and forth, sawing into the top layer. And then she hears the terrific bellow of what sounds like an elephant, followed in quick and epic succession by several dozen others.

Alice looks up. A large black eye looks right back down at her. It hovers in the air above her, blinking eclipses every few seconds, in the midst of thick, shaggy amber hair. A majestic ivory tusk juts out from beneath where the eye and the trunk meet, curls under the boat out of sight and then reemerges, arcing high in the air over the creature's head.

"No... way..."

Alice crawls on all fours out from behind the cover of the heap, back into the degrading wind that sweeps off the glacial plateau, eroding everything on the expansive plain except only the strongest, the most indomitable of things.

The mammoth takes a step back at the sight of her, sending a long, rumbling thunder through the ice again as the rest of the pack — dozens, spread out over a mile across the plain — quickly follow suit. The towering mammoth raises its trunk and issues a warning cry, again, echoed in chorus by the others; it swings its head back and forth, scraping its magnificent tusks into the ice, kicking up heavy, sharp chunks of debris, casting them into the air and onto Alice.

She scrambles back behind the trembling heap. The mammoth gives it a love tap for good measure, sending her for cover out on the exposed plain. He continues the swaying of his head, the collision of tusk against ice; when she finally stops running, too exhausted to do any more, she looks back and sees his behavior isn't to intimidate her. The mammoth clears the top layer of ice away with his tusks, and then with its long trunk rips up the prairie grass buried beneath.

Alice cautiously returns to the cover of the wreckage, and marvels. She had a brief flirtation with the prehistoric as a girl, before she settled firmly in her passion for astronomy. She never really took to dinosaurs, but the creatures of the Ice Age - the mammoth, the sabretooth, the giant sloth - all the species that stand as emblems of the world that passed with the melting of the ice and the rise of modern man 10,000 years ago — *Is this 10,000 years ago?* - always fascinated her. Her mother told her once mammoths had roamed Iowa in their heyday; someone found a skeleton.

Where? Alice asked, but her mother didn't know; she had read it somewhere in a magazine, forgot it until Alice became enamored with a tiny plastic toy of the creature that came in a plastic bag with dozens of others for a dollar at Jane's.

She wonders if any other species that vanished in her world survive in this one. *I should be writing this stuff down in case I ever go back. How do I get back? Where am I?* The cold shutters her eyes and she falls heavily against the wreck. The horns of the mammoths trumpet. Another voice joins the chorus. It calls out to the pack, and they call back in a mixture of wariness and welcome. Another mammoth approaches from the west, this one saddled with pack bags and long wooden slats like shelves, staggered on either side of it. A rider sits atop its neck, directly behind its head. Alice gapes at his wooden mask, carved into the likeness of an owl with three distinct and long feathers branching out from the cheeks, the head; he holds a long, feathered spear.

The rider scales down a rope ladder to the ground; it jingles with every step, the rhythm of the wind. He walks past all the shallow craters holding debris, body parts, the ice like a window shot full of bb's; they hold no interest for him, not even in skin. The woman is different. The woman shimmers, like the pastel sky in the winter night. Every great once in a while, the sky falls to ground in shards of women and men; he needs to get her back to the camp. He needs to preserve her, before she vanishes like the ephemeral aurora that licks the sky and is gone, hot breath in cold air.

The rider holds his spear out, cautiously; he pokes her in her wounded shoulder, just to be sure she is real.

"Please..."

"*Do kuba,*" he says.

"Please don't hurt me..."

The rider thrusts his spear into the air and a scream jettisons from his throat, so violent and sustained the mammoths confuse it for a sound of their own. The lead bull of the herd leans back on his hind legs, stomps his legs into the ground; the quake snuffs out the last flicker of consciousness in Alice, and she dissolves into the music of the startled mammoths, the rider, the organ hum of that song she heard on the radio the other day, the streets have no names. The rider lifts her over his shoulder, scales the ladder up the side of his *mamont* and places her in one of the half dozen stores that saddle the beast, three a side, repurposed, fur-lined kayaks. It's dumb luck he even finds Alice; the Yukalut people, like the Kuzar, live outside the influence of Canon, and choose to live their lives much as their ancestors did, thousands of years ago. He had only come this far south to mine the fish-rich rivers that feed the constellation of inland seas that marks at least the natural border between Canon Major and the glacial hinterlands.

Hours pass on the open tundra. Endless, myopic ice gives to a wrinkled landscape, the ice forming hexagons around pools formed in the summer and now frozen over; bare, gray rock veins through the ice, bulging into dark skeins of exposed bedrock. Three monstrous peaks cleave the horizon, as if someone tried to peel back the earth. Their knife-thin points tip toward the sky like sinking ships. The rider recites their names, *Giran, kithaba, nysad,* the three titans of the north, guardians of the gate, and knows he is home.

Somewhere in between Alice thaws and all that's left is the hard, dirty cold on the edges of her, that stubborn ice like the crust that forms over the street curbs, always the last to go in the spring. She dreams strange dreams, hundreds of them strung together in a delirious pastiche, one flowing into the other. In one she searches the jungle, an out-sized, pre-historic jungle dominated by gigantic fauna; she follows footprints in the mud, a trail of shed guns and knives, of shed clothes. She finally finds her brother Danny hiding in the brush, naked and painted in mud. She tries to lead him home, but he takes her deeper into the jungle, which turns out to reside entirely within a greenhouse on the grounds of a grand estate, like something in the English countryside.

He drags her on out of the greenhouse, down the winding paths through the manicured gardens to the rust-coated mansion quailed with parapets. Inside she finds a princess on a gigantic burnished throne that makes her look a child. White paint clays on her face, rouge and lipstick smeared, smudged, her hands pink with the residue; Alice and Danny kneel before her and the princess stands to inspect him, as if he were some animal Alice captured in the wild and returned to present to her little princess, her wig slouching, too big for her head.

The mansion dissolves with the cold, with the tissue of the dream itself. It becomes another, of Iowa. The palace becomes the new shopping mall on the old highway. Danny becomes Brian, her father, and in the funhouse mirror they have in the video arcade, Alice becomes the princess, her lips stained with bright red, running down her chin like she bit her lip, her cheeks brushed with white powder, her hair under her leaning wig short and boyish, rust red International.

"This is happening..."

Alice touches her rent lips. Her fingers come away red. She thrashes around inside the covered kayak, clawing out from under the heap of cut fish meat the rider buried her in. The smell of it saturates the kayak, making her nose curl the way it did every time she and her mother went into the fish market downtown during Lent. Bread heavy and round like river stones rumble out of a satchel atop the heap down on her. She tries to pry a bite off one, but it's too hard and her jaw aches; she uses it instead to pry open the kayak cover.

The *mamont* threads the towering stone pillars that form the gate of the Yukalut boundary. The pillars give to a rocky valley, striped by beige and brick red. Lava, ice, and the erosion of the elements have sculpted thousands of irregular, free-standing conical rocks, some strong and dynamic like pyramids, others smooth and round like mushrooms, from the husk of an ancient mountain. Most of the rocks are cracked eggs with homes inside; hearths burn within the hollowed pinnacles, giving them the appearance of lanterns. Snowdrifts sweeping across the floor of the valley gleam like silver streams in the weak sunlight, a frequent wave that never lets these tiny sandcastles get a start. People emerge from doors, appear in the cracks of their homes; Alice sees faces, strange, angular jaws, and small, deep and square eyes.

Bells jingle as the rider dismounts. The kayak cover peels back and Alice screams. He pulls her out, limbs too stiff to kick, and carries her down to the ground. Other Yukalut gather around, all of them dressed in robes and rags sewn from the hair of the mammoth; wood masks cover their faces, each cut in a different shape and expression, some touched with spots and stripes of paint, others with feathers. Wood sheathes their fingers; it also forms a kind of breast plate under the rags for some of the men and she wonders where they find it, out here in this barren wasteland. The Yukalut sniff at her, paw at her matted, snarled hair; they see exactly what the rider does, the shimmer of color that makes the sky seem bruised. They understand exactly what she is.

They point, into the village, toward a towering mound of heaved ice topped with earth in its center. The people push the rider and Alice along, terrified she may evaporate before she gets there. Alice stumbles to her knees, and they lift her up, off her feet and she is flying through the streets.

"Let me go! Get off me!"

The Yukalut race her to the foot of the mound, an exposed pingo that cracked and fell apart; half of it remains, a solid bulb of ice frosted with earth, in an annual wither on its way to becoming one of the other eroded stumps that litter the valley. The mouth of a cave opens at the base of the pingo; Alice's fear reanimates her dead limbs and she wrests free of her handlers. Claws at their wooden faces.

"No! I want to go home! I want to go home!"

They drag her into the cave, a downward slope into the overwhelming arctic womb of the earth. In the turgid dark, women start to bore into the side of the wall with the claws of polar bears, and the men strip Alice of her clothes.

IV

Razor weeds slice out of crumbling houses, stone graves sprouting spring flowers that froze with the first frost and now entombed in ice look like flecks of dust in dried paint. Joshua and Miranda crawl on their bellies through the rubble of a Yukalut home, one of half a dozen or so that topped a mushroom-like pingo on the outskirts of the village. As the structure sheared away below, it left the cluster of homes on a scalp of earth rolling up the side of the ice core's remains. Joshua looks down into the heart of the village, quiet, seemingly empty save for the mammoths taking refuge from the wind in a small herd behind the massive pingo at the village's center. Yukalut hunters stand guard outside, like wooden statues petrified in the polar air.

"What's that game? Hot potato?" Miranda says, voice muffled behind the frost-crusted scarf she wears over her mouth. She wishes she had a hot potato right now.

"I mean, c'mon."

They found the wreckage from the airship, glassy blotches of blood on the ice; they found mammoth tracks, and followed them, and the undeniable crackle of radioactivity miles beyond what they thought they would. Miranda cradles the radiometer in her palm, wipes away the frost from its touch screen interface to uncover the flashing toxic green blip.

"She has to be dead, right?"

"I feel like I've been here before," he says.

"We've never been to a Yukalut camp."

"Before."

"Oh. When?"

"I don't know."

He's been so many places, all over this world and the other, his entire life a blur of bullets and blood.

"It just seems really familiar."

"How could you even remember a place like this?"

"How could you forget?" he says, taking a moment — a fraction of a second — to take in the beauty of the valley.

Miranda turns back to the ghostly light of the radiometer. "How long do the bodies radiate after they die?"

"Years," he says. The ground sings with them.

"Where do they come from?"

"Doesn't matter."

"Do you think they took her for food?"

"The Yukalut aren't cannibals."

"What for, then?"

He imagines all the things they may be doing to her, but doesn't dwell on them any more than he does anything else.

"We should just call in a strike."

"I want to be sure," she says.

"Then you should have shot her in the head."

"There's not that many of them."

"This place is a gusher. I feel it."

"Remember Abajobir?"

"Yeah... yeah."

Joshua crawls up to a crouched position behind a section of half-fallen wall, to get a better look at the guards.

"Well. Find us a way to lure them up here."

Miranda rummages through the pockets on her utility belt. "What do you think mammoths like to eat?"

"Bratty little girls."

"Boring old boys."

She takes a compact mirror — small and slender as a nail file — in her palm. "I could eat one of those mammoth things. Or make a house out of it. I'm freezing... wow."

She puts her hand to her head. "My head..." Dark red syrups from her nose.

"Your pills," he says, and gets them from her belt before she does. He takes the mirror, replaces it with a pair of fat, white pills, and hands her his canteen.

"You need to take them every day."

Miranda holds her head in her hands. "I do..."

"Are you ok?"

"I'm fine."

"Stay back. I'll handle it."

"No! I'm fine. I'm fine, let's do it."

"You don't need to do this, Miranda."

The headaches and the nosebleeds come more often now. The last year or so, once a month; now at least once a week.

"They're going to section me."

"Just take your pills, you'll be fine."

"What's causing it?"

"I think it's the radiation," he says, holding the mirror

to the moon, flicking light at the guards below. "It makes you sick sometimes if you get too much exposure."

"But you don't get sick."

"Here they come. Ready?"

She wipes her nose clean; the blood is like dried paint on the back of her hand. "Ready."

The bell-festooned bandoliers of the guard hang loose on Miranda; so does the outer robe, already torn in half to fit it more to her size. They walk down the hill, her wooden mask bobbling around her head, and return to the guard's posts.

"I can't see anything," she whispers.

"Shh."

"It smells like bad breath."

Joshua checks his radiometer. The signal strobes stronger, and stronger still as he approaches the cave like entrance into the base of the grand pingo.

"She's inside."

"Inside what? This thing?"

Déjà vu overwhelms him. He forgets so much of his life, wills it away; he knows he's been here before, but he can't remember. His teachers taught him nothing agents ever do really happens; there's no record of it kept anywhere but in your head, and even that was too dangerous to keep, so Joshua never did. An agent keeps the peace because he is invisible. A ghost, liminal as the breath issuing like smoke from the slit on the face of her mask, as the aurora rushing overhead.

"This is a mistake," he says.

"Wimp."

Miranda disappears into the shadowed mouth of the cave, and Joshua, reluctantly, follows. The smell of burning fish oil hangs in the air like a curtain. The sea-blue walls, ice that hasn't seen the light of day in tens of thousands of years, flicker with light from torches gushing from the roots of severed mammoth tusks curling up from the ground; the skull of the tusked *mamont*, carved up with Yukalut glyphs of warning, hangs over a fork in the tunnel. Joshua stops and checks his radiometer. Green flashes back at him intensely.

"It's going crazy..."

"She's not here."

"Maybe the ice is messing with the readings."

"Let's split up," Miranda says.

"No. We stay together."

The reading comes back stronger from the left than it does the right path; they make their choice. The cave deepens and widens and the wall divides in some places to pillars thin enough for Miranda to close her hand around; others still bifurcate into arched lattices of permafrost that give them the appearance of flying buttresses. The geometrical faces the Yukalut wear in wood gaze down from the walls in ice; they descend further into the frozen labyrinth, Joshua's anxiety increasing with every echoing jingle of bells, every drop of water the torches loosen from the walls to puddles on the floor. Even masked, it's evident in his body language.

"What is it?" she says.

"Shh."

Joshua is always calm, still, detached; their orders take them to more dangerous assignments in the tribal regions of the borderless land bridge between Canon Major and Sabiria, to the desert wastes of Mars, where they are always on their own, where they are expected to remain invisible. For the average citizen of the world, to be watched is to live; for an agent of Canon, an 'eye,' to be seen is to die. Miranda focuses on his breathing, rushed, louder than she's ever heard it.

"What's wrong, Joshua?"

"I said be quiet."

"You said, 'Shh.'"

He checks the radiometer again. The levels of radiation inside the pingo spike off the chart.

"This doesn't make any sense. It's like there's a whole... army of them in here..."

Joshua struck the details from his memory, but he knows now he was here before, in this place; he knows what brought him here. He turns the illuminated interface of the radiometer toward the wall, and embedded in the glassy ice, the petrified face of a woman — her hair still perfectly long and black — stares at out him with millennial shock.

"We need to get out of here," he says.

"What is that — is that an Echo?"

"Let's go," he says, grabbing her hand.

"I'm going to find her-"

It sounds like a wreath, hanging on a door pushed open from the wind; the Yukalut man charges down the tunnel at them, pointing at Miranda, shouting in his language that no child can be inside the temple and she needs to leave. All Miranda understands is there is a man coming toward her. Her training kicks in — the switch imperceptible now to Joshua — and in a heartbeat the Yukalut is on the ground, unconscious.

She grabs the club he carries, fashioned from *mamont* tusk, to bash his brains in; Joshua grabs her wrist.

"When I tell you to do something, you do it."

"What's the matter with you?"

"I won't tell you again... wait."

He hears it, wishes he didn't; an echo from down the tunnel, as soft as the drip, drip of the melting ice. *Help*, she says, her voice nearly exhausted. *Please help.*

Miranda drops the club, and draws her gun.

"We have a mission," she says, and follows the voice of the woman her superiors sent her to silence.

They enter the heart of the Yukalut temple. Bodies form the marrow of the pillars of ice, the light fallen to earth in human form frozen and preserved for all time. A Yukalut shaman, his wooden mask broad as a shield and marvelously decorated, makes no move. He simply sits on a cushion of mamont hair, surrounded in candles of whale oil, and continues his devotion. Miranda walks past him to the most recent addition, a figure wrapped in bandages made of seal skin, sheathed in pack ice and left to cement into the permafrost.

"Help," Alice mutters.

Miranda claws the ice away from Alice's face. She peels away the bandages — wetted before applied to her skin. Alice feels nothing, the cold almost a strange comfort to her now.

Miranda removes her wooden face. "Gotcha'."

"No..."

Miranda places the barrel of the gun between Alice's eyes. "You'll appreciate this later, believe me."

"What did I do... to you?"

Miranda holds her finger from the trigger. "You're a threat," she says. "All of you are."

"Why?"

"Do you have mice where you come from?"

"Yes..."

"Why do you buy mouse traps?"

Alice barely manages to strength to close her eyes as Miranda presses the gun to her numb skin.

"Wait!"

Joshua walks past her, into the mouth of a miniature cave, his hands drawn like magnets to the curving, ceramic walls. He holds up his radiometer — flickering furious light —

and traces letters carved in the ice, words dug first with fingers
and then knuckles and then rock.

> *Our Father, which art in heaven,*
> *hallowed be thy name.*
> *Thy kingdom come.*
> *Thy wylle be done*
> *in earth as it is in heaven.*
> *Geve us this daye oure daylye bread.*
> *And forgeve us our trespasses,*
> *as we forgeve them that trespass against us.*
> *And leade us not into temptacion.*
> *But delyver us from evyll. Amen.*

The words surface the entire landscape of the cave. He
kneels down in the back corner, collects sheets of shorn bandages, now stiff as tree bark, from the floor. Her hands. She
had ruined her hands. How had he forgotten. He crumples the
bandages in his fists, against his chest, against the book tucked
within his vest pocket, weighing like a stone against his heart.
Joshua backs out of the cave, transfixed.

He collides with Miranda. "Joshua?"

"I need some charges."

"Good," she says, and hands him a pair of thermic
charges from her belt. "You do that, I'll take care of her."

"No."

"No?"

"We need her," he says, not even sure he's saying it.

"Need her for what?"

"For study."

"Our orders were to mitigate."

"They've changed," he says.

"Since when?"

"Get her out of there."

"Are you kidding me?"

"Miranda."

Bells ring furiously down the tunnel.

"Get her out," he says. "Now."

Joshua places the charges inside the cave of her words, sets the timer for one minute. He runs over to help Miranda dig Alice out of the crushed ice pack the Yukalut encased her in; once she's out, he hoists her over his shoulder.

"Move!"

Yukalut tribesmen charge down the tunnel. Joshua hurls a flash bomb into them, and takes cover behind a pillar. Light explodes in the tunnel, and then screams. Joshua knows the kind, a blind, deaf manic scream that typically only subsides with a bullet. He peeks around the corner; the bomb exploded against the back of one of the Yukalut, igniting his fur coverings. The magnesium flame consumes it in seconds and he rockets down the tunnel, searching for water in all this ice.

Joshua throws a smoke bomb next; white smoke clouds the tunnel, and he casually advances into it.

Gunfire erupts within the cloud, simultaneous with more screams. A young Yukalut, eighteen, stumbles out of the smoke, his clothes stained blood-red at his navel. He holds his hands out to Miranda, pleadingly. He opens his mouth, to plead with words, but only offers more blood. The boy thinks of his young wife, waiting for him at home for him to return and Miranda does not think. She fires and he collapses to the hull like a puppet, let go of his strings.

"C'mon!" she hears Joshua shout, and Miranda takes off down the tunnel after him, hurdling bodies in the smoke.

They emerge out of the pingo, and continue through

the streets of the village, across the valley floor and into the cover of the fallen homes on the outskirts. Light flashes inside the pingo; it belches smoke, and then like a soufflé, the whole thing collapses in on itself.

Joshua rips the Yukalut coverings off of his body, and wraps Alice in them; he opens the first-aid kit on his utility belt, and applies a coagulant to Alice's chest wound.

"Why are you doing this?" Miranda asks.

"Call in an evac," he says, as the cries of the tribe's women catch the bitter wind.

"When did our orders change?"

"Do as I say."

"We've already got ones like her for study."

Joshua grabs the phone out of her hand. "Radio One."

She grabs it back. "Don't you think I'm good enough?"

"Miranda..."

"I know I messed up on the ship. I'll do better."

"This isn't about you."

"Drowning Man, this is Radio One, come back, over."

"I can do this if you just let me," she says.

"I don't want you to — Miranda, please."

"This is what we do."

"You don't even know what we - " He catches himself at the last minute; always editing.

"What are you talking about?"

"Just do as I say."

"Why?"

"Don't ask why. I gave you an order."

Miranda jabs the receiver of her field phone to her ear. "Radio One, Radio One, this is Blue Room, over."

"Copy Blue Room, over."

"Radio One, request immediate evac from our GPS, over."

"Two to go, over."

"They gave us back some change, Radio One."

"Change? Over?"

"Copy that," she says, as Joshua holds Alice against him, rubs the sides of her chest to warm her heat.

"We are plus one. Over."

"I didn't think you two were gone long enough to have a baby, over?"

An embarrassed smile breaks on Miranda's lips. "Radio One, I'm going to tell your mother you said that, over."

"I don't have a mother, Blue Room."

"Copy that, Radio One. None of us do."

V

"Why didn't you call for reinforcements?"

Joshua shifts in his seat overlooking the arena floor, brings his arms closer in to his sides, conscious suddenly of how small the chair is, how close he is to Anaba Kin, his superior and director of all Special Operations at Division I. Anaba trains one eye on the incident report Joshua filed the night before and one on the unfolding situation below: agents lead a 9th century Viking warrior out into the middle of the narrow circle, ensconced deep inside the subterranean complex beneath the Long House, the Division's worldwide headquarters that runs over a mile beneath the bedrock of midtown Lenapolis. The spectators in the seats above and all around him — all students, subjugate agents under the age of ten — sit up and lean forward all at once, some coming to their feet for a better look. He finds it hard to distinguish the boys from the girls in their uniform fatigues and haircuts.

The few adults wear the cobalt long coats of the instructors. These agents devote their time and energy to the study of the Canon, and the teaching of the next class. Many never left the Long House, graduating directly from students to teachers and bypassing the usual domestic tour most agents are compelled to complete. Joshua did his part too, patrolling the streets, nursing the sick and elderly, maintaining the society's vast infrastructure, but his natural aptitude for difficult assignments made him the perfect candidate for solving the world's most persistent problem.

The Viking stands aghast as his escorts release him from his bonds, and then unceremoniously toss an iron sword and shield at his feet. They make a hasty retreat off the arena floor back to the gate they entered through. The Viking picks up the sword, lighter and of a different craft than his; he pulls at his ill-fitting, itchy clothes, approximations of the dress agent scholars have surmised his people wore. The students remain utterly silent, utterly rapt as the Viking staggers around in a circle around the arena. He rushes the gates. Made of titanium, they don't even budge; he scales the ten foot wall separating the floor from the stadium seating and brings his sword down on the unmoved girl sitting right in front of him.

The magnetic force field knocks him back down to the arena floor. In shock, he screams unintelligible obscenities at the crowd. The girl quietly takes notes.

"I was working an assignment," Joshua says, his voice frayed with fatigue. "I don't need reinforcements to bring in some girl, and if I do, I don't know why you brought me back."

Anaba looks sideways at Joshua, slumped in his chair, eyes bloodshot. "Didn't say you did."

"So?"

"I'm asking why you didn't call for them when you realized what it was you were dealing with."

"What was it I was dealing with?"

"Tell me again, why is this — Alice - still alive?"

"Why are these men still alive?"

Another gate opens, on the opposite side of the arena floor. Agents shove out another captive. The samurai arrived only days ago, swept off the killing fields in the middle of the defense of the islands from the invading Mongol Empire; the Division has intercepted five Echoes of this type, and their records on the samurai and his culture are satisfactory.

The situation confuses the samurai as much as it does the Viking, but he's more disciplined with his fear. The Viking has been here months, kept isolated since his capture in a cell even further below in the sub-levels of the building; Division linguists have decoded his language, harvested it for the knowledge he has of his era of history and now the Side-Time scholars have learned all they are going to from this man, so out he goes into the arena, in his faux animal skin and his manufactured chain-mail, for one last examination.

"You think Alice has information? About this Elizabeth? Oh, look at that. That's a pretty sword."

The samurai points his imitation katana at the Viking, in warning or invitation, no one can tell, and begins a slow circle around the outer edge of the arena, inexorably spiraling in toward the center. The Viking bashes his sword against his shield, makes several suggestions about the honor of the samurai's mother; he confuses him for the champion of those seated above him, but doesn't confuse what is happening. He knows from tales told by his elders the old Roman sport of gladiators, snatching men from all corners of the known world to fend against each other, against exotic beasts for their delight of the Roman people. That is what is happening to him: he has been kidnapped, not by Roman legions but some witchcraft, and made a slave to the passions of a people deprived of honor.

"The Kuzar must have believed Alice had some connection to Elizabeth. They took a huge risk in capturing her."

"Or they're just trolling for any Echo that shows up?"

"I don't know," Joshua says. "That's why she's here."

"Miranda's report," Anaba says. "You didn't think this Alice was worth bringing in alive until you found her in the Yukalut camp. At one point, you wanted to call in a strike."

The Viking and samurai clash swords. "Ooh, wow."

"The Kuzar had radiometers," Joshua says, rubbing his eyes. "They're looking for something. Someone. Anything Alice can tell us about their operation, or her connection, whatever it is, to Elizabeth can only help us."

"You were still going to call in a strike."

"I thought we could be walking into a hornet's nest."

"Did you see something in this place that changed your mind? Why did you destroy it? Not that I care about their little ice temple — well, actually I kind of do — Miranda said there were other Echoes inside. In the ice."

"That's why I destroyed it."

"That's why."

"Yes."

"You couldn't tell her that?"

"I'm the agent. She has to learn to follow my lead."

Anaba sighs, and trades the incident report for the small book in his lap. "This book. You were right to keep Alice alive. This Elizabeth. She's one, too. Obviously."

"Obviously," Joshua says.

"She must have arrived in the north, like Alice."

"What makes you say that?"

"You said you've seen incidents of this symbol up there before? This 'crucifix?'"

"Once or twice."

"Did you report those?"

"I'm sure I did."

"What if knowledge of this book is widespread in the north? This is our worst fear realized, Joshua. Think of the damage they could do if they — I can smell him up here, can you smell that? — what do you suppose that is?"

"I don't know."

"Anyways. We have to contain this somehow."

"Of course." *That's what I do. Contain. I am a container, of rebellion, sedition; secrets.*

"Did you ever work an Elizabeth?"

"They don't always have names."

"We'll pull the files," Anaba says.

"Of course."

"As much trouble as the book is, it does answer a lot of our questions about their early history."

"I don't know what interest it would be to the Kuzar," Joshua says. "Seems to have to do with the Jews."

"You read it?"

Joshua pauses. "I examined it."

Anaba lingers on Joshua, ignoring for the moment the eruption of gasps in the crowd, of blood on the arena floor. The samurai withdraws his sword from the Viking's chest and returns to a defensive stance; the Viking collapses to his knees, moaning, bloody hands held skyward. He prays for home, for *ragnarok*, for deliverance from the hell he has found.

He bleeds out. The samurai trains his eyes on the crowd. He runs at them, tries to escape as his opponent did but the force field repels him; it knocks him back to the arena floor, knocks him unconscious. Agents step onto the floor again and drag him away, back to a cell until his next examination.

"Well. That was disappointing," Anaba says, expecting more of a show from the vaunted Viking, suggested from other sources to be one of the fiercest and most feared warriors in all the history of the world he arrived from. Then again, he was just a man in coat of fake animal skin and chain mail, precisely the man that Anaba's forefathers pacified so easily centuries before as the founders of Canon spread out through the globe, bringing with them peace, health and most importantly, the Canon, to the disparate peoples of the world.

"It seems the Kuzar have every interest in the book."

"What do you mean?"

Anaba hedges. "This is a bit bigger than you know."

"It's just a book," Joshua says, laughing. "It's a bunch of nonsense if you ask me. God and angels, and whatever."

"It's not the idea of some supernatural mumbo-jumbo that keeps me awake at night, Joshua."

Anaba sits up on the edge of his seat, watches as agents drag away the body of the dead Viking, spreading a crimson trail across the marbled floor of the private arena.

"All the stuff at the beginning, gardens, apples, snakes, leave all that out — this book is a lineage. A legacy. A promise. They can only be echoes, Joshua. Not voices."

Joshua leans forward with him, lowers his voice as the hall empties of spectators. "Why? Why do they come? How?"

"We don't know."

"Is that true, or is my clearance just not high enough?"

Anaba smiles. "You want clearance?"

They exit the arena — passing a clutch of child agents on tour with a guide, explaining the honor of their being chosen, as the prophet M was chosen over a thousand years ago, to lift a savage and ignorant human race into peace and prosperity, sacrificing her desires for the good of all man - and take an elevator down ten more levels into the granite bedrock. The levels tick by on the monitor inside the elevator car, one by one until they reach their end — Sub Basement 3. The car keeps going. It stops finally; a soft electronic voice announces their location: "Department of Pneumaretics."

They exit out into a bunker like room dominated by a gently turning holographic globe of the world. Needles of light stick up out of the continents as if the earth were some kind of pincushion, tiny boxes of notes like the word balloons of Miranda's comics attached to each one. Joshua comes to the world, reads a note fixed to a position in the central region of the northern continent in the western hemisphere. *Alice*, it says. *Iowa, Carpenter. Circa 1986. United States, industrial superpower, former colony of England.* Three more Echoes have arrived since; agents track them right now.

The globe turns with his touch. The ice cap that dominates the northern hemisphere recedes, and the oceans rise. The land bridge connecting western Canon Major to Sabira disappears beneath the water. He scrolls across the burgeoning Ontarian Ocean, to the conjoined super-continent of Europa and Africa, watches as a minor sea develops in the middle of it. It replaces the entire northern half of the Saharan desert, which now occupies all of north Africa and southern Europa to the Rhine; as the waters rise, a peninsula the shape of a boot forms in lower Europa. The ancient scar of the Nile reopens, bleeds with water again and the inexplicable geography described in the book appears.

"I had my analyst up all night with this," Anaba says, tossing the book on a slender wood table as he walks past it, straight to the back of the room, and the chalkboard that spans the entire back wall. A timeline spans it one end to the other, marked every few inches or so with a critical piece of information gleaned from the brief, intense study of the book. Anaba unbuttons his overcoat and lays it on the back of a chair. He takes a piece of chalk in his hand.

"This 'Book of Common Prayer' comes from a place called England, what they call 'medieval' England, and for some reason, the language is somewhat similar to Canon."

"Except there's no Canon in their history."

"And no England in ours. The island it's supposed to be on is mostly under ice. Strange, yeah? Gets stranger. This English text is to do with the tribes of Israel."

Joshua joins Anaba at the chalkboard. The Jewish people disappeared with the Nile, as did many other peoples in that region when Canon engineers - in a clandestine bid to bring a perpetual source of power, water and food to the region - dammed the sea that separated Europa from Africa. They expected the Sahara to transform into the world's breadbasket; instead, the Sahara expanded. The people of the Mediterranean had power to light their homes but none to feed their families and as the climate changed, so did the attitude toward the Canon. The embryonic powers of the age — Rome, Greece, Carthage — saw the Canon dam as a means to cripple the Western world, forever, and with the tribes of Israel they united in an effort to destroy the dam. A brief, ugly war ended with the subjugation of the Greco-Roman provinces, and the Jewish tribes fleeing into the ever growing desert, never to be seen or heard from again.

"They didn't have it any better in the side-history," Anaba says. "But they did survive. They thrived even, from time to time. Sort of like flowers that die with the winter, I guess, but bloom with the spring."

"That's pretty."

"You think so? I thought that up before, during the display. Anyways, this gives us their entire history from this garden business to roughly a hundred years after the birth of Christ, which other sources indicate was the origin of their calendar. They split their history in two with him. Before, and after. Must have made an impression, him. So it goes with the Jews. Before him you got this 'old' testament, you got traditional Jewish people in and out of Israel waiting for their messiah, and after, you got the 'new' testament, and people who think he's already come. Their entire history hinges on this one man. And it all ends up in this England."

"England is this promised land they're looking for?"

"It would seem so. There's clearly some kind of division between the English Jew and others. The preface of the book goes on and on about the abolishment of certain ceremonies."

Joshua leans against the back of the chair. He gestures to a point on the timeline. "What's this?"

"Yeah. 'The Book of Joshua.' The sixth book of the older testament. Recounts the effort of Joshua, successor to Moses, to cross the river Jordan to the city of Jericho."

Joshua presses his thumb against the fishhook end of the J on the board, leaving it smudged.

"They besieged the city. Took it by force. Events or people move them out of the Promised Land, they come back. Flowers. Spring. With a vengeance, Joshua."

"You're afraid of people that no longer exist."

Anaba leaves the blackboard to his desk. "We evicted the Jews from Israel round about a thousand years ago, like the Romans did in their history — get this, the Romans were an *empire* over there — a fucking empire, man, how did they ever stay sober long enough for that, right? — anyways — it's not the Jews I'm afraid of. It's the idea, remember."

Anaba flips around the bulbous monitor of his computer. "This is fucking classified."

The screen projects a crude page from the web — its primary feature the image of a crown of thorns, the backdrop of passages from the book, set to the soundtrack of a very familiar voice to Joshua, crackling with static.

"My friends," a man's voice says, "Every day I hear in your voices despair. Hopelessness. I see it in your eyes. All of you feel you are alone, without tether, carried along by the rapids of this cruel Canon river. I once felt the same. What connection did I have to anyone? Any family? Any country? We are all of us strangers in a strange land, as we have been for centuries and I felt this same way you do until I found the book. And then I knew. We do have a country. A history. A destiny. I knew that we are all Elizabeth."

Anaba turns the recording off. "Recognize the voice?"

Joshua goes white. Of course he recognizes the voice. Michael. His father, his brother, his best friend — the man who made Joshua everything he is today — speaks from beyond the borders of the republic he swore to defend, over Kuzur radio frequencies. He speaks from beyond the grave.

"You said he died…"

"Of course I said he died. No one ever quits the agency. You get your discharge with your death certificate, man."

"He quit?"

"I had him in deep cover in the north. In Niurka. He lived with them, ate with them, acted like one of them for years and apparently he became one of them. It shouldn't come as any great shock, right? He was obsessed with them. I mean, he took his name - hell, he took yours - from archives on the lost tribes. And now here those names are again in this book… at least now I know what book he's talking about. This shit is all over Tangle. Every time we block it, they throw another page up. There's no locating the exact source."

"A year?"

"He was obsessed with pre-Canon cultures. He went on and on about this kind of thing. Lost histories."

"Maybe he wrote it."

"He's a traitor. Let's not give him too much credit."

Joshua leans against the desk, his legs, his hands numb. "I don't believe this..."

"You had better believe it," Anaba says. "Given the fact he authorized an Kuzar air ship to breach Canon air space to snatch Alice tells me two things: one, he doesn't need a radio to get his point across, and two, he doesn't know where Elizabeth is. He is leading naked revolt against the republic, all of it based entirely on a piece of gibberish written by a woman who may or may not even exist."

Joshua sifts through the stacks of books piled on Anaba's desk: *The Canon. The Lost Adventure of the Fourth Voyage. Pre-Canon Pacific History. Kuandra's Alephmen Anatomy and Engineering Pilot (Revised). The Path of M.*

"I still don't know why any of this matters to the Kuzar," he says. "Or Michael."

"The Kuzar have no origin. This book gives them one. The Jewish in the book wander and suffer but they get their promised land, Joshua. They get their England. And now their prophet is here, setting the Kuzar on fire with the idea they can have one, too. Imagine it. A Kuzar promised land."

Joshua looks at the blackboard, lined with a history that never happened, and at the computer, container of a voice he never thought he would hear again; he doesn't know what to think. He is not trained to think. Only to act.

"It's the idea we must fear, Joshua. An idea is like a virus. Once it becomes airborne... it's almost always fatal." He stands up, wipes the sweat from his upper lip. "That star. That fucking nova or whatever you call it. In Taurus."

"What does that have to do with anything?"

"There's a star in the book, naturally. It signals the birth of this Christ. Their messiah."

"You're paranoid," Joshua says, walking away from the blackboard. "Down here with your analysts and linguists, you read everything into nothing. You're paranoid, Anaba."

"I want this Elizabeth found. You eat, sleep and shit this until you find her, understand?"

Joshua rubs his eyes. "I understand."

"And I want her brought to me. No mitigation. I want all knowledge of this book expunged. If that means killing every last Kuzar that's put eyes on it, I don't care. I will not let this become a rallying point for any sedition against the republic. We are the one and only hope of the world. M gave to us peace and unity. Stability. Reason."

"I remember that part of my lessons."

"You're right about one thing, Joshua. Our enemy isn't the Kuzar, or even the Jews. Our enemy invades from another world. Another time. Their weapon is a virus of ideas. And there's no defense. No immunization. Our world is injured. It's porous. Weak. We cannot let it be invalid. *Invalid,* understand? This is our world, Joshua. Not theirs."

"You don't have to tell me."

"I didn't have to tell Michael."

"Just because he trained me doesn't mean I'm going to betray the agency like he has."

"Doesn't mean you won't."

"Paranoid."

"Get going. Bring me back our Elizabeth."

Joshua remains fixed between the door and the globe,

slowly turning, its face changing with every revolution.

"Why, Anaba? Do they come here?"

"I told you. We don't know."

Joshua looks at the board. The book filled in much of the first quarter of it, but serious gaps remain in the side-history of the world; the timeline ends in the 21st century. "You really don't?"

"I'd tell you," Anaba says. "If I knew."

"Right."

"You'd tell me. Wouldn't you?"

"Right," Joshua says, and leaves.

VI

Alice has never been to New York City. She only knows
it from the movies, but she knows enough of its geography to understand that the island flickering past outside the window of the rail car is Manhattan. The tongue
shape of the island is unmistakable, even if it seems a little broader, the rivers that border it more narrow; the
buildings denser, layered together, over another, centuries now of brick and steel and ruins in the empty spaces
between. Ruins of skyscrapers that fell into the scrap piles
of their successors. Their iron skeletons and calligraphic
skins stand naked under the gauzy swath of the winter sky,
the corpse ideas of the iconic city that Alice knew, realized best — best not the word, most terribly — in the spectacular steel-lattice air terminal that stands about where
the Empire State Building should. Airships launch every
few minutes from various docking prongs up and down
the spire, curling out of its sides like sconces.

Alice tries to lose herself in the grandeur of the Lenapolis skyline, in the music of the magnetic rail car she occupies
with Joshua and his little pit bull Miranda as it zips on an elevated line through buildings that open like the eyes of needles.
She tries, but she fails; the wonder of the world outside only
reminds her that something terrible has happened to her, is
happening (*This is happening*) and this is not a dream. And she is
not going home. She knows that now.

"Is this like a train, a car or what?" she says, clutching
at the belt of her wrap coat. It feels spray-painted on. They exchanged her Yukalut wrappings at the Long House for a modest
blouse and slacks, boots up to her knees.

"What," Joshua says, wiggling out of his overcoat into a
plain white dress shirt and dark suit jacket he gleaned from the
agency outfit surplus — a costume gallery stocked for any possible undercover mission an agent might find themselves in.

"It doesn't have any wheels."

"It's magnetic."

"Oh. Where are we going?"

"To find Elizabeth," Joshua says.

"But I've told you a million times. I don't know anything
about her. If I did, I'd tell you, I swear to God."

Joshua doesn't answer. He keeps his eyes straight ahead
at the procession of buildings rising and falling outside.

Centuries of skyscrapers blur together into turquoise
and violet and jade streams, Picasso painting with his pen, every
so often writing the letter M; it is everywhere in the city. Every
few minutes or so, the neon billboards of the city go blank, and
flash with bright, simple warnings: DON'T LET AN ECHO
DISTRACT YOU – REPORT A SIGHTING. EYES OPEN.
SOMEONE LISTENED, which accompanies a crude depic-
tion of a nude man sitting at a dinner table, the bodies of a

family dead and bloody on the floor about him. Eventually all the screens cycle to the image of a woman, eyes wrapped in a scarlet blindfold, bleeds into the skyscraping canvases all along the avenues. Her voice promises all those in reach of it that "You are watched." Where plasma doesn't project the blind woman, sunken relieves cut in stone do; in nearly every image she alternately ponders the world, held like a pebble in her hand, or the sky behind her, the stars all sparkling eyes.

"Who is she?" Alice asks.

"M brought reason to the world," Joshua says. "Peace."

"From where?"

It's the most famous story in the world: M, the matriarch of Canon, wandered into the Wrinkle Lakes region just north of Lenapolis over 1300 years ago, a refugee from a far-away country. The only detail she offered of her homeland — nameless, like her — was that a self-induced calamity destroyed it. What she did offer made any detail of her origin trivial; she possessed knowledge god-like to the indigenous population, and in a generation they went from hunters and farmers to stone masons; coal smiths; engineers.

The massive stone tributes her discoverers erected for her on the bluffs overlooking Keuka Lake — constructed with precision and skill to then only available across the ocean in Giza — suggest she was blind; one of them features a very geometrical M with deep, empty sockets, holding in each hand one of her eyes. Joshua prefers to think she chose her sightlessness. It fits more with her vision of the world.

Whoever she was — wherever she might have come from - M became the architect of one world, and the destroyer of others. She erased the nascent traditions of her new followers as cleanly as hers had been; she founded a new order, a new world, and set about killing the old one in the crib. Her nation swept out from beyond its borders, across the seas, into the villages and city-states of northern Europa, and then like wildfire down to the Mediterranean, where the locus of the old world was wrenched out of the new like a bad tooth. Her world still faced a daily insurgency from the past in the form of each new Echo; and because she would not always be with them, M chose from her new followers the progenitors of what is today Division I, tasked with making sure Echoes never became more than ghosts; *geists; gei.*

"It doesn't matter," Joshua says.

"Where am I?" she says. "What's happened?"

"Where you are doesn't matter. How you got here doesn't either. What matters is we find Elizabeth."

"Why?"

"Because it's the only thing keeping you alive."

"Are you going to kill me when you're done?"

"Yes," Miranda says, browsing her comic.

"Help us," Joshua quickly says, "and we'll see."

"I'll help you," Alice says, tears burning as they fall down her ice-scorched cheeks. "I just don't know how."

"Makes two of us," Miranda says.

"This is like the fucking *Twilight Zone* or something."

"What's that?" Joshua asks.

"Never mind." Alice rubs the small crater in her chest where the bullet penetrated on its way through her lung.

Joshua watches her in the rearview. "Burns."

"You've been shot?"

"Once or twice."

"Are you like a soldier or something?"

"Something."

"My brother was in the Army."

"What happened to him?"

"He disappeared, too."

For a long time, Alice thought they just overlooked him. The jungles absorbed so many young men, hundreds every year; she knew they had to be somewhere. Even after the war ended, even after the country turned its attention elsewhere, she saw Danny wandering around the wet, humid jungle in his fatigues, in an amnesic daze. The concussive force of the bomb that killed him — that they said killed him, nothing was ever found — bounced him off a tree. When he woke up, he forgot his name, which is why he didn't go back to his platoon. He walked through the jungle to the sea. He found a small fishing village and they gave him work on a boat. That's what he's doing, she told her father, a year after. Fishing. She even suggested they call the Navy to have them inspect small boats off the coast of Vietnam or Cambodia, just in case.

He slapped her. Alice didn't say any more about Danny fishing after that. They never talked about him at all again. She knows her mother will likely devote years to these kinds of fantasies about her, the last years of her life in self-delusion, the only thing that keeps her alive the prospect of Danny or Alice or both now, showing up on the front porch as young and perfect as they were on the days they left.

"Do you think he could have come here? My brother?"

"I don't know."

"How many are there like me?"

"Why are you talking to it, Joshua?" Miranda says, coming out of her immersion in Samaire at the end of a chapter.

"I'm not an it," Alice says.

"No, you're bad marksmanship."

"Maybe that gun's too heavy for a little girl like you."

"Shut your mouth."

"You need a lesson in manners, Carrie."

"My name isn't Carrie and you're not my mother, so."

"You even have a mother?"

"What are we even doing with it, Joshua?"

"We're looking for the woman that wrote the book."

"And how does she help us with that? She hasn't given us a single lead to go on and besides, Elizabeth's radiation trail has got to be ice cold by now–"

"We have our orders," Joshua says.

Miranda peevishly goes back to the comic. They travel another mile on the line into the clustered epicenter of the city, until they switch tracks to the public rail and enter the elevated terminal at the New Corinthian Theater, blooming out of a spire in the shadow of the tallest pastel peaks. Joshua remains in his seat, staring straight ahead.

"What are we doing here?" Miranda asks.

"Stay in the car. I'll be back." He doesn't move.

"Joshua?"

"Both of you stay put."

"Don't leave me with her," Alice says.

"I'll be right back."

Joshua leaves the car and drifts up the stairs from the platform to the grand theater's main lobby, hands sweating, heart racing. He fiddles with the collar of his shirt, the fit of his jacket; he hardly ever wears civilian clothes. The suit jacket, the pressed slacks and shined shoes feel as alien to him as the people do. He's never felt at home, not even among his comrades. He spent ten years at the Long House feeling like a out-of-place piece of furniture and then eight years with Michael, carried around like a piece of equipment and ever since no one has ever know where to put him, what to do with him, least of all himself. *I am not even my own man.*

A majestic relief in stucco spans the circumference of

the domed lobby, a jar barely containing the hum of anticipation for the evening's debut performance of *Amleth, or The Mad Prince*. This is her fourth production, the debut of the season; he sees her picture routinely in the society pages of the Transmission, often on the arm of a different suitor each time. Her hair is most always short, save for a cleft of aubergine that frames the right side of her face; she seems awkward in some of the pictures, tall, thin, dressed in form-hugging vest-jackets and slacks among heaps of women in billowing evening gowns and skyscraping headdresses.

He follows the music of gossip through the lobby toward the grand lounge bar that spans the outside of the theater from entry to entry, until her voice finally begins to join the symphony, its notes equally brass and bombastic, soft and melodic; in it he hears the pride and confidence of her people, extinguished in this world; the refinement of her education, she herself a walking book, a living history of the world Anaba fears so much. Joshua hears the gravity of that world, of everything it ever set on her shoulders. She carried more than her reedy frame suggests and it's there, if you listen, in the voice, in the amber eyes, like a hawk's.

"Bess," the old man says, roping his arm around her waist, slipping his hand over her ass. "C'mon, Bess."

She smiles, gamely, even as she removes his hand. "If you could deliver such a performance as promised tonight..."

"My reputation precedes me?"

"In advance, sir. Your scouts betray your position. I should think after the show you will be tired and in need of much rest before any further campaigning, and I suggest-"

"You do this every time I'm in town," he says, grabbing the slack of the belt of her waistcoat, pulling her close.

"-I suggest a more subtle strategy in the future."

She slips free again. She smooths out the wrinkles in her vest, in her smile and goes on as if nothing has happened.

"You promised."

"A wise woman never makes promises."

"Don't I take good care of you?"

"You know I adore you, Donava."

"Then come back to the hotel with me after the show."

"We shall see our mood after the performance. From the rehearsals I fear it shall be quite — pessimistic..."

The crowd parts and at the sight of him the color leaves her face. So does all the tension in her muscles; her eyes sink, her cheeks, her lips, she puddles before him; utter resignation overcomes her. She expected this, even as the years flitted away like leaves on the fall breeze that lives in this city all year round, even as he receded farther and farther into her memory. She knew; she knew he would come back, and finish the job he started nine years ago.

"My lord," she says, the quiver in her voice barely perceptible, "you are quite underdressed for the occasion."

"We're not staying," Joshua says.

"Excuse me," Donava says, stepping in between them. "Hi, there. Donava Sah. She's with me."

"Walk away."

"Listen here, buddy. Maybe you don't know who I am."

"Donava Sah. I know where you live."

Donava goes pale. "Who are you?"

"Come with me," Joshua says to her. "Now."

He puts his hand firmly on her arm and she can do nothing but follow, her limp arm held out like the handle of a tea cup as he leads across the lobby into a small, overstuffed coat room. He expels the attendant and then locks the door. She yanks her arm out of his grip. "You take great liberty with my person, sir."

"You told me your name was Bess."

"Bess Rose."

"You seem to have done well for yourself, 'Bess.'"

"One finds one's level," she says. "You told me I would never see you again, Joshua."

"You told me you'd never have to," Joshua says. "You promised me you would never make so much as a single peep."

"A single peep would be a Herculean task for even the most modest of sparrows, my lord, but I have kept my word and my anonymity. You cannot claim otherwise."

He takes the book from his inside coat pocket and throws it at her. "I don't think so."

Elizabeth opens the pages of the book, instantly wet and running ink. "Where... where did you find this?"

"That's your signature on the front, right? Elizabeth?"

"I was not going to give you my name, Joshua..."

"How many copies are there?"

"I did not make this."

"You're lying."

"I did not create this, Joshua. And I have made no copies, as you say. I have never seen this before."

"You carved these same words on the wall of that cave. You wrote it down on their parchment."

Elizabeth touches her face, the scars the ice left in her skin. "This was an exercise in sanity, Joshua..."

"There wasn't enough there for all this. You wrote it all out, after. After I left you here and you promised me you would never stick your head up out of the ground, you wrote this thing down and you gave it to someone."

"No, I swear."

"You wrote it, like one of your plays. For the stage."

"No... no. I... I wrote it down. In the cave. All of it. He kept bringing me parchment."

"Who did?"

"I had to do it, you understand. I was torn from my world, Joshua. My faith and understanding in all things, I had to find them. This was the only way I knew how."

Her formal education as a young girl consisted of such exercises, handwriting essays and sometimes entire short books from the Latin or Greek and then after Grindal let her fiddle with something else for a couple of weeks, back again, from memory, exactly as it was in the original. Her first such effort was at the age of 11, a New Year's gift for her step-mother Catherine, *The Mirior or Glasse of the Synneful Soul.* She bound the manuscript the same as she did her copy of the Bible, in canvas; embroidered the cover in silk stitch, a heartsease in each corner. By the time she had ended her education, quoted the Bible with a priest's ease. She recited its prayers as she awaited potential execution in the Tower, as she walked toward her destiny in Westminster Abbey, the day of her coronation, and as a strange light fell over London on a tepid spring day three years into her reign, obliviating the spires and steeples.

"It has been my companion through all the upheavals and unforeseen shifts in my life... I latched onto every proverb and verse for ballast. I intended nothing more."

She frowns at the way the penmanship deteriorates at the end of each chapter, generally the end also of those exorbitantly long sessions, ten, twelve hours of nothing but pen, paper and memory; her hands ache just thinking about it.

"There were only a couple pages in the cave..."

"You went back?"

"Who gave you the parchment – the shaman..."

Elizabeth issues a long sigh, and sits on the attendant's

stool. The memories of those first days here in this other world
— the sights, the smells — flood back into her mind. She spent
weeks in that camp, enchanting the Yukalut enough with her
beauty and her words to forestall their entombing her in their
temple of ice; she tried to escape, and they flogged her with
twisted strands of seal skin braided with polar bear teeth. They
mummified her in the ice, but the shaman, beset with a vision he could not and never did explain to her, excavated her
before she froze to death. He brought her food and water; he
told her all the stories of his people, he told her of the vision
he had when she arrived, one that convinced him she must live,
and for days and nights Elizabeth listened. When he slept, she
carved the stories of her people into the ice. She wrote them in
her own blood and vomit on the sheets of seal skin he used to
transcribe his visions.

And then Joshua came, a boy then. Now, he looks like
the withered, blackened ruins of something stronger; a scar
travels from his lower lip under his chin, another from his
right temple up into his hair, black, shrapnel shot with gray.
The eyes, shot through with carbuncle and shale.

"Why didn't you take the book with you?" he says.

"I do not recall you giving me the option of packing
first," she says.

He came, gun in hand, to kill her as he had done Alice
and countless others before. She squatted in the corner of her
tiny cave, chiseling the morning prayer, and he put the muzzle
of his gun to the back of her head. He can't fault Elizabeth for
his hesitation; it existed before her and it's the only reason she's
alive today. He lingered on his decision long enough for her to
turn around, and for him to see her face. No one taught him
about love at the Long House, not his teachers, the staid books
in the library, the girls he trained with, neutered of impulse as

he was. When love finally found Joshua in the Yukalut cave, its education of him was instantaneous, and complete.

He made himself forget her, as he forgets everything else but Elizabeth resisted oblivion, as she has always done and she lived in his memory, a fragment, a shard, a flicker and now here he stands, face to face with his treachery, hand in hand with Michael's. *I am not my own man.* How did the book get into the hands of the Kuzar? Joshua will never know; the shaman died in the explosion that brought down the temple.

"There are copies of this circulating in the north. They are looking for people like you. They're looking for *you.*"

"Who looks for me?"

"Aren't you listening?"

"You are very hard not to hear sir," she says, opening the pages of the book, "but hard to understand. Speak plain."

"The Kuzar. Northern insurgents."

"I have not read of such things in the transmission."

"There's a lot they don't cover."

He bends over, places his hands on his knees like someone who has been running for miles.

"You come as a shock to me, sir. As you always must. I am quite upset. I had forgotten this."

"How could you forget?"

She shakes her head; she's forgotten even that. "I have come to accept my circumstances, impossible as they are. I have forgotten much, even my most brazen hopes."

"You don't forget things like this."

"You do if you mean to," she says, closing the book, holding it to her heart. "I have tried so very hard to forget that world. These words. What other recourse did I have? I had to put the past aside. The solace it gave me carried me only so far. I had to acclimatize myself to this new world somehow. A crutch can be both a help and a hindrance, you must surely know. I have made a new life for myself..."

Applause erupts from inside the theater as the curtain rises on *Amleth*. Elizabeth blinks tears, the totality of what she has accomplished unrealized until she just gave voice to it. "The years passed, and so did the hope of my ever... why do I explain. You cannot possibly understand."

"Why can't I understand?"

"Do not insult my intelligence, sir. I know well the circumstances of your... *club*, and you did not have to choose to relinquish your identity. There are not words enough in expression to serve my sorrow and here you are, professing that you understand? Tell me, sir. Tell me from where you came from. Who were your parents, then?"

"I don't — I never knew them."

"From what line are you? What tradition?"

"It's irrelevant," he says.

"Then what of your history with the agency? Tell me of it. Tell me of your education and your teachers. Your comrades, you must have had many among your campaigns."

"That's classified."

"Yes. They made that cut for you clean as the head from the block. No history. No identity. You do not possess even the compulsion to yearn for them, so how would you, exactly, understand what it is I have done, or that I may feel?"

"Maybe I don't, then," he says.

"No, you do not. Are you going to kill me, Joshua?"

"I'm supposed to bring you in."

"You will have as much to explain as I."

"Bargaining. Again."

"I fear neither death nor my enemies."

"The theater is the perfect place for you," he says. "You're very dramatic, you know that?"

"I am a Tudor, sir. The dramatic is in my blood."

He can't bring her in; then he'd have to explain why he didn't in the first place, nine years ago. He can't kill her. He couldn't then, and he can't now. He leans into the mass of coats and jackets along the wall without realizing it is a rack; he sinks into the emblems and styles of fashion and society, pulls on the arm of one coat to keep from falling any further into the void and the coat comes off its hanger and he slips. He falls to the floor on his ass, under an avalanche of coats, of varied lives he can only imagine.

He throws the tangle of coats from on top of him as fast he can, thinking she will use the opportunity to slip out of the room but there she is, kneeling before him.

"You never wear a dress," he says. "To a show."

"These frocks of yours are not fit for princes."

Prince. He remembers the word from his studies. A son to a king, a male heir to the throne of the embryonic fiefdoms that existed before Canon philosophy made the ideas of divine right and monarchy obsolete. That is why Anaba fears the book so much, because it has a prince, a king, a kingdom for the people of the world to inherit. Divine right perished with the rise of the republic; so did ideas such as legacy and tradition, whether they were personal, familial, or national. In Canon power belongs to everyone and no one; there is no need, no desire, no want for saviors or heroes or miracles, for tradition or faith beyond the Canon; for fairy tales.

"You have been spying on me," she says, removing the last slack arm of a coat from off his head.

"Keeping tabs."

Elizabeth caresses his hair back into the place, brushes the scar across his chin.

"You come back from the hunt, scarred like an old hound. Such a young face... such an old soul. How many more of me have you encountered, Joshua? How many of them did you spare?"

He says nothing.

"Or am I the only one to inspire such mercy in you? Somehow, I doubt it. And me, jealous."

"You have to come with me," he says.

"They will kill me in the end, so you may as well now."

"I'm not going to kill you, Elizabeth. But they will. You know they will. It's not just me looking for you."

"Where do I go, then?"

"Away. I have to send you away again."

Elizabeth puts her hands to the sides of her neck. "No, I am not well for travel. I feel warm... not myself."

"You're fine."

"I must return to my apartment first and pack. I will need to supply myself for this journey-"

"I'll buy you new clothes," he says.

She has put many men to many flights of fancy, but this one she thinks has a death wish. "I have made my life here."

"I'll get you a new one."

"You cannot just... walk into my life after nine years and make such demands of me as these. You are not my keeper."

"I am," he says. "I've kept you alive for those nine years and if you want to live — you want to live, don't you?"

"Yes."

"Then you'll do as I say."

Elizabeth clutches the book to her heart, finds that center of herself that never falters, no matter the trials and tribulations of the tempest that has been her life from birth.

"What will I be now? Who shall I become?"

"I'll leave that to you."

"And what of you?" she says.

He stands up out of the mess of coats. "What of me?"

She touches her hand to his cheek.

"You compromise yourself for my benefit. You compromise the oaths you took. Your own life, I do not understand."

He doesn't, either. He never has.

"We have to go. If the agency doesn't find you, the rebels will. I can't protect you from both of them."

"My life must always be plots..."

He takes her hand in his. "Come with me."

"They will put you to the axe for this, Joshua."

"I think it'll be more like a firing squad."

"Where shall we go? There is nowhere on earth beyond the eye of your organization."

"No, nowhere on earth."

Fear and wonder collide on her face. "We cannot just flit away from the surface of the earth unseen."

"I didn't exactly plan any of this."

"Sleight of hand is one of the most essential tools in any dramatist's arsenal," Elizabeth says, and opens her small pocket purse. She places her mobile phone to her ear, her eyes glassing as a voice comes on the line.

"Henry? Henry, it is Bess," she says, a smile cracking on her lips, loosening her tears. "Yes, yes, it goes very well. Henry, I need you to do something for me. I need for you to contact Meeley. Tonight, at once. For how many?"

She looks to Joshua. He holds up four fingers, to her surprise and disappointment.

"Four. Yes, I know. Tell her I will double her usual fee. Good. And Henry? Henry, please see the dogs are fed, will you? I may not be back. Until late. No, there is nothing else.

That will be all for you, Henry. Thank you."

She drops the device back in her purse. "Four?"

"Who's Meeley?"

"We need to be at the Exchange in half an hour."

VII

Outside the theater, lights atop the lamp-like pedestals on the street corner, on every corner, flash madly, as do the holographic skins of the neighboring buildings.

ECHO PROTOCOLS IN EFFECT. EYES OPEN, EARS COVERED.

"What is this?" Elizabeth says.

Joshua rushes to the rail car, finds it empty. "Where is she... where did she go?"

Miranda comes around the corner, dragging Alice along with her. "She ran out of the car."

"I told you to stay put," Joshua says.

"Sorry... I just — what did I do?"

Joshua goes to the pedestal, opens an access panel in its base and deactivates the cluster of hyper-sensitive radiometers nested in its crown. The flashing light atop it dims, and the manic screens of the buildings go blank.

"We've got it taken care of," Joshua says to a startled

THE BOOK OF ELIZABETH

bystander. "Thank you for remaining calm."

Joshua ushers everyone back into the rail car and speeds away back on to the intercity rail even as Elizabeth negotiates the cramped space inside with Alice and Miranda.

"You should have stayed in the car," he says. "That alert went straight to the Long House."

"They all do," Miranda says. "Who the hell is this?"

"This is Bess. Bess, this is Miranda. And Alice."

"Accomplices," Elizabeth says. "How delightful."

"You're English," Alice says, to which Elizabeth smiles with guarded appreciation.

"Take the wheel for a second," Joshua says to Miranda, and takes a small syringe from his utility belt. He reaches into the back seat and pokes Alice firmly on her shoulder.

"Ow! What the hell, man?"

"This will muzzle you for a while," Joshua says, chiding himself for not having done this before they left the Long House. Gamma rays suffuse Echoes at the time of transfer; while it's only on the level of typical background radiation, Division I developed and installed extremely sensitive equipment in virtually every corner of the world.

"What's the big deal? They know we have her," Miranda says, sliding back over to the passenger seat.

"That reminds me," he says. "It's time for your pills."

"Oh yeah," she says, and takes them from the tiny box on her utility belt. She swallows both without water.

"And what ails you, my dear?" Elizabeth asks.

"Who is she, Joshua? What is she doing here?"

"She's coming with us."

"Coming with us where? Why?"

"Orders," he says and Alice knows now that 'orders' is the excuse Joshua makes for any and everything he does not

86

want to discuss. She knows from the nervous way he keeps glancing in the rearview at the English-accented woman beside her, from the nervous, possessive way Bess palms the book, not quite the Bible but the Book of Common Prayer of the Church of England, that they are not looking for Elizabeth anymore. She glances at Joshua, and so much of the fear that has hardened within her since her arrival evaporates into hope.

"Does she not know, Joshua?" Elizabeth says.

"Know what?" Miranda asks. "What don't I know?"

Joshua looks back at Elizabeth. "You keep quiet."

Elizabeth's eyes wax at his hubris — though she can't fault for him for not knowing his place — as much they do at his dilemma. He has told the child, his partner, nothing.

"Miranda, these orders are need to know only. You know how it goes sometimes. You just have to trust me, buddy."

Miranda crosses her arms fiercely across her chest, and aims her angry pout directly at Joshua, who wilts under it as a flower would a lamp; he can't go back. He'll have to take Miranda with them, or — if only someone else had responded to Alice. Then he'd never know; no one would ever have known.

"And you?" Elizabeth says to Alice. "Are you following orders as well, or are you merely along for the ride?"

"I'm Alice," she says. "From Iowa."

"I am not familiar, my dear."

"So where are we going, anyway?" Miranda says.

"Clockwork," Joshua says.

"Back to Mars?"

Alice vaults up between the two front seats. "Mars? We're going to Mars? The planet? We can do that?"

"Elizabeth is on Mars?" Miranda says.

"It is where she will be," Elizabeth says with a resigned sigh. She rubs her neck again; she can feel it swelling, feel the ache in her throat. "Alas, I am finally removed from thy world, Lord. Though I fear not into your Heavenly embrace."

"Why do you talk so funny? Are you one of them, too?"

"Miranda. She has information."

"You've been to Mars?" Alice says. "For real? No way. So? What's it really like?"

Joshua guides the car uptown, toward the titanic mooring mast in the city center. "Cold. Just like here."

"Elizabeth is on Mars?" Miranda asks again. He says nothing. "The rebels would know, wouldn't they?"

"These rebels are on Mars?" Alice asks. "I thought they were Eskimos or something? From the north, you said?"

"It's a long story," he says. "Canon influence — agency influence — isn't what it is here."

"So it would be safer there," Alice says, looking into the rear view mirror. "For someone like Elizabeth."

Joshua looks into the mirror, into her eyes. "Yes. It would be safer. For someone like Elizabeth."

"She could have been hiding there years," Miranda says.

"She could have."

"You think they show up on Mars, too? The Echoes? Or just here? What if they showed up out in outer space?" She laughs. "All naked and stuff. One minute you're doing whatever and then the next you're a popsicle."

"I don't know if they do, buddy."

"Would you suffocate or freeze first?"

"I don't know."

"This Elizabeth chick must be pretty sharp to give us the slip. She has to be getting help from someone."

"She has to be," Elizabeth says.

Alice holds her hands to her head. "We're really going to Mars? Don't fuck with me. You have no idea what a big deal this is to me. You're not fucking with me, are you?"

Joshua draws in a deep breath, leans back in his seat. "I am not fucking with you, Alice."

The car rushes into the canyon of chrome towers that gleam a strange electric pink, their curving lines reflecting their own light, reflected again off the drowsy clouds. Passenger airships three times the size of the Kuzar air ship appear in and out of them every few minutes, like flying whales in a sea of cotton candy; Alice watches one trail away into the east, and wonders if Iowa is out there somewhere west, even if slightly askew. Of course it isn't; Iowa isn't some place these machines fly over. Iowa doesn't exist.

They arrive at the Transportation Exchange. The cabin of the rail car falls into shadow as it passes under the steel girders of the eastern pylon, one of four supporting the mooring tower. Inside it, lights glitter like diamonds sparkling in the walls of a mine, deep in the earth. Elizabeth looks up through the web of light and steel, the peak of the tower dissolving into the clouds and her mind drifts to scripture as it so often does; *Then they said, 'Come, let us build ourselves a city, and a tower with its top in the heavens, and let us make a name for ourselves; otherwise we shall be scattered abroad upon the face of the whole earth.'* Overhead, beyond the steel calligraphy, beyond the scatter of light, the oval shapes of airships great and small dock and undock, arriving and departing to and from the great cities of the world, the many varied worlds of the Lord.

"We're going to Mars in a blimp?" Alice says. "You have blimps that can do that?"

Joshua shrugs, leans against the glass wall of the elevator car, not impressed in the least at the harried nimiety outside as Alice is, as even Miranda still is. He looks across the car at Elizabeth, who looks at nothing.

"I can't believe this," Alice says. "There's no fucking way, this is a dream or something. It has to be."

"It is far from a dream," Elizabeth offers, her eyes closed now. "It is a nightmare of wish fulfillment and wonders, beneath which lie the traps and snares of all our most personal desires. Is that not right, Joshua?"

He says nothing.

"Is this the future?" Alice says, returning to her breathless gaze at the circus of activity outside. "Do you guys have time travel? Can you take me back?"

"No, no, and no," Miranda says.

"How do you know, though?"

"It's a one way trip."

"And that's what you people do," Alice says, feeling her heart skip. "You kill us, so no one ever finds out."

"It's what we usually do," Miranda says.

"I want to go home."

Alice turns away from the others, to hide her tears. Elizabeth gently places a sympathetic hand on her shoulder. The longing for home, the decapitating shock of being ripped from her world and left naked and alone in the next have never really left her; they've only become less heavy. Elizabeth carries nothing that doesn't serve her. Fear, doubt, sickness for home - she left them on the side of the road as unceremoniously as she did her faith. She focuses instead on the positive. In most every way, this world stacks up better against the one she left, beginning with its freedom from all the diseases that dogged hers. The war. The hunger. The human strife that dominated the history of her world from its very beginning. The indoor plumbing can't be overlooked, either. Yet what this world makes up for in the basics it lacks in the details; Canon lacks charm. Soul, she would say. It lacks England. Christ. It lacks a sense of struggle; achievement. The great ideas, the great works and the great moments in the history of this world did not come with the human suffering they did in hers. Blood did not slick the path to progress. Canon came ready-made. Pre-fab. And still, it came with freedoms she would never have imagined, not just for everyday people, but for herself.

She smooths her hair back behind her ear, and then holsters both her hands in the pockets of her slacks. She stands at the window with Alice, gawking open-mouthed at the menagerie of ways out - only the one road out of town in Carpenter - and Elizabeth smiles. She belabors her dismay with Joshua, and this is no easy thing, walking away from a life she has diligently cultivated over nine years; but Elizabeth has spent most of her life moving from one situation to the next. From before she can remember, she passed from the care of nurses, ladies-in-waiting, governesses; she moved from the house of her baby brother Edward to her step-mother Catherine Parr's, and for a time after the death of her father the King, the house of Parr and her new husband, Thomas Seymour; after the death of her brother she moved again, this time from Hatfield House to the Tower of London, always a new house, always a new role for her to play: princess to prisoner, sister to usurper, bastard to heir.

She did not expect her reign as queen of England to last either, with so many plots at home and abroad to either marry or kill her, but she did not expect to leave it in this fashion, whatever fashion this is; what happened to her, to Alice, remains beyond her understanding. But she survives, as she always does, as she will now, as Bess, on Earth or Mars.

The elevator continues up through the mile-high neck of the Exchange. Joshua finds the wait excruciating. The silence is pregnant; it wants for something to fill it, but more words are the last thing he wants. He wants to get to Mars with as little said as possible. He wants to drop Alice and Elizabeth in Clockwork, into their new lives, and get back — he can never come back. He taps his fingers against his elbows, a hollow sound like someone tap-tapping their straw against their cup. He looks around the car, smaller by the minute and Miranda is sitting on the floor, reading her comic, unbothered; Alice passes the time staring; Elizabeth does not look. She does not move. Elizabeth stands utterly still, eyes down, hands clasped, monkish and still.

She is the ocean, calm on her surface but deep, turbulent underneath, and more turbulent still the farther you go. The darker. Colder. The pressure intensifies. Crushes everything. What is inside her. What does she keep, what does she know; to write a book of that length, of that much complexity from memory and then to claim to merely forget it; what other treasures and stores of knowledge does she possess? Elizabeth is nothing but secrets. He could tell her anything. Everything. She would never betray him. She would not even remember herself. His story would only become part of the vastness within her, the unknowable beauty. And she is beautiful, strangely; her face. She has the most unique face he has ever seen, he can't stop looking at it. The nose is long and thin, like the rest of her, the eyes deep and piercing; he has never found any woman attractive, but Elizabeth confuses him. She has since the moment they met.

Elizabeth opens her eyes and he shifts his gaze, down toward the floor, and Miranda looks back up at him, confused, her comic forgotten. He rubs his eyes, looks away.

The car finally runs out its string and the doors open onto a windswept catwalk. A small, squat air ship, its gondola situated atop the hull like a conning tower, gently drifts into position; the docking clamps lock and the very tip of the air ship's nose cone opens out into a hatch.

"We're going to Mars in this thing?" Alice says.

A lithe woman in an aged leather jacket and leather skull cap, the two halves of the chin straps hanging down the sides of her face like rabbit ears, crawls out of the hatch and eases down onto the catwalk. They have a look, agents; no matter what clothes they disguise themselves in. It's a look they share with soldiers, nurses; a look of frayed fatigue.

"This some kind of trap?" she says.

Elizabeth steps forward. "We have not been properly introduced, Meeley. I am Bess."

"Nice to meet you, Bess."

"I apologize for the short notice, and for any confusion. Our circumstances are quite... sudden."

Meeley lifts her goggles from her eyes and removes her gloves, one finger at a time.

"Stands to reason. Henry said I'd be taking four this time. Didn't say one of them was going to be you."

"Henry is not aware I am one of your passengers."

"What's with the Eyes?"

"I have agreed to double your fee."

"You may want to triple it," Meeley says. "Especially considering that this is lining up to be my last run for you."

"Whatever you require."

"I don't even want to know. Everyone, get on. We've got ten minutes to make rendezvous with the air ship tender."

"The appropriate funds will be remitted to your account once your passengers have been safely conducted to Mars, as per our custom," Elizabeth says.

"So long as it's good when I get back."

"Custom?" Joshua says to Elizabeth.

"And what shall your fee be?"

"An agent can't be bought."

"With money, perhaps."

Joshua stows the natural impulse to question who Meeley is, what kinds of runs she makes for 'Bess' — he's pretty sure he knows — but Miranda can't hold back any longer.

"These people are all Echoes," she says.

"Let's go," Joshua says.

"But they're smuggling Echoes to Mars."

"And maybe they did Elizabeth."

"So we're going to report them after we find her?"

"This is where I get off," Meeley says.

"No," Joshua says. "There's no problem. No one's reporting anything. No one's getting arrested."

"What?" Miranda shrieks.

"I have your word on that?" Meeley asks.

"If I wanted you in custody, you would be."

"But Joshua!"

"We have our orders."

"You have to tell me!"

"I can't, buddy."

"Don't you trust me?"

"Buddy," he says, and puts a tremorous hand to her cheek. Miranda winces; something is wrong. It's out of character for him. Protocol. Something is very wrong with all of this.

A man in a tattered and grimed jumpsuit steps out of the nose cone hatch. The strong wind on the landing platform whips what remains of his white hair up into bands of cirrus.

"Tell them to find some other way," he says.

"William," Meeley says, in warning.

He continues down the steps onto the platform. "You can't let them on board. You can't trust them!"

"Go back inside and finish the launch prep."

He looks at Alice; too young. Elizabeth is too different, alien in the same way Meeley and the other crewmembers are. The other two though, the man and that mouthy little girl, they look just like the agents that showed up at his door a week after he and his wife came home from the hospital, the two that conscripted their first and only daughter. They had named her Ophelia; she'd be 35 now.

"They're thieves," he says. "Thieves and butchers."

"I'd keep your mouth shut if I were you," Miranda says. "You're a traitor providing aid and comfort to the enemy."

"Miranda," Joshua says.

William laughs. "Miranda. That's not your real name is it? Bet you don't even know what it is–"

Miranda grabs his arm, twists it behind him and drives his elbow into his back until he's on the platform, screaming.

"My name is Miranda!" William cries out in pain. "You hear me? You hear me, old man? I know my name!"

"Miranda, stop!"

"You're under arrest," she says, "for sedition."

Joshua grabs her away. "I said stop!"

She spins away from William on the whirlwind of emotion swirling inside her; the anger chases the tail of her hurt pride, whips around so fast she feels dizzy.

"I'm sorry," Joshua says. "Please, if you'll just let us aboard. There'll be no trouble."

"Right," Meeley says, and kneels down to help William. William, broken first from the loss of his daughter, broken last by some demonic version of her, refuses it. He rolls over onto his hands and knees, staggers up to his feet, and walks off the platform toward the entry into the tower.

"Where are you going?"

There is nowhere to go. His wife is dead; she had left him years ago, after Ophelia. She couldn't take it, the fear of another baby, another loss. These trips back and forth to Mars have been stretching out the thread of his life, a silent prick in the skin of the bastards that undid his life but to go there now, to go with them would be disintegration. He will go home to his empty home in the city and spend the last few months of his life allowing the vacancy of his house to permeate him, until there is nothing left within but a heart too old and too weak to support the body it inhabits.

"William!" Meeley cries, following after him. He never answers. He enters the tower, and disappears. "Great... there goes the best air ship engineer I ever had. Actually, he's the only air ship engineer I've ever had. Bess..."

"The fee has increased again, yes."

"You shouldn't have done that," Joshua says to Miranda.

"He's the enemy."

"How is he the enemy?"

"You heard him," she says, conscious suddenly of how loud her voice is in the utter stillness that occupies the platform. She looks at Alice, her face riven with abject fear; she looks at 'Bess,' gently massaging her sore neck, looking over at Joshua with something like contempt.

"I know my name."

A name is all we've got, he told her. He gave her everything. He trained her, raised her to be a soldier and she is the perfect soldier. *What have I made of you buddy.*

"We have our orders," Joshua says, his voice weary. He just wants to sleep. It feels like he hasn't closed his eyes since they arrived back in the city, and before that he didn't get more than three hours a night rest in Clockwork, every day and night on the move, on the warpath. And now they are racing right back to the front, into the belly of the beast.

"But-"

"You're going to arrest everyone who disagrees with some part of what the republic does? You'd have to arrest me."

She opens her mouth in protest, in disbelief. No words form, and none leave her lips.

"If you'd just listen, instead of just reacting at the slightest thing. You never listen to me."

"I listen..."

"You disappoint me, Miranda."

He stands in wait, in silence, for the next few minutes as Meeley finishes the final preparations left undone in William's departure. Miranda doesn't say another word either, doesn't return to the comfort of her comic book. She stands in line behind Joshua, eyes cast down at the cold steel of the landing platform, her heart pounding with shame.

"Everyone get on board," Meeley says, and leads the way into the ship through the hatch.

They eek down a thread-like catwalk that runs down the spine of the ship, through a web of rings and longitudinal girders that recalls the iron lattice design of the tower outside; majestic shafts of moonlight slice down through the windows in the hull above, giving the interior of the air ship the appearance of a cathedral. Instead of balloon sacks for helium or hydrogen as Alice expected, the musculature of the ship contains four porpoise-like liquid-hydrogen fuel cells, each imprinted with a muscular logo: Da Vinci Industries.

"Has one of these ever blown up?" Alice asks Joshua as he herds her back to the rest of the group.

"An air ship?"

"Because it wouldn't burn like the *Hindenburg*. It would just go. You know, poof. Just like that."

"What's the *Hindenburg*?"

"I'm scared. She scares me. She shot me."

"It's going to be all right, Alice."

"Why are you doing this?" Her voice falls to a whisper. "You're helping us, Elizabeth and me. Aren't you? Why?"

He takes her by the arm. "We're falling behind."

"Thanks. Anyway. Thank you." He nods, uncomfortable with her sincerity. "Am I ever going to go home?"

"No," he says.

Simple as that. "Oh. Are you sure?"

"I'm sure."

"What caused this? I mean, what happened?"

"No one knows."

"Do you ever wonder?"

"No."

"If you could find a way... would you? Help me get home?"

"If there were a way," he says.

Alice feels some measure of relief; at least she has this, she has him, on her side.

"Aren't you scared of her?"

"Who?"

"Miranda."

That expression, that dismissive snort and smile, flits over his face. "Why would I be afraid of her?"

"Why won't you tell her what you're doing?"

"That's not why I'm afraid," he says.

"So you are," she says. "Afraid."

"I'm afraid for her. Not because of her. I'm afraid of what she'll become."

"Jesus, Joshua. Of what she'll become?"

They come to a ladder running vertically through the ship, and follow Meeley up into the cramped gondola. A young woman dressed in the same kind of baggy, gray jump suit William wore waits for them at the bottom. Kitzer's eyes flare at the sight of Joshua, and the same resigned terror that fell over Elizabeth in a flash frost does her.

"I know, I know. Eyes. We're being paid not to ask questions," Meeley says. "This is our patron, Bess."

"Thank you," Kitzer says. "Thank you so very much."

"It is nice to meet your acquaintance as well," Elizabeth says, to this day unaccustomed to the abundant presence of Moors in this world. Elizabeth never once left England; God or chance delivered her from it and all of its limitations nine years ago, but nothing could deliver her from the relentless shock of the world outside the apartment Joshua found for her in Lenapolis. The building itself awe-inspiring, seventy stories tall, its jumbled contents of people of all hues; the sky full of machines, the streets unconscious veins of activity, they never stopped flowing with cars and people and buses and trains; the city around her, stacked with structures impossible for her to comprehend.

"Just so we all understand," Meeley says. "This is my ship. And my rules. Do we understand?"

"We do," Joshua says.

"Hello," Kitzer says to him, eyes intently on his, her voice to Alice a kinetic fusion of Germany, sharp and stout, and the South, flowing and melodic. "I'm Kit."

Joshua merely nods in acknowledgement at the caramel girl, her hair a shock of frizzy black radiating out from her head like an opulent cartwheel ruff, and moves on to investigating the flight compartment of the gondola.

Meeley takes her place at the helm, and begins the process of undocking from the tower.

"Wait, where's William?" Kitzer says.

"He took an early retirement," Meeley answers. "Kit, go get the cargo bay ready. You're engineer now, by the way."

"What kind of benefits come with that?"

"Increased risk of serious injury or death."

"If only my mother could see me now."

Kit leaves the cabin through the back. The ship detaches from the docking cone, and the web of steel expands outside the windows. Alice stands at the forward window of the cabin, hands and face against the glass.

"I'll never get used to this..."

"You're from the Midwest?" Meeley asks.

"Iowa."

Meeley smiles. "I saw my first air plane at the Iowa State Fair when I was a girl."

"Really? When was that?"

"Had to have been aught-seven, aught-eight."

"Aught? Like — oh-eight? 1908?"

"Right."

"Jesus... but when did you come here?"

"Five, six years back. Hell of a thing. I'm flying along over the ocean and there's this light outside — like northern lights, but it was the morning. And everything just disappeared. My partner... I never saw him again."

"I don't understand... how could 1908 have been five years ago? I'm from 1986."

"Never met someone from the future before," Meeley says, her voice becoming melancholy. "Five years. Here I am thinking five years I've been gone and maybe they're still look- ing for me. Maybe he still has hope. And here you are, from eighty years hence, and I'm still gone."

"I'm sure they're looking for you," Alice says.

"Is five years here five years there? Is there still there? You know what I'm trying to say? I don't know. I ended up on solid ground here. Wherever here is."

A chill comes over Alice; her mother may already be dead. Brian. The world may have gone on for decades without her, her disappearance only a tiny blip in the local paper, if the world back home still exists at all. The air ship banks to port, and then climbs steeply. The clouds rise around them, flowing up the skin of the ship like water did her body in the bathtub back home, after long days of nothing and nowhere and morning shows and soaps and trips to the store and dinner and him on her and they surface to a startlingly clear sky.

"Mostly it all looks the same from up here," Meeley says. "A little more white and a little more tan. And the flying, I can't complain about the flying. But it's not home."

"Are you from Iowa too, then?"

"All over. Nebraska, Iowa... I'm a mutt."

"It's good to know it's not just me."

"It's not," Meeley says. "When you get where you're going, you'll see. There's hundreds of us."

Joshua covers Miranda's mouth with his hand.

"Mars... it's amazing. I still don't know how we're going to get there though, in this. Not that there's anything wrong with this, but it just doesn't seem like a space ship."

"It's not. The space ship is up there."

Alice stands at the arched windows in mute shock as a gargantuan trimaran-shaped craft transits the moon. Other ships — each roughly the size of this one — swarm around it like pilot fish do sharks, their tail lights blinking red and yellow furious at the cluster of traffic trying to dock with the ship. One by one they fall into line, and enter the gaping mouth at the fore of the central fuselage - itself roughly the size of an ocean liner back home — the whole of it suspended between cretaceous twin hulls, each much more sleek and aerodynamic than anything Alice has ever seen.

"*Liza Blay*, this is *The Sally Gap*. Transmitting our permissions on your channel, over."

"*Sally Gap*, this is *Liza Blay* Control. Permissions received. You are number four for docking."

"Number four, over and out."

The Sally Gap takes its place in line, and drifts gently into the maw of the *Liza Blay*. Docked air ships line either side of the enormous docking bay, housed in claw like carriages; passengers debark via the nose cone hatch onto catwalks that vein the rounded walls of the hangar bay.

Alice holds her hands to her face, shakes her head in astonishment. "This is the most... amazing..."

"I need you all to go back to the cargo bay now," Meeley says, keeping a careful eye on the slowing ships ahead.

The four of them — Alice, Elizabeth, Joshua and Miranda — funnel through the hatch out of the cabin, past the small mess and crew quarters with room enough only for tiny, stacked bunks, and down into the cargo bay that occupies the majority of the ship. Stacked bundles of logs fill the entire bay. Kitzer walks across the top of them, ducking under the ceiling, and then climbs down to the deck by a rope.

"What's all this?" Miranda says.

"Fine Irish timber," Kitzer replies. "They don't have a lot of natural wood on Mars. Came as a shock to me, too."

"This is your cover? You transport wood?"

"Not just wood," Kitzer says, turning to the axed end of a bundled cluster of logs behind her. She knocks on the end of the center log, producing an odd, hollow sound. She knocks it again, just once, and end of the log pops open like a lid.

"In you all go," she says. "Children first."

Miranda leads the way with a fierce grimace and Alice brings up the rear; she squeezes into the dark, slender tube, a deceptively meager beginning to what promises to be — what Alice hopes will be — the voyage of a lifetime.

VIII

An hour passes. The air becomes heavy, warm, tinged with nervous breath; it reminds Alice some of the concrete tunnels built through mounds of earth at the playground. She crawled through them until she got too big she couldn't fit. There's this gap in her life of four or five years where she stopped going to the park, doing childish things; she barely remembers anything about those years now. When did Danny go to the war? '68? '69? Then she went back to the playground, at thirteen or so, with Brian, with other boys. She hears the ruffle of hard, dead leaves about to fall; the jangle on the rusted chains of the swing set in the cool fall breeze. A cold hand slides inside her coat, under her sweater, onto her skin.

Voices intrude on her memory, from outside the log. A man's. Meeley's. They exchange just a few words, all of them muffled behind the wood, and then are gone. Long minutes pass. A loud knock shudders through the log, startling all of them; light pours in as the hatch swings open.

"You're good to come out now," Kitzer says.

Elizabeth hates to fly. She's only done so once before, a few scant weeks after her arrival here nine years ago; the experience left her much as it does now, weak, light-headed and sick to her stomach. She reclines on the small bunk in the compact quarters she shares with Alice, the back of her hand over her forehead, the palm of the other on the side of her neck, where it's been virtually since she left the theater. Elizabeth thought at first she would enjoy the freedom flight offered, the gentle behemoths on display daily in the skies above so inviting to her, but on her first — and to now, only — trip aboard a modest sightseeing ferry that circled the city, turbulence jostled the ship so violently it threw the entire congregation of passengers from one side of the cabin to the other. Elizabeth slammed against one of the support beams running diagonally through the cramped cabin and she did not let go of it until the ship returned safe and sound to its mooring mast back at the Exchange.

The *Liza Blay* hardly feels as if it is moving at all, yet there is much turbulence within her; she feels thrown like a rock a child has dropped into a tin can. The sound she must make, with all the rattling and conflagration within her, with all the carefully organized aspects of her life here thrown into the air, thrown into one another. She moans, and it hurts to. Her neck must be swelling horribly now; she holds her hand to it, presses against the weight forming there and the sound she must make. The indignity of being brought low like this only compounds the situation. *I am the queen of England. I fear neither death nor my enemies. I fear nothing but the Lord my God and please Lord, deliver me now. Please.*

Alice stands at the miniscule portal in the cabin wall, unabashed wonder on her face as she looks out onto the other ships docked inside the hangar of the *Liza Blay*.

"I want to go out there."

"Please, do not suggest such things."

"Are you like sea sick or something?"

"Do I yellow?" Elizabeth says. "I must be a sight."

Alice leaves the portal, leans over the bunk to examine Elizabeth. "No, you're fine."

"I must look horrid. I am faint. I fear I shall vomit. Please place the ice pale near me, I shall need it soon."

Alice takes the bucket off the floor — whether it's an ice bucket or a bucket for something else, she's not sure - and sets it on the floor beside the bunk.

"I think you're just a little queasy is all."

She reminds Alice a little of her grandmother, a grand Southern drama queen who found no peer after moving to Iowa from Alabama in 1946 with her new husband, fresh from the war. She fainted on every momentous occasion in American history subsequent (though remembered with remarkable detail exactly where she and what she was doing the day Kennedy was shot, the day Bobby Kennedy was shot, the day they landed on the moon, etc.) and she abandoned consciousness at every single event in the Vale family as well, including both the announcement of Alice's pending arrival and the actual arrival itself.

"You seem to be adjusting well, my dear," Elizabeth says.

Alice shrugs. "The free trip to outer space helps."

So does the fact that her brain simply hasn't registered the enormity of what's happened to her. Two days ago she stood on the back porch of her house with its drafty doors and peeling paint contemplating her future as part of the furniture and now here she is, in a world where Carpenter doesn't exist, on a space blimp that doesn't have Goodyear on the side of it but the ubiquitous symbol of Canon, the eye, its infinite iris stretching back along both fuselages.

"I'm pretty sure at some point I'll wake up, and 'You were there, and you too...' Except you weren't there. Back home. None of you were. It doesn't seem real, yet."

"Yet will never arrive, let me assure you."

The hangar bay loses its hold on Alice, and she sits down in the chair — dollhouse size it seems like, along with everything else in their quarters — opposite the bunks.

"Do you think this happened to everybody?"

"Joshua intimated we arrive with some regularity, but this world is not populated with the citizens of ours, merely transplanted. We are alien here. And we are uncommon. Wherever all the good and many people of our world went, Alice, the balance did not venture here."

"Jesus..."

"Please do not take the Lord's name in vain."

"Oh. Sorry."

"It is a comfort," Elizabeth says, relaxing her hand a little from her neck, "to finally meet another that shares my affliction. It has been a... solitary experience."

"You're helping people, though. People like us. You're paying Meeley to smuggle us to Mars."

"I have deliberately never met the acquaintance of another in our condition, both for their protection and for mine. I merely hold some modest investment in Meeley's lumber enterprise that I made through a reputable broker."

"You sound like you won't even admit it to yourself."

"I can be held to no account for what I do not know."

"You must be lonely."

Alice doesn't know — thank God Elizabeth thinks, that now, she won't — the soul-consuming fear and isolation that she has, the belief that this is personal, that this grand scheme is for her benefit, a hell stylized to suit only Elizabeth Tudor. Yet this world departs from her notion of Hell in many ways. It does offer these technological wonders, frightening as they may be at times; it offers brief moments of joy and satisfaction, and despite the nagging, unshakeable fear - realized today - of turning a corner, running into Joshua again, Canon offers a freedom that England never could. She is free of the destiny cast in stone in the moment of her conception, a forked destiny that ends either in crown or casket; the thread of her life has been severed. Elizabeth is slave now only to circumstance, and its mercy; she is free, so long as she remains conspicuous, to follow her passions.

"You wrote that book. You're her, right?"

Elizabeth pauses. "Yes. I am her."

"You're English. Like old English."

"I am confident we can burn away most if not all of this voyage exchanging our tales, and while I am eager to know yours, I do not feel quite up to it at the moment."

"Let's go get some hot tea. Mom says tea always helps."

"Yes, if you would bring me a pot, that would be divine. Two sugars, please. You may also find a cup for yourself."

Alice chuckles. "No, I mean, we can go get some. Together. There's kind of a kitchen out there. Maybe they'll let us go see the rest of the ship. Do you think they would?"

"I am not well enough to walk."

"C'mon," Alice says, getting up and going to the bunk again. "It will do you some good to get out and walk around."

She takes Elizabeth by the arm. Elizabeth snatches it back. "Do not touch me."

Alice steps back. "Sorry."

"It is not allowed for you to place your hands upon my person without my permission."

"Ok." Alice holds her hands up. "Sorry."

Elizabeth takes a breath, removes her hand from her forehead. She regrets her tone, too hostile; Alice doesn't know that she is the Queen of England. She doesn't regret her admonishment, however. A fact is a fact. She is the queen, regardless of her situation. Monarchs even in exile are due the same respect they would be on the throne and Elizabeth forgets much but not her royal disposition or its distance, despite the fact that there is little to no practical difference between her and any other person in Canon.

"Do not be sorry," she says, sitting up on the bunk. "I am an old maid, rooted in her habits. You must forgive me."

"It's no big deal."

"Yes. As you say. Shall we? Tea sounds lovely."

Elizabeth extends her elbow, for Alice to take in the European manner. Alice smiles appreciatively, and they exit their quarters into the gondola arm in arm.

Joshua sits outside, on a metal chair between their room and the one he and Miranda occupy next door.

"Where are you two going?" he says, out of his sleepy slouch in the chair at once.

"For tea," Elizabeth says. "You may supervise, but Alice and I seek a more feminine affair. Besides, I do not think it practical for us to escape from the ship while it delivers us along at such great speed, and such great height."

"Fine. Whatever. I'll be here," he says, and leans back in the chair, his eyes shut almost at once.

"And where is young Miranda?"

"No," Alice says quickly. "She's not — feminine."

"Resting," Joshua says.

"Then we shall leave her to it."

"Can we go out into the rest of the ship?" Alice asks.

"Absolutely not."

"We shall dress ourselves as members of the crew," Elizabeth says. "No one shall be the wiser, I think, if Meeley instructs her colleagues to remain aboard."

"Meeley can bring you back tea."

"We shall not go through customs until we reach Mars. Our identities are practically anonymous until then."

"It's too risky."

"Oh, let me Joshua," Elizabeth says, the tone of her voice softening. "I will likely never again have the opportunity to witness such wonders as those beyond."

Joshua reluctantly reaches into his pocket. "One hour," he says, and stands. He stabs a nickel size plastic device — a homing beacon - to the collar of Elizabeth's blouse.

"One hour and that's it."

"Good evening, sir."

The two women slip into the dungy coveralls like Kitzer and Meeley wear, and then debark the ship out into the hangar bay of the *Liza Blay*. They exit it on to the spacious promenade deck that runs continuously around the circumference of the *Liza Blay's* titanic gondola; encapsulated inside a glass dome, it provides a remarkable view of the sky above. Conductors lead clusters of passengers along the promenade — pointing out the signs giving direction to the museum, the gymnasiums; the myriad restaurants and cafes and shops; the main theater where Aytanya will be performing her retinue ("A most prodigious talent," Elizabeth says); the main dining hall; the lounges and nightclubs including the Zero G club where passengers can entertain themselves after hours — weightless — and of course the glass bottom deck.

Alice and Elizabeth walk side-by-side down the immaculate corridor to the elevators. They go up nine decks to the spectacular dining hall, swathed in ivory and brass, terraced into three levels that descend into a crescent shaped veranda — a temple of glass, with pews of leather loveseats and couches - that forms the rump of the gondola. A waiter leads them to a small, cloth-covered table on the starboard side, beside the generous window. Elizabeth is used to grandeur, but not like this; a cold, gray dampness permeated the palaces of her kingdom, alleviated only by candle or torchlight. And the smell; how could she forget the stench of London town, especially in the spring when the river would come over its banks and flood the sewers running under the city. The entire city stank, of fish and shit. Of decomposing heads of criminals and traitors, stuck on pikes.

Alice gazes out onto the world, curving beneath her, as Elizabeth returns to touching her neck every few seconds.

"It's so beautiful... I never believed I would ever..."

"Do they not have such inventions in Iowa?"

"Not exactly. We have airplanes. I guess you know what those are. Helicopters. And the shuttle. Goes into space. Not to Mars, but... I think it's pretty sweet."

The waiter takes their order, and then only a minute later brings a pot of tea, and two cups, upside down on porcelain saucers. Alice smiles as she turns her cup over, remembering the hours she spent in her room as a girl, having imaginary tea with the set she stole from old man Jane.

"This is nice. This is really nice."

"Yes," Elizabeth says, as she waits for Alice to pour her tea. "Tell me of Iowa. It is foreign to me."

"You're like from the past or something, right?"

"Yes. For you. I heard you say 1986."

"Yeah. When do you come from?"

She does not remember the exact day; it was October, 1562. An early autumn breeze rippled through the gauze wings of the majestic ruffle arcing around her neck, the ochre rays of the setting sun sparkling like diamonds in its bejeweled web as she walked her private gardens of Hampton Court just before twilight. She walked the cobblestone paths among the manicured trees and decaying flowers, kneading the same dilemma over and over again in her mind, the dilemma of Mary Stuart. It kept Elizabeth up at night, the prospect of an ambitious Catholic - attractive - queen on her back doorstep with the support of not just Rome, but Spain as well.

It kept her advisers up late as well, though not always of their own volition; she often summoned Cecil to her quarters at midnight or later to seek his advice on which direction to take with Mary. When he left her, sometimes at one, sometimes later, he often left confident she had absorbed his council and that the matter was resolved. In the morning, he invariably found she had changed her mind again.

Elizabeth found no *via media* when it came to Mary; on one hand, the Queen of Scots was her cousin, and a woman alone on the throne like she was. She suspected they had much more in common than apart and that was borne out in the hopeful letters they exchanged that year, delicately negotiating a meeting between the two women. Mary sought to ensure her place as Elizabeth's successor, as Elizabeth sought to mitigate Mary's passion for the crown. Mary threatened her security in every way. She aggressively sought a husband and consequently an heir, both of which Elizabeth denied not only herself but her kingdom. She would not marry. She could not. Her choices were either unacceptable to her or to her councilors, and any choice compromised her rule; she made a decision, early in her young reign that marriage would make England weaker than if she remained celibate and so she took for her husband the only suitor whose needs outweighed hers.

She never pined for marriage. She had pangs, as everyone does, for companionship, for mere human touch and she did find it occasionally, with Dudley and when his presence in her privy room attracted too much attention, she found it among the only people admitted there. So she looked forward to a meeting with Mary, to meeting someone, perhaps the only someone, who understood her lonely position. Mary seemed to long for the meeting and the reconciliation as well, going so far as to tell a go-between that she wished either she or Elizabeth had been a man, so marriage could bring peace.

"She is said to be quite beautiful," William Cecil said, walking beside Elizabeth in the gardens that night. "Though I understand the nose diminishes the overall effect."

"I shall have to examine her then," Elizabeth said, rubbing her side, sore suddenly. "And judge her quality for myself. I shall not betroth myself to any one without first making an inspection. A prince must maintain his standards."

"Indeed," Cecil said, laughing. "But Your Majesty, in all seriousness, this meeting must be postponed. A year at least, until the Huguenot situation is resolved."

"This 'situation' as you describe it in France has delayed our meeting a good deal already."

"She seeks the hand of Don Carlos of Spain. Such a union would give the Papists an intractable foothold in our realm."

"I have advised her that such a match would jeopardize our friendship, and indeed, any possibility of succession."

"She must not succeed you, Your Majesty."

"If she agrees to terms, I am not opposed to her—"

"Why do you continue to indulge this fantasy? Everything you and your father have fought and risked mightily for would be squandered if Mary Stuart ever came to power here."

"I will have assurances from–"

"Your Majesty, we must not concern ourselves with the future. We must focus on the moment."

"Do you believe the moment is ever not my concern?"

Cecil charged ahead, knowing if she spun off on a tangent as easily and often as she did off the main paths of the garden into darker, lonelier avenues, they would be in the garden sometime after supper, with the moon high above them.

"She actively supports the Catholics of France in their struggle against the Huguenots, who need I remind you, are rightful allies of ours."

"You are always reminding me, Cecil, of things I have perfect memory of."

"You seem to remember things too well," he said, pulling his cloak tighter over his shoulders. "You would do well with forgetting certain things. They hold up your decisions."

Elizabeth sighed. She thought once seeing all sides of an issue suited a queen; however, her deliberations had only grown since her ascendancy four years prior. Cecil provided sound, sage advice; nevertheless, on the most important issues that confronted her, the question of Mary Stuart, the need to marry and secure the throne, she found faults in his council. Anyone would, chipping away at it for hours into the night.

That was always Elizabeth's problem; Cecil thought no one came to the throne more prepared, more ready to rule than Elizabeth, save perhaps her father. Her short years provided her enough near-death experience to make her scrappy, swift, and most of all, political in the most acrobatic sense. But she was young, only 25 at the time of her coronation. Worse, she was a woman; that handicapped in the minds of her own court from the start. She had the potential, he saw it clearly from the moment they first met, for greatness; but she needed sharpening.

Focus. He honed her intellect, her wit, making her razor sharp but she continued to, on her own, in the hours she kept with no one but God and he feared she was whittling herself, thinning the royal blade so much it would break at the lightest of blows from another.

"We must send men to France in support of our allies."

"Yes. Yes, we must," she said, cradling her side now. The trees rustled with the increasingly brisk breeze.

"You cannot meet with Mary Stuart," he said.

"We must come to some accord with her. For my sake as well as England's. Even you know that."

"Appeasement cannot be our tactic in this matter. Her alliances to Spain and France make her most dangerous. Any concession to her is a concession to Rome."

"I will not have war in England over faith."

"Then I would advise - again - meeting with her at all. The woman is as likely to slit your throat as kiss your hand."

Elizabeth touched her hand to her forehead. It was damp. She felt warm, dizzy. "Then I shall have her inspected also for the concealment of weapons upon my examination of her qualities, Cecil. She shall be quite naked at the end."

"She is quite naked now. If she does not consent to signing the Treaty, then you must consider her as you do the Countess Lennox. The only place you should meet Mary Stuart is at the Tower, my lady. You must eliminate her threat."

"Am I not attempting to do so?"

"Enchanting as you are, Your Majesty, I do not expect the Queen of Scots to be as amenable as your other suitors, regardless of the examination you submit her to."

Elizabeth drifted against him. "My lady?"

"I am not well," she said. "I shall retire, I think."

Several of her ladies came running to her side from

their huddled, clustered position well behind them.

"Mary, run my bath," she said, and Mary Sidney left ahead of the others to do just that. "I just need to relax."

"Yes, rest," Cecil said. "You tax yourself with too many burdens. Do not keep yourself awake tonight with all your considerations. Think of nothing, my lady."

"For your sake, Cecil," she said, leaning on her ladies as they led her back to the manor. After walking only a few yards, she broke free of them and strode into the main house under her own steam. She took her bath, and feeling the fever dissolve into the warm water, she took again to the gardens only this time to come down with a terrible chill.

She went to her bed, the fever back (it had never left) and now running out of control. Cecil summoned a physician, who diagnosed her condition as smallpox. Elizabeth laughed him out of the room, as she had no spots — "I am not a leopard, sir" - but Cecil felt his blood go cold. Smallpox ran rampant throughout England and Europe, killing thousands, disfiguring more; his queen could be on her deathbed and she had no heir. England had no security. His first thought, as any good Secretary of State's would be, was who would succeed her, his young, beautiful queen, if God in His wisdom decided to remove her to Heaven at this worst possible moment. There were no good choices.

"My lady, I leave you to your rest," he said.

"I am merely weak with the prospect of marriage," she replied, and her ladies gasped. Elizabeth smiled. "I shall wake a man, and take for my wife the Queen of Scots, and peace shall be upon my kingdom. I shall give you many sons, Cecil."

Cecil approached her bed, tentatively. The queen's eyes were yellow. He held his hand to his side, clutched in a fist. "You are tired, my lady. I will see you in better spirits in the morning, I have no doubt."

"Do not despair. I may yet forestall my expiration. I am still debating the implications of my death upon my soul. No doubt my ruminations shall delay the inevitable."

"No doubt."

"I shall deliver the earth from the strife of our warring Christianity. Rome shall not fear London and London not Rome. I will wake in a better world, as a better prince."

"There are no better princes, Your Majesty," Cecil said, and withdrew from the room. He did not allow himself his tears. He immediately went to his office to draft a letter summoning the other councilors to Hampton; the succession had to be decided, and swiftly from the looks of it.

The history books Alice read as a girl barely touched on this moment, perhaps the most precarious of many such scares in Elizabeth's life; they focused instead on the great achievements of her reign, nearly fifty years during which England flowered into its Golden Age. Shakespeare. The defeat of the Spanish Armada. History splinters at this moment; if those events ever did occur, they do now only in Alice's memory. Elizabeth fled from consciousness, and England, on a curtain of light that fell over Hampton as it did all London. It seeped in through the windows, under the cracks of the doors; it filled the long corridors of the palace so swift and thick women screamed that it was on fire.

In an instant, the strange mist of kaleidoscopic light ripped Elizabeth from her sickbed in England in 1562 - from her destiny as the greatest queen England would ever know - and it tossed her like garbage, weak and near-death into the frozen wasteland of a North America that never saw Columbus; never Washington; never Lincoln; never independence.

IX

Elizabeth wandered in the miasma of her sickness, stumbling between rocky fingers of turgid canyons, their walls razor sharp from millennia of wind erosion, riddled with pebbled craters worn minute caves she found refuge in. She believed she had died, and faced now the crucible that Christ did, that all souls must, crossing the desert; that this one was of ice only buttressed her fear that she was in Hell. She believed she had to do so, and reject all temptations, to walk into the light of the Lord, circling the circumference of the sky for the duration of day. She walked, for miles, for unknown hours, her mind empty of any thought but reaching the light, her reward. If she slept, she doesn't remember; only vague flashes of curling up in a fetal ball against the indescribable cold, against her demons that came out in legion with the stars, ever come to mind when she thinks of it.

The ghost of her father, so large he eclipsed the sun; the banshee cries of her sister Mary: "Bastard!", "Whore!", echoing through the labyrinth of the gorges and canyons, through her bones, and through the valley she had descended into; the specter of her mother, headless, walking back and forth in front of the tiny cave Elizabeth sought refuge in.

Whispers issued from her cleaved neck. "Elizabeth," the flayed voice of Anne Boleyn whispered. "Make me a son."

Elizabeth shielded her eyes with her arms. "Though I walk through the valley of the shadow of death, I will fear no evil... I will fear no evil for thou art with me..."

The headless figure of her mother trolled in front of the mouth of the cave. "Become for me a son, and soothe the king. Be for me a prince of England and restore my head to its perch. Elizabeth. I cannot see my way until you do."

Elizabeth ignored the pleas of her mother, of all the ghosts but their voices left her scarred, far more than the craters of the smallpox that still ravaged her body. She held out against the denial of her faith, her gender, and when the sun rose in the mornings she continued her pilgrimage across the ice so cold it melded to the soles of her feet, her nakedness obscured under a crust of clayed, dry earth.

She blacked out. When she woke up, the Yukalut were burying her in ice within their temple. Time passed; the shaman freed her. She wrote the book, in ice. All Elizabeth had been was frozen, shattered and left in the north. Joshua found someone else, someone broken and reconstituted, a collection of fragments that don't fit as comfortably as did they before. *This must be an angel,* she thought, this beautiful creature that carried her out of the temple into the day, the sun behind him like the ambient glow of the Lord.

Elizabeth clasped her hands together in prayer. *Oh Lord,*

she said, but God or Joshua did not hear her. Her voice expired somewhere back in the arctic desert, shred on screams extracted from the needling demands of dead Anne. Joshua held his hand away from the holster strapped to his thigh. This woman, his mission, Case Designate: Unknown, Case #: 062-33-B612 quivered and quaked with trauma he could only imagine. She seemed as utterly small, as utterly fragile as the newborn his radiometer had led him to in the forests of Celtica four years before; as utterly innocent. He looked over his shoulder, into the Yukalut village. Toward the mountains and the city beyond them. No one had seen her. No one knew she existed, except for the agency and its orbiting satellites, primed to detect any fluctuation in gamma radiation on the surface below. His superiors did not require a body; he knew that from prior missions. All they required was his report, and his word, unimpeachable, that he had done as so ordered.

Joshua lifted the sun-goggles back over his forehead, cracked open the ice-crusted shall coiled around his neck and draped it over her shoulders. He knelt down before her, trembling now with confusion as much as delirium and he took the flask of water from his utility belt and put it to her lips. They broke open into deep crevices with each soundless word. He poured some water into his palm, rubbed away the layer of grime and frozen skin on her face into long, black rolls of dirt that fell from her cheeks like leeches.

She was beautiful. More an angel than she thought him.

"It's ok," he said. "Don't try to speak. I'm here to help you. I'm going to help you now."

He lifted her up into his arms. She weighed hardly anything. Elizabeth looked up into the face of her redeemer, her savior, and convulsed with dry, heaving sobs.

Take thee into thy arms oh Lord, she tried to say, *your humble and most grateful child. Thank you. Thank you.*

Joshua dismissed her appreciation by looking away, down at the ground. He didn't want thanks or praise. He didn't want any other means of appreciation she might offer as some of the others had, later, after he eased them from the shock of their situations into their new lives. Joshua wanted nothing except for answers to questions that formed like weeds between the stones of his foundation and that with each passing year, forced apart the seams with their unchecked growth, their death and decay. The inevitable rebirth that flowered from it compromised a lifetime of construction, the powerful, robust architecture of the Canon agent, but no less susceptible to nature than any work of man.

Joshua walked out of the village. "What's your name?"

"They called me Bess," Elizabeth says, fingering the cleft of her hair framing the right side of her face. A pet name for their Good Queen. Outside the spacious windows of the dining room of the *Liza Blay,* the clouds part ahead of the regal pearl of the full moon. Below, the earth curves, shrinks; Elizabeth has known for nearly a decade now from photos, its true shape; but for the first time here is proof that the world is something beyond which she can conceive.

"It is not flat," she says, as if an afterthought.

Alice smiles a little, thinking maybe Elizabeth is putting her on. "You didn't know that?"

"Elizabeth did not know."

Elizabeth Tudor died with the world she left behind, a flat world, carved like a pie in her mind into the divisions of man. It took a long time to undo the idea that Joshua was an angel, that the tall, lithe and clustered numbers of hyaline glass towers in Lenapolis were not the dwelling of God. She did not imagine that in Heaven, though, there would be enclosed carts to ferry passengers and cargo down concrete laden avenues without the aid of any beast; she didn't imagine a sky clouded with what she believed had to be boats, long chrome tubes propelled by something other than wind or oar.

If it is Heaven, it is wonderful; if not, it is terrific.

She wondered when that word — terrific — stopped meaning what it meant. Something that terrifies. People exclaim it when met with something positive, and as she walked the streets between towers alive of with images of the living, Elizabeth thought people said 'terrific' when confronted with a situation like this one, a situation both terrible and wonderful at once. The afterlife then wasn't a place or abstraction but the mind of God; God sees all and on every spire of thought in His head she was witness to all God's thoughts. EYES OPEN, EARS CLOSED. SACRIFICE. INTEGRITY.

I am a thought in the mind of the Lord. I see through the eyes of God, and know creation as He does.

'Bess Rose' took up residence in a small apartment, humiliatingly small for someone accustomed to excess even in her most dire conditions - her various 'cells' at the Tower and after in Woodstock were in truth luxurious, considering — located in a government housing project on west side of the Danis River. Joshua made her promise never to breathe a word to anyone about her true identity — *They'll kill you,* he told her. *Who?* she asked, and he said, *Men like me* - and well-practiced in the art of disguising her true nature, Elizabeth took to this new subterfuge like a baby to water.

The easy part was her accent — along with her language, conveniently similar enough (Joshua, for the first time, questioned why). After she chose her new name, he minted it with a fabricated Bio-ID print he subcutaneously planted on her thumb. He ran it under his scanner and the print instantly delivered a

history and biography for Bess Rose of Seneca Towers, Unit #489;
she lived all her 30 years in the city, born to parents now dead,
no siblings. It listed her place of work as the Grand City Library,
where she shelved books (Elizabeth didn't mind this so much at
first, once she actually started working there; eventually her natural disposition led her away from any kind of manual labor to
a more familiar lifestyle, provided for by a variety of wealthy pa-
trons invested in her talent — translations of ancient works of dead
civilizations subsumed into Canon and then gradually, her own
plays — and more importantly, her beauty).

And then, after Joshua led her around on a tour of the
neighborhood, of her new life, all the time Elizabeth nodding as if she would remember, as if she could focus at all, he
dropped her back at the front lobby of her apartment and without any preamble told her, *I can never see you again.*

"You cannot leave me," she said, grabbing his sleeve as
he turned and began to walk away. "Do not leave me alone."

"I have to."

"I order you to stay."

He smiled. "It has to be this way. You won't ever see me
again, I promise. You don't want to. If you do..."

He couldn't make her understand then, any more than
he could himself. "Don't worry. I'll... I'll be watching."

She took his hand in hers, placed it against her cheek.
"Angele Dei, qui custos es mei."

"What does that mean?"

"Do not go."

Joshua placed his other hand to her face, cupped it and
brushed away the tears with his thumb. The impulse to kiss her,
to hold her at least welled up within him and again he shoved it
back down. He let go of her, turned and disappeared into the
anonymity of the alien city, its voices and faces.

Elizabeth — Bess — began life anew.

"1562... geez," Alice says. "I still don't get it. Meeley was from 1908, and you... how can we all disappear from different times and all end up here in the same place?"

"Such things are beyond our understanding. Let us not tangle ourselves in the threads God weaves for us."

"Ok..."

"Tell me of England in this time of yours, Alice. Tell me of Iowa. You speak my language, are you a subject?"

"Subject? Oh. Like English. No. Iowa is part of the United States. Which was a colony of England. Well, 13 of them were. Like two hundred years ago. But then there was all this stuff about taxes and whatever and then we kind of went our separate ways. But we're still friends."

Elizabeth rubs her neck. "Colonies... in the new world?"

"Right."

"Our ambition in that realm was only a glimmer at the time of my — departure, and here in but a few words you provide both the rise and fall of our fortunes there. I do not understand this, Alice. I do not understand how history could have survived the injury it sustained in my time, to continue on to yours. Does your history not record my disappearance? What comes of England after me?"

"I don't know... were you important?"

Elizabeth lets out a sharp laugh. "Was I?"

"Elizabeth... wait. Get out!" Alice lowers her voice to a hushed whisper. "You're — you're her?"

"Indeed."

"So, were you really like a virgin the whole time?"

Elizabeth drops a cube of sugar into her cup, stirs it once (wishing now she had ordered a beer instead) and then sets the spoon on the saucer as she waits for the tea to cool.

"Still too hot."

Alice sips at her tea, still scalding hot on her tongue. "So, uh... why do you think he's helping us? Joshua?"

"We must not question his mercy," she says, glancing out the window for a brief moment before returning to her study of the dinner crowd. "Lest any exposure to light evaporate it."

"Right," Alice says. "Right."

But you know why. He's been helping you since you got here. He's been protecting you. There must be a reason.

"He's kind of cute."

"Hmm?"

"Joshua."

"He is blessed, in all the appropriate places."

"He likes you," Alice says, tentatively, stirring the pot. "I can tell."

Elizabeth finds that she can't suppress her smile. It has been years — if ever, truly — that she has been able to enjoy the company of women. As queen, an entire retinue of women and girls orbited around her, charged with her meals, her clothes, her wigs; she didn't talk with them like she does Alice now. That was impossible. Kat Ashley remained her friend and confidant even after the coronation, but Elizabeth gradually withdrew into her role as queen and later as the Virgin, wife only of England, mistress to no one but God.

"Joshua does not see me in such a fashion," she says. "He is wedded to his country. He is chaste. And devout. One must admire his devotion... one cannot help but appreciate it."

"He's risking a lot, though. Helping us."

"'The grasshopper shall be a burden.'"

"He never said? Why?"

Elizabeth doesn't bother to respond. She made her point before. She waits for the tea to cool and when steam no longer rises from the surface of it she lifts the cup to her lips. She takes one curt sip and then sets it back down.

Alice nervously arranges and rearranges the placement of the cup, the saucer, the spoon, more conscious with each passing second that she is seated at a table with royalty; her manners have totally sucked to this point. She's probably not even supposed to look the woman in the eye. She sits up straight. She unfolds the napkin and lays it across her lap. She makes sure to keep her elbows off the table. Her jaw clenches. She forgets the will, the mechanism to speak.

"Your tea will go cold," Elizabeth says, after Alice sits prone for nearly two minutes, her only movement the barely perceptible rise and fall of her belly as she breathes.

Alice nods and takes another sip of tea, careful to mimic the way Elizabeth does it, lifting the saucer with the cup.

"What did you do, Alice? Back in Iowa?"

"Nothing. Laundry."

"You were a wash girl?"

"I guess."

"You may look at me when speaking," Elizabeth says. "You will not turn to stone."

"Ok."

"You harbored ambitions, though. For the heavens."

"I wanted to be an astronaut. I want to be an astronaut. I'm talking like I'm dead."

"And this ambition of yours — it is obtainable for a woman? In your time?"

"Oh, yeah."

"What dreams may come."

"Yeah. No shit." She covers her mouth. "Sorry."

It was Elizabeth's birthright — depending on the mood of those in charge — to reign, but the role of monarch was never something she could aspire to. She was a prince, her father's daughter, but kings ruled England. Women did not serve to occupy the throne single-handedly, they were not capable; women of the line served to provide their husbands their kings sons, future heirs of England. The penalty for not fulfilling that duty, their one and only duty, was often severe. Elizabeth has lived here in this world for nine years, seen equality among the sexes she could scarcely imagine in hers. That it did exist there, for Alice at least, does not give her satisfaction. It frustrates her. In this world she has found her freedom from the moors of her society, but not her heart; the ideas, the perspective of 16th century England, remain firmly in place, strict as the bone-lined corsets of her gowns that left gorges in her skin.

"You know of me, Alice."

"I read about you, in high school. Just a little in World History, but I remember. We watched that movie with Vanessa Redgrave. I forget who played you, though."

"Movie? You mean cinema?" Alice nods. Elizabeth smiles; one of the best things about this world have been its films, and the cathedral of the magic lantern that projects them. She attends the theater as dutifully as she once did church, daily, taking in the sights and sounds of the world.

"I was the subject of a film?"

"A couple, I think."

Elizabeth smiles with delight. "Who did this Redgrave woman play then, if not me?"

"Mary. Um, you know. Queen of Scots or whatever."

The smile evaporates. "What?"

"I think that's her."

"Why should she be subject of any film? What came of my cousin Mary Stuart? Did she — did she succeed me?"

"No, you — you don't know, do you? Maybe I better not

say. In case we ever... you know. Go back."

Elizabeth leans back in her chair, dangles her arm over the back. "How long... how long did Her Majesty reign? Did she marry? No, of course not. We decided long against that. Did I leave my country well? What does history say of me?"

"There's no record of you - I mean you never disappeared. You lived and you — this never happened to you."

"Rue that you ever came to me, Alice. Before, I thought England ended with me, but now I know not only did it continue on, I did as well. How is it possible for one to lead two separate lives? Is my soul split somehow? Is yours?"

"It kind of fucks with your head."

"As you say."

Alice leans back in her chair, gazes out the window at the strange star in Taurus. "I think whatever happened, it happened to us at the same time. I mean, I was in 1986, and you were in 1562 or whatever, but it happened at the same time. You know what I mean? History was fine from you to me until something happened, somewhere. I don't know."

Elizabeth nods. "If all time is a line, from alpha to omega, someone has brushed that line with their hand. Smeared beginning and end together in such fashion as to make one indistinguishable from the other. And through that confusion we may say they have a drawn a new line. However, it is not as clean and tidy as our author intended."

"You think someone did this?"

"I cannot say."

"You must worry about your people."

"They do not suffer," Elizabeth says.

"Oh."

"Only my vanity. No, the people of my country are relieved, from the shackles of our world."

"Like disease and stuff?"

"Disease savages the body. I speak of the soul. My country is — was — divided in two, between London and Rome, Catholic and Protestant. It was my only hope that a single city did not chart the course of man — and a single church. I sought a middle way, but I feared none could ever be found. I am relieved to know that I was wrong. Here in this world, God does not divide us. God does not exist. Perhaps this then is Hell, but God forgive me, it is a tolerable one."

Alice wants to ask what she means — if she means what Alice thinks she does, and if so, why she wrote the book then - but such questions seem too personal to ask of a queen; she goes back to her tea, the thieved toy set forever pricking in her memory, like thoughts of home. You can take the girl out of Carpenter, but never Carpenter out of the girl.

"I'm sorry — I just have to ask: you don't think of like God and stuff, religion, as a disease, do you?"

"Is it any different, Alice?" she says, resting her head against her hands. "In 1986? Does God divide men less?"

"More. Seems like," Alice says.

"More. How could it be more. It is not God I despise. You will never hear such blasphemy from me. It is the fault of man. We corrupt and distort the word of God to serve our base aims. We are sinners, Alice. You and I. We know our shame as Adam did. The people in this world... they do not know their shame. They are innocent. They exist in a paradise without age or time. All the burden of our history... erased. See what they have accomplished. Joshua... we walk in a godless land and yet, there are angels that walk among us."

Alice rubs her chest, thinks of Miranda planting the barrel of the gun against her skin and pulling the trigger.

"I don't know... angel might be too strong a term."

"An angel's perspective is quite different than a man's."

"A queen's, too. I guess."

"I do not expect you to understand."

"I guess I wouldn't."

"Tell me, Alice. Are you a child of Christ?"

"I'm Catholic, if that's what you mean."

Fatigue allows the frown to slip through. "Rome's reach extends even into the New World, then."

"The Pope came to Des Moines a couple years ago. There were so many people... I've never seen so many people."

Elizabeth fixes on the web of lights strung along the eastern seaboard. Rome did not diminish in its power; it expanded its influence. England lost its colonies in the New World; she fears England in Alice's time is little more than it was in hers, a solitary outcropping in sea of red.

"You really think of them that way? Like they're better than us?" Elizabeth means to answer, but Alice rolls along her train of thought. "I mean, maybe they have fancier stuff and they have cures for all these diseases back home, but — I'm not religious or anything, but - I think they could do with a little good news, you know? I mean, this is all-"

"I do not understand — you are not religious?"

"Not really. I can't even remember the last time I went to church. Probably when we got married."

"And this is tolerated?"

"It's no big deal."

"You seem quite free, Alice."

"If you say so."

"I do."

"But like I was saying, this all seems great maybe, but — he just up and grabbed you out of your life. Told you were going to another planet for Christ's sake — sorry — and she — fuck her.

She scares the hell out of me. There's nothing angelic about her. Demonic, maybe."

"We no longer inhabit the world of men. Ours now is a world of angels and demons. Gods and monsters."

"It's like Orwell or something."

"I do not understand."

"Like — I mean this is all great, but it's because — it's like in the olden times, you know. The Spanish Inquisition."

"Precisely. Precisely, that is my meaning. The tree of religion causes considerable damage when it takes root. The roots expand, and upend everything above and below."

"But — what I'm saying is, this place is just like that. This place is no different than when the church controlled everything. There's just no church. What's the difference?"

"The difference is man must be governed. What forever complicated that governance in our world was religion. Religion is only perspective. God, you see, has none."

"These people's god is blind."

"Precisely."

"I just don't get how someone could write something like you did, and think the way you do."

"I do not 'get,' as you say, how someone can choose not to practice their religion without penalty, nor do I 'get' how you are able to pursue a man's occupation, let alone a man's most brazen dream, and yet nevertheless, merely wash clothes."

Elizabeth exhales a long, tense sigh. These are her choices. These are her only choices.

"I cannot divorce myself from God," Elizabeth says, the strain naked in her voice, "though I must, if I am to survive. For God has divorced Himself from us. Perhaps He has left us, or exiled us; perhaps He has forgotten us and in so doing, time and tide became confused. We must make what we can of our circumstances. We cannot change them; we can only endure. I cannot account for how or why, but we have been given a new Eden. The apple remains our challenge. I planted my seed in cold, dead ground, and yet it has borne fruit.

"My only hope is that there is no hunger in our garden."

X

Blood streams out of Elizabeth's nose, on to her lip. She dabs it away with a napkin.

"Excuse me," she says, and reaches into her pocket for a small pillbox. "I am late in taking my medicine."

"I guess you are sea sick."

"I am that. However, this is unrelated." Elizabeth takes two of the fat, white pills with her tea. "Iodine. There are after effects of the radiation we are exposed to in the transfer from our world to this one. This radiation apparently has a negative effect on the humors."

"Geez... it's like fallout or something."

Elizabeth closes the pillbox and tucks it back in her pocket. "You will present symptoms in time as well. Not to worry. There are remedies. I shall warn you now, for women, it makes menstruation somewhat... irregular."

"Shouldn't we be trying to find out what happened?"

"As I said, it is beyond understanding."

"It's like a dream or something. A fantasy, you know? Mars." Alice fingers the tea cup, traces the delicate curve of its tiny arm. "I don't know. If someone shows up with a pair of ruby red slippers, I guess we'll know."

Elizabeth wonders what the significance of ruby slippers is, but she wants off the subject. "Hmm."

"Shouldn't we try to see if there's a way back?"

"There is no way back."

"But if you could?"

Elizabeth takes a deep breath, and then releases her hands from their fierce clasp, so tight her fingers have gone red. She leans back in her seat and signals the waiter.

"A deck of cards," she says as he approaches. "We shall pass our time not in deliberation, but in leisure."

The waiter goes to fetch a deck of cards from behind the bar and Elizabeth relaxes enough to smile.

"You play cards, Alice?"

"Solitaire."

"Sounds French."

"I don't know."

"I prefer Taroccho myself, but I imagine it will be as lost on you as your French pastime. I fear for your Iowa, my dear, with its Papist and French influence – Des Moines? – ah, here we are," she says, as the waiter returns with the deck. He places it gently on the table and then withdraws again.

"Such manners. A man born for the court, I should think. I shall teach you a game I have learned here. It is a game of wager. We do not of course have funds to bet, but we shall gamble. What do you suppose we bet, Alice?"

Alice shrugs, with a smile threatening to blossom on her

lips, and leans forward. "Every hand I win, I get to ask you a question. And you have to answer. Truthfully."

Elizabeth shuffles the deck, sliding the cards in and out of each other over and over. "Do I seem false to you?"

"I'm just curious. You're Queen Elizabeth, you know?"

"Hmm. And then what shall be your penance?"

"I don't know. Up to you, I guess."

Elizabeth completes her shuffling and sets the deck on the table. She cuts it, and then leaves the halves alone.

"I am curious, too. About the world I left behind. If I win a hand, you will answer for me any question I ask."

"I thought you didn't want to know."

"Then you must play your best game, my dear."

"And the game is?"

"They call it poker."

Alice smiles and cracks her fingers, appalling Elizabeth's sense of decorum.

"Good thing we already agreed to the terms," Alice says. "If I knew we were playing poker, you'd be out of your clothes in like fifteen minutes. So, c'mon. Deal."

Elizabeth picks up the cards. "You are familiar with this game? And in Iowa you wager your clothes?"

Alice collects her hole cards. "Me and you are going to have *so* much fun on this trip."

Elizabeth deals out the cards. "It is to you."

She hears the waiter welcome a new guest; she looks to the upper terrace and sees Joshua there.

"Do sit down," Elizabeth says as he approaches. "Alice intends to deploy a method of poker in which the players wager their clothes. Apparently in Iowa, apparel is at a premium."

"No, thank you."

"What other clothes do you own, aside from that bleak

uniform? Is it not the same one you wore when you met me? Variety would do him well, don't you agree, Alice?"

"Doesn't have to wear anything."

"It's been an hour," Joshua says.

"We have only begun to play," Elizabeth says.

"Play in your room."

"Perhaps privacy would suit Alice's game more, unless we are to include the waiter and other guests as well. I am not opposed to the idea, mind you, though such a conference would have to be governed by certain rules."

Joshua grabs the cards out of her hand. "I'm not playing any games, and you two have mingled enough. Go back to the ship and stay there. Don't talk with anybody. Just stay there until we get to where we're going. Ok? Let's go."

"Your manners leave much to desire, sir."

"I can hear every word you say."

"What?" Alice says. "How?"

"His device, no doubt," Elizabeth says, stiffening into a regal posture — nose up, neck back, countenance of barely held toleration. "Planted upon our person."

"You're out in public gabbing like people may not be listening," he says, planting his both his hands on the table and leaning down low with his voice so no one hears.

"You exaggerate," Elizabeth says.

"Go back to the ship."

Alice stands up to leave, but Elizabeth remains in her seat. "Go on, dear. I will catch up."

Alice blazes a trail from the table, arms crossed all the way up the stairs and out of the dining room. Joshua steps aside so Elizabeth can follow, but she refuses to concede her seat. She folds her hands in her lap and fixes her gaze out the window at the sky, nauseating as it is.

"I'm not asking."

"You will ask," she says. "And I will consider."

"You're not — you're not a queen anymore."

"I am God's anointed queen, sir. I should like to see your credentials before you make impositions on His."

Joshua takes the open seat. "Sounds to me like you don't place much stock in your God anymore." He picks up Alice's hand. A pair of nines. "We should go back. It's just Alice and Miranda back there."

Elizabeth collects her cards from where Joshua left them on the table. Ace of hearts, queen of diamonds.

"What shall we wager? Clothes I think are less wise in our case," she says, looking up from her cards a moment to gauge his reaction (indeterminate). "Prior to her endeavor to remove me from my clothes, Alice suggested we wager answers. I shall bet a question, and you its answer."

"I think you missed the part where I said we're going back to the *Sally Gap*."

"Where was young Miranda when you rescued me?"

"This is your question?"

Elizabeth deals out three community cards, and then turns them over one by one. Two of clubs, seven of spades, queen of hearts. "Only idle conversation. I stay."

He sighs. "The Long House. We spend the first five years there until we begin our field apprenticeship."

"And before me?"

"Are we getting to your question yet?"

Elizabeth deals out the turn. Jack of hearts.

"We are near. Do you have anything to bet?"

He shakes his head. "I'll stay."

She deals out the last card. Five of clubs. "Have you anything to bet now? I imagine if you had anything of value in your hand, you would have supported it before."

"I'm not really playing, so."

"I am. Does she know?"

"Know what?"

"The girl," Elizabeth says, impatiently. "Miranda. That is my question. Does she know the truth?"

"What truth?"

"The pills," Elizabeth says, and reaches into her pocket for the pillbox. "Does she know what she takes them for? This radiation that accompanies our exchange between worlds quite dissipates in the near term, but, and I do believe this is the technical term, *trace elements persist*."

Joshua acts for a moment like he doesn't know what she's talking about, but the more secrets he hides, the less able he is to keep them all sufficiently under wraps. He folds.

In her quarters on *The Sally Gap*, Miranda goes back a couple pages in her book and takes in, wide-eyed again, Samaire's epic battle in the streets of the city with the monster from beyond the Threshold. The monster, equipped with too many arms and no eyes senses only heat; the electric generators of the major buildings makes its belly rumble with hunger and its peels open the towers, knocks them over into staggering piles of concrete and steel to get at their delicious centers. It feeds off the house-sized generators embedded in the foundations through suckers in the palms of its many hands. Then, as the energy courses through its massive body, its fish scale skin begins to shine like water does, spoiled with oil; the nameless creature, freed from its ancient sleep in an icy tomb in the north after a melting of glaciers, continues its rampage through the city.

The local police and the agents they called in to help fire bullets and missiles, but they do little more than annoy the monster. The heat from their artillery allows it to either avoid them or destroy them, depending on its mood, which varies from minute to minute. Then Samaire arrives; armed with only a sword, leapfrogging from roof to roof. The creature sees her — the energy she exudes — and it nearly kills her. She quickly covers herself in mud — broken water lines everywhere - and so she's able to approach it, and then scale it like a mountain. Samaire ducks the flying bullets, the falling debris and the thrashing of the beast; she climbs the back of its neck, down the slope of its nose and then she stabs her sword into a gaping, slime-encrusted nostril. The monster screams and she dives, purposely, into its mouth.

She slides down its throat into its belly and from there works her way through the bile to its gigantic, undulating heart. She sinks her sword into it, splits it open from top to bottom and almost drowns in the deluge of blood. The monster topples dead into a skyscraper and the city is saved.

Miranda leaps from her bed in her cabin and draws her knife from its sheath in her boot. She jumps back up on the bed - the monster - wrestles with the pillow - its head - and makes phantom stabs into it until she pries open its mouth and winnows down its throat, under the covers, to its unseen heart. It's only then, when she finds nothing to serve as the organ she needs to bleed, that she remembers in her version of the story, the vintage story archived at the Agency, the monster couldn't see Samaire. She was just another girl.

In this new version of the story, Samaire exudes the same mysterious energy the monster does, that all things from beyond the Threshold do. The blood of the Others — the nameless, faceless race that lives beyond the Threshold and who unleash the continuous cycle of cataclysmic monster attacks on the city (not the people of the city themselves and their wasteful ways, as before) — flows in her veins. Her mother was human, shipwrecked on the other side of the Threshold, but her father — Samaire isn't human. Completely.

Despite her heroism she's unwelcome in the city, a freak of nature; the same is true in the Threshold, where even among the most sympathetic of her father's kin, she's a traitor at best. Samaire calls nowhere home. She has no family, no friends, only the occasional company of a young scientist, Cody, who tries to help her understand her singular power. She fights every day to find a balance within, between the woman of the city and the monster of the Threshold.

Miranda lies still under the covers, the search for the heart stalled; her breath comes back off the sheet and blanket hot and dampness collects on her cheek. In the older stories, Samaire is more a pet of the scientist, who is older; he finds her on the fringes of the Threshold, a nebulous lost world that lies beyond civilization, behind a veil of thick fog. He explains to her, once she's older, that her father was a scientist, too; the two men were colleagues and friends and her father went on an expedition to explore this strange part of the world with his wife and newborn girl in tow. The ship carrying them disappeared, and all hands were presumed lost. Years later, the scientist went looking for the wreck, prompted by new clues to its whereabouts, and inadvertently drifted past the Threshold. There he discovered Samaire and all the horrors she had lived with, alone, for a decade.

This version of her origin now leaves Miranda cold. She loves the idea of Samaire, if not more than human, other than; she identifies more with the young, powerful girl that can't ever fit into normal, everyday Canon than the girl who was simply lost at sea and then recovered. Nothing separates the old Samaire from her peers, except her heroism; not everyone understands her, but they adore her anyway. Her arc through the stories in the archives is one of earning their respect and approval, and gradually becoming one of them. The elder scientist Cody acts more like a doting father who teaches her how to read, how to speak correctly and how to behave properly in society. The younger, handsomer Cody in these stories acts more like a big brother. He looks out for her. Tries to make her better, but a better version of the person she is; he doesn't try to change her. He loves her the way she is, wild, free, unique. He's the only one who can understand her.

The original — the former — Samaire wants nothing more than to learn where she came from and who she was. The newer — the correct — Samaire could care less. Origin is trivial. She is her own beginning. The world spins out of her, not underneath her. The world as it was before Samaire, a world without monsters, without super-human power, no longer exists.

Miranda emerges out from under the covers. She wraps her arms around the pillow, squeezes it tight. She often does things no one understands, not even Cody; sometimes he gets angry with her, or disappointed when her behavior doesn't match up with what he expects from ordinary people. Sometimes she doesn't know how to act with other people; she has been alone in her own private world for her entire life. The manners and customs of others are only clothes to her; things she puts on, for whatever adventure or assignment she might be undertaking. They laugh, cry, caracole their bodies together in fitful motions and all of it fits as well on her as small shoes. Miranda hugs the pillow tight, her cheeks wet now. She hears the door open and shut in the cabin next to hers. No voices. Only muffled whimpering. The woman, Alice.

Miranda crawls off the bed, wipes her face dry with a sharp, vigorous swipe and goes outside into the corridor. The chair Joshua sat in between the two rooms sits empty. He must be off somewhere, with that Bess woman. Nothing about her makes sense. Joshua told her she is accompanying them on this mission because of 'orders'; normally that's good enough for her, but Bess occupies too much of Joshua's attention. He never looks at women. He never looks at any one. It's just been the two of them, for years now. She hates the company they have become; Joshua acts different. Suddenly what she does — what he taught her to do — disappoints him.

Miranda knocks on Alice's door. A moment later, it opens. Alice cringes. "Christ. What do you want?"

"I need a heart."

Joshua looks out into the blue, the burgeoning sunrise splintering it into many shades, indigo, periwinkle, violet.

"No," he says. "She doesn't know."

Elizabeth sets her cards down on the table, fixes her eyes on him. "What have you made of her, Joshua?"

"I did the best thing for her."

"Did you?"

"What do you know about it?"

"She is a child, with too much power and no sense of responsibility."

"If it wasn't for her, you'd be dead right now."

"She is the very creature you taught me to fear."

"No," he says, shaking his head. "She's a soldier. She does her duty and she does it well."

"Indeed. She is such a good soldier you cannot tell her the truth of what you are doing. What would happen if she were to find out? Would she murder Alice and I? You?"

"That's not what I'm afraid of."

"What do you fear, then? That she will learn the truth?"

"What truth is there? She was just a baby. What was I

supposed to do? Leave her out in the cold to die? Put my hand over her mouth? Put a gun to her head?"

Elizabeth doesn't flinch. "You are a lord of mercy."

"I'm a fool."

He takes the tea spoon from Alice's cup, taps it manically against the saucer and then the rhythm escapes him and he throws the spoon against the cup. It bounces off, end over end across the table into the deck of cards, spitting drops of tea all over it, all over the white tablecloth.

He stands up. "C'mon. Let's go."

Elizabeth dabs the tea from her hands with a napkin and then when she's sufficiently ready, she leaves her chair and follows behind him through the dining room. They exit onto the ventral promenade deck; some children in their nightclothes lie on the floor with their chins in their hands, their noses pressed against the glass, breathlessly watching the world turn beneath them. A boy points out all the little cities twinkling below to his sister. He knows all their names. Someday he will go to all of them, he tells her. It's important to go to all of the important places.

Joshua yawns, rubs his face as if trying to massage the fatigue out of it. Elizabeth never left England. Since her transplant to Canon, she has never left Lenapolis. Joshua goes and goes. There is no end to his travels, no rest. His mission never ends and likely will not until his death; he scrambles from continent to continent, world to world, wherever the orders of his superiors take him, running himself ragged with exhaustion and now he scrambles that much more to keep his secrets, many and multiplying, from them. He never asks why. He only follows his instincts, in everything. They are not the same. She would like to think so; on the surface it seems so, but she questions everything, and always herself.

"Joshua," she says, as he heads up the stairs. She stops at the foot of them, hooking him, drawing him back.

"What?"

"You have been to all the cities of the world."

"Most. I guess."

"It must give you a great sense of freedom," she says, inching back to the windows. "Of boundlessness."

He winces, as weary to entertain any more conversation as he is wary of where any of her words lead. Words to him are bait, pinches of sugar the poor boys of Clockwork sprinkle on the adobe steps of the old city in summer to lure out the red army ants circulating in the colonies beneath so they can step on them. They pop like grapes, they're so big.

Joshua descends back down the stairs, and they continue down the promenade. "It's all a blur," he says, shrugging. "I don't even know where I am half the time. Miranda knows."

"Do you ever want more?"

"More what?"

"Do you ever wish you could escape, Joshua? This life of yours. Yes, I know what you mean to say. You are a soldier. A servant. And I do not deny it. You are a servant to your master as I am to mine. But do you not wish? Ever?"

"For some light to sweep me out of my world?" They exchange looks. "If you plucked me out of your world and put me in yours, what would be different? I am what I am."

"You did not choose this life."

"They chose me for a reason."

They approach a small chapel of M. Joshua pauses a moment, looks in at a lone woman kneeling before a statue of M, blindfolded as always; she holds out her hands, at once as if in offering, and in emptiness, eyes in her palms. In one iris, a clock, cleft in two; in the other, the world. M did not choose her destiny as the world's savior, but she did not reject it, either. She delivered countless ideas for technologies and medicines as if she were a living fountain of knowledge, a god on earth in the guise of a teenage girl; in return, she did not seek wealth or land or the usual desires of men. She only asked that her subjects — the world wide, within a generation — serve her as completely and unselfishly as she did them. She asked they be taken, as she was, from their homes, never to return; to serve, always.

"They can't have known your facility from birth," Elizabeth says, trying to draw his attention back to her. The enigmatic M never struck her as the ideal of feminine power; the icon portrayed in art and literature down through the centuries is too meager a figure to command such respect.

"They can't have known yours, but you were still going to be queen from the moment you were born regardless," he says to her disappointment, and her fear. "We don't choose our lives. Life chooses us. We can't unmake who we are. You're a queen. I'm a soldier. People are born. Simple as that."

"I am not a queen now, as you are quick to remind me."

"You know what I mean."

Elizabeth turns from the panoramic, dizzying view of the shrinking world below. She looks on him, on the inscrutable facade he presents to the world. If there is another life caged within him, waiting for the chance to spread its wings, he isn't aware of it; he's barely aware of the life he does live. All the places he has seen. All the people he has encountered, all the stories he must have stumbled through without absorbing; stories cling to most like spider webs. On him, they're fine as smoke. His is only a narrative in scars.

"Miranda," she says, to his chagrin. "Was she born a soldier? She is so callous. So very cold."

"She's a better soldier than I am. Yes, she was born to it. I know she was. I know."

"Well. I am not born to Mars, my lord, so you will have to educate me. Or perhaps Alice. She seems more equipped for this than I. She seems to almost relish her circumstances."

"As if you don't."

"Do I?" He smiles. "Hmm. There is nothing to relish about being banished to another world. No. I shall have to learn a new way of life, again. I am able, but not as spry as I once was. Or as young. I do not think I shall fetch any pretty young thing that comes along now. I must prepare for my future. I shall require property, and an income."

He laughs. "You can get a job."

Now it's her turn to laugh. She falls against him, latches her arm to his. "And what would I do? What skills do I have to earn my way?"

"You're skilled, believe me."

"I would wobble on my legs like a newborn colt if I had to learn a new trade. No, I fear I am too old. I must remain plain to the colonists. As you desire."

"You can still write. I've read your poetry."

"Poetry does not pay the bills in any world, sir."

He discreetly tries to unhook himself from her, but she doesn't let go; instead of prying loose, he ends up dragging her with him from the windows to another set of stairs.

"Your apartment seemed to suggest otherwise."

"There are some who appreciate yet the written word."

"Is that what they appreciate?"

"Can you?"

"What?"

"Appreciate," she says.

"I think my value is pretty much what it was in the beginning. Disposable."

She squeezes his arm, laces both her arms around his now. "You are a fine vintage, sir."

"Elizabeth." He no longer attempts to be delicate; he pries her hands open and pulls his arm out of the noose of hers. "Elizabeth, you need to go back to your room."

"What fret can be such modest affection?"

"What are you doing?"

"Perhaps you find young Alice more to your liking."

"I find sleep to my liking, so let's go."

"She quite enjoys the view of you, from what she says."

"Let's go."

She reaches to touch his face. He flinches. "Has there ever been a kind hand put to you?"

"Stop."

Her fingers brush against his skin. "Beautiful Joshua... you struggle so. It tears you apart."

"Elizabeth."

"I suffer the same," she whispers. "I suffer."

Joshua gives in; he caresses her face, her chin, brushes her lips with his thumb.

"Stay with me this time," she says.

"I can't."

"All that you claim you cannot do, you do in any case."

"I'm not a traitor."

"You are what you are."

He grabs a fistful of her hair. His breath flutters heavy and fast on her skin; his lips hover over hers and his teeth flare and she thinks he might actually bite her; the tension in his face is such she thinks it might break but he does not kiss her. He relaxes his grip on her hair, slides his hand down the back of her neck, over her shoulder, down the valley between her breasts all the way to her navel.

The stairs above creak with movement. Miranda stands there, a red round couch pillow in her hand, riven.

"Joshua," she says. "What are you doing?"

He steps away from Elizabeth as if falling into line. His eyes, fixed on the deck, blaze with shame and anger. "She was being uncooperative. Take her back to the ship."

Elizabeth smiles wise as she begins again her ascent up the stairs. Miranda stares daggers at her as she passes.

Joshua points to the pillow in her hand. "What's that?"

"It's a heart," she says, crestfallen. "The heart of a monster. I cut it out for you."

The chandelier hanging in willowy crystal from the ceiling of the mezzanine rattles, singing like wind chimes as a thud shudders through the ship; Elizabeth locks her arms around the brass banister at the top of the stairs, terrified.

"What is happening?"

The boy lying on the floor with his sister, naming all the cities he will visit in his future, sits up on his knees.

"There's another ship out there."

XI

The Kuzar ship scarabs across the moon. The audacity. How did they ever find them; the alert Alice set off at the theater in Lenapolis. It's the only way they could possibly be tracking them. The Kuzar have tapped into the Echo Detection Grid. That, or they have someone inside. The thought mollifies Joshua; what if they do have a mole inside the Long House? Then someone there knows where he is right now. They know what he is doing, and who he is doing it with.

A warning shot — nothing more — streaks into the flight path of the *Liza Blay*. The passenger ship obediently banks to port, out of its orbital trajectory and Joshua clings to the railing of the stairs along with everyone else. The ship slows. If only the captain had sped up; the Kuzar certainly have no intention of destroying the ship. They could never have caught him. They have no means to follow into space.

This is exactly what they wanted.

A second ship, a sloop-dirigible, small and swift, punches out of the opaline cloud cap below them. A series of overlapping plates of armor flows from its bow to its stern, capped by a black, arrow-shaped crest that sheathes the ventral side of the nose cone. Twin cannons jut out like fangs from the underside of the cone. They spit light and smoke expands from them, clouds of ink in water; the shells impact the rudder of the *Liza Blay*, and the ship stalls.

Smoke filters into the ship. Screams pop like fireworks. Joshua grabs hold of Elizabeth and shoves her like a plow into earth all the way into the nearest passenger cabin. She trips over the shoes passengers have left outside their doors to be shined by the stewards in the night; Joshua doesn't stop to pick her back up, just drags her by her arm and deposits her on the bed with so much force she flops back off it awkwardly onto the floor. He slides the door shut behind him, barricading it with his body, denying her the view of the corridor filling with men, women and children jolted out of their sleep from the escalating commotion below.

"Who are they?" Elizabeth says. "What do they want?"

"You," Joshua says.

"What?"

Miranda leans against the door; she marvels, mouth agape at the sound of the carnage unfolding outside. The welfare of the passengers, the brashness of the attack doesn't even enter into her mind; all she sees is the comic-book size adventure in front of her. She only sees her and Joshua throwing back the boarding party, and then leading the reprisal, boarding the ship that no doubt has breached the hangar bay, capturing it and its outlaw crew, just the two of them, together.

"They have no idea," Miranda says, breathlessly. "They have no idea what they've just done."

"No, they don't," Joshua says, but referring to the passengers. The Kuzar are here for only one thing. Elizabeth clutches to the bedpost, one hand to her throbbing neck. They risk everything; open war. Annihilation. Such passion; for a person. An idea. It makes no sense to him. Alert klaxons sound throughout the ship, and then abruptly stop; they've taken the bridge. The Kuzar will stop at nothing to find what they're looking for; they've proven that beyond any doubt.

"We have to get off the ship," Joshua says.

Miranda and Elizabeth together: "What?"

"There's too many of them."

"We can stop them," Miranda says, with naked eagerness.

Agents operate under cover, out of sight, their works and their consequences invisible to the outside world. Staying means fighting. Fighting means making a battlefield of a ship with no means of self-defense. It means two against twenty. Thirty. A hundred. And if — even if — they did somehow throw back the Kuzar, there would be the having to explain later just what two agents were doing on a domestic flight to the Martian colonies, and just who they were traveling with.

"No. We have to leave."

"What about the people?" Elizabeth says.

"This is our mission. You're the mission."

"I thought Elizabeth was our mission?" Miranda says.

"She is," Joshua says. "She is. And we're not going to keep to it by staying aboard this ship. There is nothing we can do for these people but increase the risk of them all getting killed. There's only two of us, buddy. There could be a hundred of them out there. We're leaving."

He opens the clasp on the pack housing Miranda's field phone — his back on *The Sally Gap* — and winds the dial.

"Joshua to *Sally Gap*. Come in." He hears only static.

"They're jamming every frequency."

Miranda takes the receiver from him. "They can't jam ours. I'm calling the Long House."

"Don't."

Miranda looks at him, desperate. "Why the hell not?"

"Our mission is secret," he says, desperate as she is. "Classified, ok? No one — no one knows about it, Miranda, not even other agents. We can't let anyone find out."

"That doesn't make sense."

"We don't have time for this now. We're leaving. So get moving now, or I will leave you here."

"This is not dignified," Elizabeth says.

"It's survival," he says, no more proud of what he's about to do than she is. "Which you should understand."

"So where are we going then?" Miranda says. "There's no getting to the *Sally Gap* with all the Kuzar in the hangar."

Joshua closes his eyes, pounds his gun against his forehead, pounds out flints of memory. The company of air ships in the hangar aren't the only way off the *Liza Blay*; the designers outfitted it with a variety of auxiliary craft — sightseeing boats for sojourns to the moons of Mars or the orbital resort, as well as maintenance craft designed for patrol or repair - housed in the connective framework that marries the passenger gondola to the twin outrigger fuselages.

"Follow me," he says. "Stay together. I'll take the point. Miranda, you've got the rear."

"We're really not going to fight them?" she asks.

"Miranda!"

She flinches, jolted out of her fantasy, and herds Elizabeth into the middle of the room between she and Joshua. He leads the way out into the corridor, a tour through pure, living, breathing panic; crew and passengers alike seek cover or escape anywhere they can find it. Joshua pushes through the thrush of panicked passengers toward the elevator lobby; it's like walking headlong into 100 mile an hour winds. Screams cascade from below; they score every flickering light, every distant sound of gunfire. People pound the elevator doors, desperate for them to open as much for relief from the crushing weight of the mob behind them as from the Kuzar.

He shoves through the gridlock of bodies. Twists arms. Elbows ribs. A woman, suspended between the girth of one man and the height of another, stares at him with vacant eyes. There's nowhere to go. He seizes Elizabeth, throws her over his shoulder, and using a light fixture as leverage, climbs up and over the crowd. Miranda spiders after him and together they flop and wobble over the undulating mass of passengers out of the lobby to the promenade deck. They run across the mezzanine — clear mostly, save for a few running the way they came - and Joshua encounters a Kuzar in the midst of them.

The Kuzar points his machine gun at Joshua in the same instant Joshua deflects it away and wraps the gun strap around his throat. He strangles him dead and drops him to the floor.

It emboldens Miranda — she searches for another Kuzar, but they disappoint her with their local scarcity. The deft dispatch of the Kuzar proves finally Joshua's — any agent's - lethality to Elizabeth, until now only suggested; he is an angel, merciful and just, able to mete out judgment with a single touch. If he wanted to, he could strike down all these heartless invaders. Turn them in seconds to the salt pillars the wind and cold of their ever north has been slowly doing for decades. He could deliver the passengers from their fate. He chooses not to. For her sake. For the lie they share.

Joshua ushers them down the starboard promenade through the gondola, down the stairs and down deck after deck until he exits at E Deck, where the gondola connects to either outrigger. He rushes through the kitchen servicing the luncheon room there, and on into the compact alleyway of crews' quarters; the storage rooms that serve now as hiding places and finally the maintenance ports that take him into the heart of the starboard connecting hull. Joshua leads the way across the axial gangway, a high, narrow pass of cold steel threading the hull from the gondola to the outrigger.

They crouch along, moving sideways, until the claustrophobic passageway blooms into a small auxiliary bay.

Half a dozen Kuzar wait for them.

"Shit."

Miranda raises her gun; Joshua stays her hand. Frustrated tears blaze down her cheeks as the Kuzar march them all together with dozens of other passengers back to the promenade at the ends of bayoneted rifles. The Kuzar force them into the grand dining hall; there they organize the mewing passengers into rows of a hundred or more, spanning the width of the colossal hall. In the chaos, they find Alice.

"What are you doing here?" Joshua says.

"I'm sorry... they were coming in and I just came looking for you... I didn't know where else to go."

An Alephman throws over tables and chairs to make room, every brash action maximized to intimidate their captives. Joshua mourns for the people that chose this voyage. Not for their lives, spared to this point, but for the obvious truth that the whispers of the rebellion in the northern territories are true, that for all that shines and sparkles in Canon there are still corners where dirt and dust and debris collect; Canon, the great example of peace and prosperity in the world these last thousand years and more, won't be spared the fissures of war, the lines that betray her age.

His grief will have to wait. Squads of Kuzar roam the crowd of passengers, each taking their time examining them with radiometers concealed in their hands. The Kuzar soldier nearest them, a row ahead, waves it awkwardly in front of the dumbstruck passengers like a can of spray paint. He sweeps through the row with Alice, Elizabeth and Miranda.

"Don't let them take me," Alice whispers.

"Just breathe," Joshua says.

The Kuzar passes the radiometer over Alice. The device returns nothing. He next examines Elizabeth, no different, and then Miranda. She looks on in mute disgust as he strikes out and goes to another Kuzar on the foyer, his face obscured behind an outsized gas mask, the air hose curling like an elephantine trunk to a boxy oxygen container. He checks the radiometer for defects, but there are none.

"That shot you gave me," Alice says to Joshua.

"Yes, dear," Elizabeth says. "We are quite invisible."

The two Kuzar converse with each other, and it seems with someone else, someone in their ears; then, the masked Kuzar descends from the foyer, and holds up his hands. A hush falls over the dining room. He places a beat-up, antique radio on top of the banister.

"We seek only the prophet Elizabeth," Michael announces, his voice broken with static and hard to hear. "Joshua. Spare the passengers and crew of this ship any more disaster. You know what I am doing is right. You know our cause is just. If you didn't, you wouldn't be here. Come forward, Joshua. Join me. I ask you, as a friend, and brother."

"What is he talking about?" Miranda whispers.

"Surrender Elizabeth. If you do not, I will execute every passenger we do not identify as an Echo until you do."

Elizabeth's hands unlock, slide from behind her head

down to her neck, sore and swollen.

"I must come forward," Elizabeth whispers.

"No."

"Joshua, be reasonable."

"We have to find a way out of this."

"They mean to murder innocent lives."

"They already have."

"It is your duty to protect them," Elizabeth says.

"My duty is to the mission."

"I will not be the cause of this."

"Joshua," Michael's voice bellows, "this is your last chance. Don't make these people suffer for your pride."

The masked Kuzar descends back down into the dining room. He begins his search anew in the front row of passengers, now armed with a different type of radiometer.

"What's that?" Miranda says.

"I don't know. I haven't seen it before."

The Kuzar scans the first passenger, a young man. The radiometer doesn't buzz. The Kuzar shoots him in the head.

Screams multiply, drowning out Elizabeth's confession; Joshua grabs her and shoves her deeper into the crowd. The Kuzar, seeing and hearing nothing in the way of surrender, continues to canvass the front row, one body at a time.

"Stand behind me," Joshua whispers to Miranda.

"What?"

"Behind me. In the row behind me."

"Why?"

The Kuzar completes the first row. He steps over the body of a woman and sweeps the radiometer up and down the passenger beside Joshua. Joshua places his hand firmly on Miranda's stomach and pushes her back behind him.

The Kuzar inspects him next. Joshua stares into the

glass eyes of the gas mask as the rebel waits for the result; the scan comes back negative, and the Kuzar — his breathing heavy, compressed — lifts his gun to Joshua's head.

"Wait," another Kuzar says. "This one."

He reaches between Joshua and Alice, grabs lurking Miranda and pulls her out front and center.

"You missed this one."

The Kuzar puts the radiometer to her. Joshua puts it into his nose. He wrests the submachine gun away from him and horrified screams explode along with a cloud of red mist; two more rebels drop before they even realize what is happening. When they do, the Kuzar spray the dining room with bullets. They cut down the decorative trees, the brass pillars, the marble statues standing sentry at every level of the terraced hall, the passengers in between. The sea of people crashes to the floor, leaving Joshua standing alone in the middle of them. He takes dead aim at the windows of the hall in the distance with the gun he liberated from the Kuzar and fires.

A scream louder than any uttered in the ship so far envelopes the room, along with a gale force wind that rips everything not fastened down from the floor and out the gigantic hole he placed in the window into the sky. Kuzar, crew, passengers — mostly passengers — disappear.

Elizabeth and Alice hook their arms around the spindles of the railing that trails the central stairwell, but even they rattle in their places; dishes, forks and knives become weapons as they fly through the air out the fissure. Joshua crawls toward the stairs — the table he and Miranda hid behind long gone — and the four of them form a human chain, climbing over one another step by step, flight by flight until breathless and exhausted they reach the landing. Shield doors drop over the windows and pressure returns to the hall; ears still ringing,

Joshua pulls his company up on their feet — never looking back — out of the hall into the promenade.

"Where do we go?" Alice says. "Where do we go?"

"Back to the escape pods," he says.

Alice looks back at the dazed people spilling out of the dining hall. "Wait," she says. "Wait for the others."

He doesn't. He leads them back through the chaos toward the outrigger and the auxiliary bay. The Kuzar collected in the dining room; none remain to guard the patrol craft now.

Joshua opens the cockpit hatch to the nearest bubble shaped patrol boat and turns to Elizabeth. "Get in. Hurry, c'mon." Miranda follows and — "Wait. Wait, where's Alice?"

Joshua looks down the passageway. "Alice?"

No answer comes but the rush of air. "Where is she? Did you see her? She was right behind me, did you see her?"

"You must go back for her," Elizabeth says from inside the mouth of the lifeboat. "Joshua, please."

He looks to Miranda. She shakes her head. *You made a decision. Now stick to it.* He doesn't need Alice. Only Elizabeth. For what? What is he doing? Is it just for her, or is it for every woman he's been sent to mitigate the last thirteen years? If he doesn't leave now — right now - the Kuzar will find them, jettison the boats unused; if they don't, the squads of agents that will arrive soon to perform the rescue he should be conducting himself certainly will.

He wipes the sweat from his lip with his gun hand, bends over, rests his hands on his knees; he's so tired. Always tired. He looks down the passageway. At Miranda.

"I'm going back."

"What?"

"I can't leave her. I'll be right back," he says and starts down the passageway. Miranda follows after him.

"No, you stay here."

"No!"

"I need you to stay and protect Bess. If they-"

"They won't! They can't."

"Then you have nothing to worry about. If they do, you need to get — you need to get Bess off this ship to safety. You need to take her somewhere no one is ever going to find her. And you can't — you just have to trust me right now, buddy, you can't ever tell anyone about it, okay?"

"Then you stay!" Miranda shouts. "If you won't tell me what's going on, then you stay here and guard her! Who was that guy on the radio? Why does he think Elizabeth is with-"

Elizabeth slips her hand around the bar spanning the inside of the patrol craft hatch cover, closes her fingers around it tight, wonders if it can deflect bullets.

Why so much consternation over lying to her; her entire life has been a lie. "Buddy..."

"Don't call me buddy."

"Miranda... you have your orders."

"Orders? Don't give me your fucking orders!"

"I promise," he says. "I promise, when this is over, I'll explain. Ok? Everything."

"Where are we going? Who is she?"

"We don't have time for this!"

"I'm calling in support," she says. "This is open war now. The Kuzar have no idea what they've-"

Miranda looks to Elizabeth, cowering inside the pod. "They think she's Elizabeth."

"Miranda, I can explain-"

"She's a decoy, isn't she?"

"What?"

"We're luring them out in the open. The Kuzar. These

Elizabeth cultists. This is what headquarters wants."

"Right," he says. "That's right."

"You could have told me," she says.

"And I will. I promise I will. Now you have to protect Bess. She's all that matters. Miranda, you're..."

Joshua lingers in the passageway a moment, the words so heavy on his tongue it can't move. It will have to wait. The truth has waited this long. He has no time to lose.

He goes back, inside of fear. Inside of death. This is what it looks like, the promenade walls riddled with bullets, speckled with blood. He is inside rage. The Kuzar take out their eternal anger at their Canon oppressors in base, barbaric fashion. People are what they are. He is a soldier. Elizabeth is a queen. And the Kuzar is a beast, a man low and unrefined, incapable of being brought up. A living fossil in need of a helpful shove toward oblivion. So he obliges them. He comes across one looting the pockets of a dead man at the bottom of the fore stairs. Joshua places the nozzle behind the Kuzar's right ear and he slumps over, like he fell asleep on his knees. Blood spurts out his head like a fountain, one, two, three times, and then fizzles into a relaxed flow.

Upstairs, the Kuzar comb through the passenger cabins for Elizabeth. Each one is its own trap. Alice certainly didn't go back up there, if she had any choice. The Kuzar sweep each room, zeroing in on her with the specially attuned radiometers and Joshua inches back down the stairs, painted to the wall, toward the boy he shot. Another Kuzar is bent over the body.

The other man, middle-aged, face scorched by wind and cold and streaked by tears, makes no attempt to confront Joshua. He only cradles the body of the younger man, wails madly, slams his fist so hard against his chest it reverberates in his sobs.

"What do you have to be sorry for?" Joshua says, moving down the stairs cautiously.

The old man continues the barrage against his own body. Joshua moves to point-bank range. The Kuzar reaches out, guides the barrel of the gun against his forehead. He shouts. Pounds his fist. Implores Joshua to pull the trigger.

Joshua looks down at the man, at the blood-soaked boy — just a boy — in his arms. His left eye bloodshot and swimming. The man closes his trembling fist over his heart, pulls it away as if he pulls it out of his chest and he holds out his open palm — empty — for Joshua to behold. Joshua flinches. He sees Miranda, on these same stairs not a half hour ago, holding a pillow. A heart she cut out of a monster for him. He sees Miranda dead in his arms. Her life destroyed. His. This is her only destiny. Either he will die or she will die or the both of them and what would it be to live without her; before he found her, he was just a soldier. Thoughtless. Chosen. Branded. An instrument. With her, with all the choices that followed, beginning with her name, he became something. *What have I become.*

He looks down at the Kuzar — this creature he thinks incapable of exceeding his origins — and Joshua comes undone. She cut out a heart for him. He had none of his own.

He will tell her everything when he gets back. They will live in truth. Free of fear and doubt. Joshua yanks the gun from the old man's hand. The gun feels heavy; he forgot how heavy it felt in his hands, the first time he ever held it.

He takes the radiometer off the boy and leaves the man to weep. To plead for death. Joshua races through the E deck, searching for any sign of Alice's radiation signature. The lights flicker; the sound of sporadic gunfire echoes through the corridors, rife with Kuzar. Joshua wastes ten minutes going on and off the deck to avoid them and then a flicker of ghostly green light on the radiometer; it takes another minute of exacting caution to descend a long, winding ramp that spirals into the center of the ventral deck, and rings the glass portal in the ship's belly that provides a breathtaking, unfettered view of the earth scrolling past below.

Alice stands on the far side, leaned over the chrome rail. Joshua checks the room. No one else.

"Alice?"

She barely looks up at him. "Hi."

"Alice, come on. We have to get out of here."

She stays where she is, transfixed almost by the view of the curved earth, city lights arranged in constellations shaped like organs, lungs, hearts, livers, or nonsense geometric shapes she saw spray-painted on the sides of railroad bridges in Carpenter, some so densely they resemble the globular clusters that lurk on the fringes of the Milky Way; all the cities of the world patterns blinking in and out of sight from behind swaths of ambergris clouds.

"You came back for me."

"Don't make me sorry, c'mon."

"You left them. You left all those other people..."

He should leave her. He should solve his problem once and for all and put a bullet in her brain.

"Why did you come back for me?"

"Alice."

"We got separated. I didn't know where you went, so. And I wanted to see this when we first came on board."

"You've seen it, so let's go."

"Why is this happening to me?"

He runs around the ring to her, seizes her arm. "Alice!"

"Ok," she says. "Ok."

He hurtles out of the viewing bubble back up the ramp

with her, abandoning the caution he took earlier. They pass the old man, still holding the younger one dead in his arms. He shouts at Joshua, crashes his fist into his chest and Alice stares at him, bewildered, for the brief moment he's in sight. Joshua traces his path back to the axial gangway, the path he's blazed twice now already, his whole life going over the same ground, again and again, burying his secrets. Exhaustion creeps up on him, dogs him when he can't afford it to and *You'll sleep when you're dead. Just keep moving.*

Ten minutes. Ten minutes or more since he left them. The wake of a jet shudders down the spine of the air ship. The patrol drones that orbit high above the continents, monitoring all activity below, have arrived; in just a few minutes — even less, more than likely — a Canon destroyer-dirge and an entire legion of agents will follow.

Cold air nips at the back of Alice's neck. Joshua stops halfway down. A Kuzar lies across the passage, blood trickling down his mask out of a bullet hole in his forehead.

Joshua aims his gun forward. "Miranda!"

No answer. He continues forward, pausing only to check the myriad nooks in the labyrinthine metal framework of the ship's interior. He never should have left them. Never should have let Elizabeth out of his sight, not with the rebels combing the ship with radiometers. The rebels cut all the auxiliary craft free from their moors, shoved them out the open hangar bay doors. Blood slicks on the deck. Her blood.

His breath freezes in the air into crystal clouds, to his lips as soon as it leaves his mouth; he crawls out into the hurricane inside the open auxiliary hangar, grabs hold of a cut metal cable flapping loose madly in the wind.

"No..."

"Joshua," Alice says. "What are we doing here?"

He activates the radiometer. "Please... please..."

Two signals — very faint — come back, both of them moving gradually toward the liner's primary hangar bay.

He grabs Alice's hand and takes off, again. The Kuzar are in retreat; the ship belongs to ghosts and survivors. He runs free across the emptied promenade into the main hangar. A trio of Kuzar drags Elizabeth and Miranda — limp and trailing crimson slush — into their sloop. Joshua fires down on their captors from the catwalk, but it's too late; the Kuzar sloop retracts its planks, and departs the hangar bay.

The sloop emerges into a cloud of anxious shell fire from the arriving destroyer-dirge. The sloop is too close to the *Liza Blay* for the gunners to differentiate; the shells collide with the *Liza Blay's* hull and the rest plays out in seconds: fire licks at the pierced skin of the starboard outrigger fuselage, melts into the superstructure, into the fuel cells.

Meeley jumps up and down at the hatch to *The Sally Gap*, signaling for Joshua and Alice to get it moving or else; Alice grabs him and drags him from his stupor to the ship.

Meeley debarks as the fuel cells rupture. The terrible cold ravaging the interior of the *Liza Blay* vanishes, along with the ship itself. As Alice promised, the liquid-hydrogen simply ignites, creating a titanic cloud of fire that spits everything within it out at extreme speed.

White smoke trails off a single yellow shoe as it streaks past the control cabin of *The Sally Gap*. It spins madly end over end around some invisible axis in its toe, a meteorite, one of millions; the myriad pieces of debris exhaust their upward velocity after a minute or so, submit to gravity and then arc down in a cloud that that takes the shape of a willow tree. Alice remembers Brian, the day of the *Challenger*, saying how it was 'cool,' the odd Y-shape the contrails of the booster rockets formed as they flew off like chickens with their heads cut off. *People are dead,* she said to him, holding the slack of her sweater like a lifeline.

He shrugged. *Still cool,* he said.

The fireball becomes the supernova of a star; a cloud of gas and dust and metal, seeds of the future like the star in Taurus, a brilliant loose iris in the sky and the cloud of fire above produces millions of infant stars. The twisted, melted metal girders that formed the shape of the ship, the gloved hands, the capped teeth, the gold watches, the leather bags and metal trunks, the small pets trapped in their cages, the forks and knives, the tea sets, the Alice's, the Joshua's, the Elizabeth's and Miranda's, all of them will fall back to earth, coalesce into a larger whole, compress and fuse in diamond forming temperature to create the new, the next, the cycle endlessly repeating; we are stars, Alice thinks. We die in space and time and we die always, and forever, and never.

Alice Vale, 24, alone, very far from home, mourns her near miss with touching the face of God; right before she finds too much beauty in disaster, reality stages a final, sobering comeback. The nose cone of the starboard outrigger, reduced to its skeletal form, falls out of the cloud, crumbling as it does, trailing ribbons of flame. The fire ball diminishes. The winds stretch it, thin it out like dough and soon it's indistinguishable from any other cloud that papers the earth. She is not a star. She is just a woman, flying faster than she falls, falling forever through time.

"What now?" Meeley says.

Joshua points a bloody finger toward the fading point of light far in the distance ahead.

"We go after them."

XII

Miranda, still at swim from the blow to the back of the head she sustained on the *Liza Blay*, finds a shore of consciousness. Mildew and must hang heavy in the cold air. Water stains the ceiling, rotted through; wedges of moldy plaster and insulation litter the floor. They cling to her face, the wet blood in her hair. She tries to wipe them away; her hands are tied behind her back. Her entire body hurts. She tries to get her bearings. Deep cracks line the walls, growing with each brief spring; melting ice drips in through the leaky roof, down into the cracks, where it freezes again and expands. A Kuzar man eclipses her view. Eyes blazing.

He rams his boot into her stomach. She rolls over to her other side and another man is there; he kicks her and they both kick, and stomp and jab. They have been doing this for — she doesn't even know how long; she barely remembers arriving here, in eroding Niurka, the city victim as much of the indurate climate in the Ice Garden as the economic choke-hold Canon has on the entire northern contested territories.

The men continue their assault. She kicks at their knees and they grab her legs and throw her against the wall. The door opens. A man in a long dark overcoat enters.

"That's enough for now," he says. "You'll have to forgive my men, Miranda. They don't like agents much."

Underneath the coat, Miranda spies a glimpse of a Canon agent's uniform. "They like you just fine. Traitor."

Michael gives an impish smile; the perception of a child, delicate as it can be, is often the hardest thing to undo.

"You're under many false impressions, agent."

"You're under arrest," Miranda says.

The men laugh. Michael only smiles.

"Thousands of Canon civilians are dead because of you."

Some of his advisors warned him — strenuously — against such an aggressive move. With no presence on Mars — and no means of getting there - he simply couldn't risk letting Elizabeth slip through his fingers and losing her forever. If she is Elizabeth; she must be. She has to be, or else he will have wrought Canon's inevitable, blind justice for nothing.

"That was never my intention."

"The only good intentions are ones you keep to yourself."

"Why were you taking Elizabeth to Mars?"

"Who's Elizabeth?"

"The woman in the next room."

"Why don't you ask her, then?"

"I did. She's spent the better part of the day denying the fact the sun is up, despite standing in broad daylight."

"Good for her."

"She's Elizabeth."

"I bet you wish she was."

"Is she a decoy?"

"Miranda. Serial number M-1347. Subjugate agent."

"Joshua has taught you well," Michael says.

"Another chip off the old block."

"The perfect soldier."

"Not like you."

That smile, again. "Is that right?"

He nods to the guards. They scoop her up off the floor and ram her into the wall. Plaster and ice fall on her head.

"Why were you taking her to Mars?"

"You can ask Joshua when he comes to get me."

One of the guards punches her in the stomach.

"Joshua is dead," Michael says. "He died on the ship."

They drop her to the floor. "That's a lie..."

"Talk. Tell me the truth, and it will lessen your pain."

"He's not dead," Miranda says.

"Joshua is... Joshua was an excellent soldier. And a good friend. I wish he were... I wish I had his help."

"He would never help you," Miranda says.

"Perhaps. But he was no help to Anaba, either."

"What are you talking about?"

"Bring her in here," Michael says to the guards.

They leave the room, and return a moment later with Elizabeth between them. Her face pales at the sight of Miranda, bloody, bruised, curled up on the floor.

"Tell me the truth," Michael says.

"I told you, I am not who you seek."

He gestures to the guards. They lift Miranda against the wall again, and deliver a blow that knocks the air out of her.

Elizabeth merely shakes her head. "This is amateur. I have weathered far better than you, sir."

"I'll kill her."

"She's a child."

"She's a soldier," he says. "And this is the only language she understands."

"Precisely. You speak it loud and clear."

With a gesture, the men release Miranda to the floor. She roils in pain, but never utters a single word or whimper.

"I'm not who you think I am. I am reformed."

"Yes," Elizabeth says. "Instead of murdering one person at a time, you have graduated to murdering scores of them."

"Canon guns destroyed the *Liza Blay*," he says.

So much violence. So much death, in her name; in the name of God. If only she had never written the book. If only Joshua had followed his orders. If only the whim of God — all she can attribute these perverse circumstances to — had left her in London, in 1562, to her own war of faith.

"Of course. It is never the match that burns down the house, but the fire. You have something of a king in you, sir. Yours is the light of your nation, and yet never you burn."

"God is the only king here."

"I think Him quite absent."

"You know of God. Of what I speak. You are Elizabeth. You are the one who brought the presence of God to us."

"My name is Bess Rose."

"Why do you lie? You are home. Among your chosen."

"It is unfortunate that your mistake comes at such significant cost. I gladly would have clarified any misunderstandings for you via telephone. My number is listed."

"We hacked into the Long House mainframe. I've read all his reports. Including his most recent assignment, he mitigated an Echo in the north exactly four times. The first one was nine years ago. How long have you been here?"

"I have been here a few hours."

"You're an Echo," Michael says. "The radiometer doesn't lie. I seek only the truth. I lift shadows."

"You have cast your people in darkness. Surely the Canon reprisal will be swift and indiscriminate."

"Why was he taking you to Mars?"

"It was as much a mystery to me as to you."

"Has he been hiding you this entire time?"

"I am quite obvious."

"Was he defecting?"

"The only defect here is your hospitality. I should think that as your guests, it would not be too much to ask that Miranda and I have a place to sit."

"Of course. You are my guest."

"And a cloth. For her wounds."

"Get a rag," Michael says. "And some ice."

One of the guards leaves, and the other leads the two guests into another room in the structure. Michael pulls out two chairs from an uneven table, and sits Elizabeth. Miranda falls into hers. Michael takes a bottle of whiskey from a rickety cabinet. The building shakes with the passing of a diesel truck outside. Dust sprinkles the table top.

"My people are frustrated. Angry. They seek peace. You can give it to them, Elizabeth, with the truth."

Elizabeth looks at the remaining guard, still glowering at Miranda, his restraint as barely held together as the building they inhabit. "Truth is not always a guarantee of peace."

"Perhaps the truth then is that Elizabeth is a myth. A legend no different than those in the Bible."

"Myths are often void of facts."

"And often based in truth."

"What does it matter?" Elizabeth says. "What does it

matter where he was taking me or why?"

"Because I have spent the last five years looking for you. Because I have spent my entire life in search of you. The faith you have given me. Because I spent ten years raising that boy… and because he found you first."

Michael pours a glass of whiskey, and hands it to Miranda. "Drink this. It will warm you up."

Miranda spits it out. "It burns…"

He pours himself a glass. "Drink it."

Michael offers a glass to Elizabeth. She declines.

"I am sorry for your ignorance," Elizabeth says. "And I am sorry you have killed your friend. You will not assuage your guilt or dispel your questions with further violence. I suggest you release us both and apply a deeper read to the book that you have so indiscriminately shattered lives for."

"This is a terrible tragedy, one I fear will have… unfortunate repercussions for my people."

"These aren't your people," Miranda says.

"Of course they are. As they are yours. As all people of the world are your kind, agent. And your charge."

"Kuzar aren't Canon."

"The Long House has invested decades of blood and treasure in insuring that they are indeed Canon. If they hadn't, why else would we be here? What would it matter what a small group of people did or didn't do up on the edge of the glacial threshold? They are your people, as they are mine."

"You're a traitor," she says.

"So you've said. I have only taken back my identity, agent. Now my people take back theirs."

"Joshua's going to come and find me. And then he's going to break you in half. You fucking traitor."

"They call us Eyes," he says. "And we're the most blind

of anyone in Canon. You'll see, agent. You will live in truth, before the end. I will give you your sight."

The guard returns with a cloth and some ice. He sets it before Miranda on the table; she swats it away.

"I found this also," one of the guards says, and hands Michael the worn, tattered copy of the book of Samaire. The musty smell of the paper takes him right back to his youth. His fellow students at the Long House used their days off — one a week, beginning with their tenth year — to shadow field agents, a tradition that led nearly all of them to the men and women they would eventually spend the last seven years of their training with. Michael spent the many of the few precious days to himself to explore the city, to stroll the avenues in search of the young girls he was told to avoid. His uniform impressed them, only slightly less than his lean, fit body and good looks. He came across stalls in the Kuzar ghettos selling their odd foods, and some - if you said the right thing, or gave the right look - their odd literature.

He read the books and magazines the others had no idea existed, developed a passion for the world beyond the campus where he had spent nearly every day and hour from his arrival there as an infant. Some days he never wanted to go back; after he finally did spend time shadowing with the agent he would eventually apprentice with, seeing the world beyond as it really was - not as they said it would be - he never did.

"I'm surprised such a thing would interest you, agent."

Miranda takes another sip. "Joshua let me read them..."

"Ah." He goes to the table of contents, searches for the story he remembers most. The secret origin of the Threshold.

"I don't know if I like it," she says, trying to focus on something other than the ribbons of pain that arc up her spine, through every nerve in her body, into her teeth, and the fear, like a slow trickle of sweat down the back of her neck, that he's dead. They killed him. He went back for that worthless bitch and got killed. Left her alone. All alone.

"No?"

"Everything's different... Samaire's different."

"I actually quite prefer this version," Michael says, studying the images of Samaire listening to an old man, a native of the coast bordering the Threshold, as he relates the long-lost tale of how the world became divided. The old man sits on a boulder on the shore as if it were a lotus.

"The stories aren't so different. It's the details."

Detail was meaningless, until she read the book; what did it matter the when, the where; a job was a job. No trace of anything she or Joshua ever did remains after they've done it. It's like they never did it at all, so what does it matter; it's gone, even from her memory. Then she read the book and suddenly detail meant everything, the color of her hair, the difference in attitude between her Samaire and his and what color shirt was he wearing? He always wore his uniform. Didn't he? He had something else on the ship. What was it? What did he say to her? He was trying to say something.

"Have you read the origin of the Threshold yet?"

Miranda releases a sigh of frustration, like a gush of steam from a broken pipe. "It doesn't matter."

"It doesn't?"

"She doesn't care," Miranda says, looking down at the floor, trying to evade him, the pressure building up inside her. "It doesn't matter where we come from."

"Where *we* come from?"

"You deaf, or what?"

Michael pockets her reaction for later. "In the archived stories, it was the scientists that did it. Well. They had a fancier title. They were philosophers. Poets of technology. Seven of them lived in a gigantic tower they built from the machines they had created throughout the ages, and they continued their experiments uninterrupted for decades — centuries, maybe — until one day, one of those experiments went terribly wrong. It cast the whole planet in this terrible fog, and let loose the horror of their misguided work to haunt the gloom for all time."

"Wow. Neat."

"It was, actually. Now, the experiment that threw the world into darkness also destroyed the philosophers' tower. It fell to earth and where it did, cities sprang up out of the debris. This one island formed the whole of human civilization. The fog, the Threshold and all of its shame, surrounded it on all sides."

"Is there a point to all this?"

Michael drifts toward the far wall, to the gorge torn open in its center, a Grand Canyon in brick. He traces the edge of the ever-growing crack with his hand.

"It was a story the professor told Samaire. She never questioned it. Now this newer version — sorry to spoil it for you - Samaire wants to know how the Threshold came to be."

"She doesn't," Miranda says. "She doesn't care."

"You seem averse, agent, to any talk of beginnings."

"They're meaningless."

"Why?"

"All we have is — our names."

Michael fits his hand into the crack, reaches as deep in as he can. "He named you. Didn't he?"

"Don't. Don't you dare."

"As I was saying. Samaire goes to a man who lives on the beaches in the north. He's lived there all his life, on the edge of the Threshold and everyone says if anyone knows, he does. So she goes to see him. And he tells her the story. In the beginning, the fog that shrouds the world beyond the Threshold covered the entire world. You could see nothing; no forests, no cities, no oceans nor mountains. The world was just a smooth, gray orb. A glass jar, filled with smoke."

"There was no tower?" Elizabeth says. "No philosophers?"

Michael holds up his hand. "There was one tower, so tall it rose over the veil of fog, over the clouds, over the earth itself. And at the top of the tower, a tree grew. The old man told her that one tree stood where they built the tower; the builders removed it and preserved it, believing a story they were told, maybe by an old man on a beach, that the tree would live forever, so long as no one ever ate from it. And so long as the tree lived, so did the people of the tower."

Elizabeth chuffs with barely suppressed laughter.

"Is something funny, Bess?"

"Familiar. Do go on."

"As our friend 'Bess' already suspects, someone did eat of the tree. And the tree died. So did the tower. It crumbled, and fell into the darkness below. But where the tree fell, a garden grew. That garden spread over the earth, its plants and flowers breathing new life into the world, clearing the sky. The fog retreated, and the Threshold was born at the place it stopped, just off shore of the garden island the survivors of the tower made their home."

Miranda shakes her head. "So?"

Michael flicks away the flaky edge of the crack in the wall. He rubs the residue of dust between his fingers.

"So. Who built the tower?"

"We did. The people of the city, I mean."

"But the Threshold existed before the rest of the world."

"In your — I mean — whatever. It doesn't matter anyway."

DARBY HARN

"But if that's true, the only people that could have built the tower lived under the fog. Beyond the Threshold."

"That's impossible," Miranda says.

"Right. It must be. Because the Others have no intelligence. No skill for something like this."

"Exactly."

"The Threshold is home to monsters and demons, not scientists. Not philosophers."

"It's bullshit."

"You know," he says, wandering back over to her, "Samaire thought so, too. At first. But then, it made sense to her. Where did the power of the Others come from? Her power?"

Miranda blinks. She never gave any thought to where. It didn't matter; Samaire's power was her own.

"Why do you think she wanted to know?"

"Who cares."

"Don't you think she wanted to know who she really was? Where she really came from? She never felt at home in the city. Even in my stories, she always wanted to go back."

"She doesn't belong anywhere. Only with Cody."

"What if she does belong somewhere? In the Threshold? What if she came from someplace else? Other? Before? Do you know what happens after she leaves the beach? All her life she battled the creatures of the Threshold, for her own survival, for the city's. After she leaves the old man, she decides to defend the Threshold from the men that seek to destroy it. She embraces her beginning. The world's."

Michael takes a long, hard look at Elizabeth, not oblivious to what he's doing; she looks away, toward the crack in the wall, to avoid his eyes. Miranda's.

"Let me show you," he says, gently placing his hand on Miranda's shoulder. "Let me show you the truth, agent, and then you can decide for yourself where your loyalties lie."

"My loyalty is to Canon. To Joshua."

"I know where you came from, Miranda. I know the truth that Joshua has hidden from you your entire life."

"Don't," Elizabeth says, despite herself.

"She must know the truth," Michael says.

"Leave her be. For the love of God, she is but a child."

Miranda trembles with rage she can barely contain. Fear drives Canon policy; it has since the beginning. Michael sees now that that fear has hardened; it has metastasized into raw, inarticulate anger. This little girl has no cause to be so angry. If his instincts are right, Miranda has no idea yet what anger is. Michael takes a radiometer from his pocket.

"I doubt you've ever seen this model, agent. It registers even the faintest traces of gamma radiation, which persist in Echoes for decades after their arrival."

He turns it around, so she can see the display. Elizabeth thinks it is like the sun dying, Miranda's face.

"This is a trick..."

"It's not a trick. He found you, just like he said. An infant alone and naked in the cold. Only he knew to look for you. I can imagine his reaction at discovering the radiation signature he was tracking was from a newborn. I would have had the same difficulty in carrying out my orders."

"You're lying... you're lying to turn me against him."

Michael shakes his head. "The radiometer doesn't lie. Now, lest you think him less than the impartial soldier he is, remember, he couldn't just make up a newborn candidate for an agent. There had to have been someone, some baby girl, whose place you took. And what happened to her, do you think?"

Elizabeth utters a sound of pure disgust; his is the cruelty of boys kicking dogs.

He goes on, steadfast. "Maybe he left her with her parents. Maybe he left her with a new family. And maybe to preserve the lie, he collected her from her home as ordered and then left her in your place, out in the cold."

The outer facade Miranda presents remains intact, but Elizabeth can tell the collapse is well under way inside. Gravity takes hold. Nothing can stop it now.

"They would have known," Miranda says, grasping for any vine of hope. "At the Long House, they would have known right away. I'd be filthy with radiation."

"Unless you masked it."

"How?"

He unclips the pillbox from her utility belt. "Regular doses dilute the radiation in your body. They prevent cancers from forming. Over time, only a device as sensitive as this one would detect any lingering traces."

The tempest of disbelief inside Miranda dies out over the land of cold, hard fact. He lied. Joshua lied to her. To Anaba, to all the agents he has served beside. He has been helping the Echoes since at least her arrival as an infant a dozen years ago. Probably longer. Deceit always looks younger than it really is. He is a traitor, and if the look of guilt and shame on Bess's — Elizabeth's - pale, damp face is any indication, a collaborator. Joshua betrayed Canon just like Michael did. More so. Michael at least had the guts to stand up for what he's done. This whole mission has been a sham. Just like her entire life.

"But he loves you," Elizabeth says, triggering the tears Miranda has so fiercely tried to hold back. She trembles with sobs so violent she almost chokes on them. Her jaw, her teeth ache in the pain of them; it's nothing to compare to the hurt expanding like an iron balloon inside her heart.

"Everything he has done, he has done for you. He loved

you, more than his own life. Of all you doubt at this moment, do not be in doubt of that."

Michael kneels beside her. "It's not my intention to hurt you, agent," he says. He gently rests a hand on her shoulder. "Only to show you the truth. The truth is often difficult. Complicated." He looks back at Elizabeth; she seems as adrift as Miranda. "But still we must stand for it."

"You do to her what you mean to do to the world," Elizabeth says. "You destroy innocence. Peace. For what?"

"What of our innocence? Our peace?"

"The Kuzar were ignorant until you came along. Their struggle is only worse now, and sure to become more so."

"Why do you defend them? Why do defend her? This is all for you. You've opened all of our eyes, why close yours?"

"I cannot see in the dark," Elizabeth says.

"Miranda. Tell me the truth. She is Elizabeth."

Miranda looks across the table. Elizabeth rubs her neck, faint and warm with the fear let loose in her. Why lie. What difference does it make, how this started; where it was going.

"All we have is our name," Miranda says.

"Yes. And what is her name?"

"Bess."

That smile. "He taught you very well. Gentlemen."

The guards converge on Miranda and drag her from the chair. They herd her, like a wet worm in their hands, out of the room and out of the old schoolhouse.

"Where are you taking her?" Elizabeth says.

"What does it matter to you? Why does she matter?"

"She is innocent."

"Hardly."

"Killing her will not change the fact that your innocence, sir, is also in considerable question."

"I need your help, Elizabeth."

"We are all of us beyond help."

"You can help me. And you can help my people, this world, by telling the truth."

"The truth is you are gravely mistaken, sir."

He smiles. "The truth is, you are Elizabeth. You wrote the book. And in doing so, you breathed life back into our people. Until we found you, the Kuzar had been a wandering, lifeless shell of a people. A shadow of who we were."

"And who were you then, sir?"

"All we have are our names," he says. "I am called Michael. My mother... meant for me to be Yuriah. I named my first apprentice Joshua, but his parents had a name for him, too. One they mourn to this day. You were once Elizabeth as you are now Bess, as we who are now Kuzar were once Jew."

"What?"

Michael extends his hand to her. "Take a walk with me, Elizabeth. I want to show you something."

XIII

Majestic columns of light pillar the infinite tundra as day breaks. Shadows of clouds race up the versant slopes of the cragged, ice-besieged mountain range ahead. Meeley fires the dorsal thrusters of the air ship, giving them more altitude. Joshua paces the cabin; they're losing even more time. The much slower speed of this older ship compared to the Kuzar sloop has cost them hours they didn't have.

"Where are we?" Alice says.

"Trondek mountains," Meeley says, carefully minding the cloud-capped peaks scrolling past below. "This is some of the most treacherous terrain in the world. Golly..."

"You can drop me outside the city," Joshua says.

"I will, seeing how we'll be shot down if we go in."

"I don't know what the Trondek mountains are," Alice says. "Is this the North Pole or something?"

"We're near the Arctic Circle," Joshua says. "Niurka will just be on the other side of these mountains."

"If it's still there," Kitzer says, biting her nails.

His phone vibrates on his utility belt. The Long House has known of the *Liza Blay* for hours now; long enough for them to have responded to the attack. He knows like Kitzer does that attack will be directed entirely toward Niurka, the arbitrary capitol of the loose Kuzar confederacy that clings to a difficult existence in the relatively ice-free valley beyond the mountains; the valley exists in the rain shadow of the Trondek, preventing much of the moisture that locks the north under ice from taking hold. The "Ice Garden," as most Canon call it, also bridges the continents of Canon Major and Asia; it's formed a desolate oasis not only for wildlife, but for the disparate people of the world — the Kuzar, the Yukalut and their varied kin — and most dangerous of all, for ideas. Joshua expects — fears — they will come over the mountains and find the valley afire, shrouded in smoke.

"I need to check in," he says.

Kitzer and Meeley share a look. "Are you going to give us up?" Meeley asks.

"No. Drop me off outside the city. Then I want you and Alice to get as far away from here as possible."

Joshua charges out of the compartment into the cargo bay. He leans against a cluster of Wicklow timber, hands on his knees, every thought pressing against the inside of his head; she's probably dead. They probably killed her.

Alice sits next to him. "You're not getting rid of me that easy," she says.

"You can't come with me. It's suicide."

"Joshua..."

"No."

"What if," she says. "What if?"

"I'm going to find her."

"Elizabeth means a lot to you."

"Miranda," he says. "I'm talking about Miranda."

"Right… and if you do? What are you going to do then? Your people have to know what happened to the ship. They're going to ask questions. They're going to know we were there."

"I'll figure it out."

She sighs. She edges closer to him. Warm again. She rests her head on his shoulder. He retreats, as much as he can, and paces the valleys between the stacks of logs.

"Why are you helping us, Joshua?"

He says nothing, and then — why bother now? "Miranda."

"What about — oh. Shit. Her? She's? For real?"

"I found her… she was just a baby, and I couldn't… ever since, I struggled with what they… I did the only thing I could for her, and now she's… she's like them. Like me."

He feels less defensive now than with Elizabeth. She figured him out; unraveled the lie just like he expected Anaba or any of the others to do years ago. He fought her, fell back on his instincts to survive but Alice isn't trying to trap him. She isn't bargaining for something else. He asks himself, for the first time, why. Why never mattered before. The years passed and he kept stuffing everything he couldn't deal with — his sympathy for this child, for these people he indiscriminately dispatched for years before, the first on an assignment when he was only 10 years old — underneath why. His love for Miranda, then concern as she displayed the same traits he saw in other agents, a sense of entitlement, a sense of superiority to the people they were sworn to protect and he questioned, for the first time, why he was different. What was wrong with him.

"I don't know what's right," he says. "Anything I do is wrong to somebody. Nothing makes sense. None of it."

"Joshua..."

A loud, urgent buzzing startles them both. His field phone furiously vibrates on his utility belt.

"Don't say anything."

"What is it?"

"Don't say a word," he says, and takes a deep breath. He detaches the receiver. "This is Joshua, go ahead."

Anaba's angry voice screams over the speaker. "Where the fuck are you?"

Joshua sighs. "I'm not exactly sure."

"Why haven't you been answering?"

Joshua moves to the end of the cargo bay. "I've been observing radio silence."

"Do you have any fucking clue what is going on? No, don't answer that. I know you do, because you and Miranda were on that ship. So let me ask you another question-"

"I was following intelligence that Elizabeth might be on Mars," Joshua says, knowing as he speaks the words he is destroying any hope of ever hiding her or Alice there.

"What intelligence? Why didn't you share this with me?"

"I didn't know there was anything to share yet. We were interrupted on the way there."

"Don't get fucking cute with me, Joshua. A thousand people are spread out all over the damn ocean. They're telling me there's still bits of them coming down and I've got men in boats pulling the fingers and toes out of the water and what do they find? No, wait. You already know the answer to this too, don't you? What the hell, Joshua? The fucking rebels raid a passenger liner, a passenger liner you and another fully trained and armed Canon agent happen to be on and you don't think it rates a call back to headquarters?"

Joshua rubs his forehead, tries to find the words. The

explanation that will make sense.

"Joshua?"

"Look, Anaba, it all happened so fast. I did what I could, and then... there were hundreds of Kuzar."

"You didn't radio for help."

"They were jamming the signal."

"The crew fired a distress buoy easy enough."

"My utility belt doesn't come with one of those."

"I'll have R&D get cracking, then."

"Look... I'm as upset as you are. I don't know how we survived, but we did. They have Miranda."

"The rebels have Miranda?"

"Affirmative."

"Then who's *we*?"

Joshua pauses. "I meant — I don't know how I survived."

"Because I assumed — and you correct me if I'm wrong — the reason the Kuzar went to all this trouble was the same reason they thought it was worth the risk to send a ship into Canon airspace. They want Alice." Joshua can hear in Anaba's voice the strain to keep his cool; he can also hear that it's a losing battle. "You mean to tell me they attacked and destroyed a passenger ship of innocent civilians, and then fled the scene with an agent but not the woman they came for? Is that what you're fucking telling me, Joshua, because you don't sound one hundred-percent confident, soldier."

"They have Alice," he says, looking at her, fear and confusion in her eyes. "Miranda, too."

"Why did they take Miranda?"

"I don't know."

"Where are you?"

"Somewhere in the north. I commandeered a civilian air ship the *Liza Blay* was tendering to Mars and I am pursuing the rebel sloop. You haven't responded yet?"

"Your transponder isn't working."

"It got damaged along with my field phone."

"I thought you said you were maintaining silence?"

Joshua winces. Any other time he'd be nimble as a cat, dancing from lie to lie but he's exhausted. He feels heavy. Frozen inside and out, with fear and uncertainty.

"I am — I was — I meant it was damaged, but I was able to fix it. I just wasn't using it. I didn't want any rebels getting wise to the fact that I've been shadowing them."

There's a long pause on Anaba's end. Joshua looks at Alice, waiting nervously as he is for the next volley. Sweat beads on his forehead. He wipes it away with his forearm.

"Anaba?"

"There's a lot of pressure here, Joshua," Anaba says, his voice absent now of all of its bluster.

"I'll find Miranda and Alice, I'll get them back."

"That won't be necessary."

Joshua's heart skips. "Why not?"

"I will recover them both."

"You will?"

"At 0800 I will be leading a task force into the city."

Alice covers her mouth.

"A smaller force — a covert operations unit would be better suited to recovering them."

"This isn't a rescue, Joshua. Not to say the evacuation of our fellow agent is not the highest of my priorities — now that I've been duly informed of her capture — but we cannot allow these people to continue to harass our way of life."

"We need more information-"

"Fuck more information. No. It's over. The Kuzar, all of these strays have done nothing but empty our cupboards and fill our house with stink and filth. We're putting them down, once and for all."

Joshua falls back off his knees, leans against the splintered logs. He sits there, head slumping, one hand with the phone to his ear, the other over his eyes and Alice crawls to him, rubs his shoulder, his back, puts all the weight she can into holding him up. The facade falls away. She sees now the effort, the lifelong struggle he has fought against the forces within and without, a daily, hourly war between the training and the principles that hold him up and the human instincts, the gravity of the human heart that drags him down.

"You sure that's wise, sir?"

"If it weren't for the fact that I'm personally going to retire Michael — and that we have to rescue Miranda unharmed — I would just nuke the place and be done with them."

"People will ask questions."

"We're reporting the loss of the *Liza Blay* as an accident. We'll ground some flights, muster up some technical problem and have it fixed. Civil war will destroy Niurka. There won't be any survivors to say otherwise," Anaba says.

Joshua takes the phone from his ear, looks at the digital readout on his watch. 0730. "There's more than just Niurka. Destroying one city and all of its people won't solve your problems. As a matter of fact, I guarantee you'll have more."

"Oh, I know I will," Anaba says, the stress gone from his voice now, replaced with something like anticipation. "I quite imagine we shall have numerous uprisings all across the north. Even in Canon cities where we have minor Kuzar populations. And they will all have to be dealt with publicly, and resolutely. The people will see the rebels for what they are, and our cities will be clean. Our world. Finally. You know, this tragedy may have been a blessing."

"What about Elizabeth?"

"What about her?"

"You still want me to find her."

"Won't matter in a few hours. There won't be any one to care one way or the other about this woman or her book. If she turns up, we'll handle the situation, but I don't think she's going to be much of an issue going forward."

Alice holds Joshua tight now. "What are my orders?"

"Hold tight. Enjoy the local color. We'll have a substantial presence in Niurka within the hour. Rendezvous with us at one of the checkpoints we'll be setting up."

"Anaba?"

"What?"

"You were searching for my transponder signal."

"As I said."

"So you were searching for Miranda's, too."

"Stands to reason."

"You didn't pick up the signal?"

Anaba pauses. "Hers must not be working, either."

Joshua activates his tracking device. Miranda's signal picks up strength as they clear the mountains.

"I see."

"We'll find her, Joshua. No worries. Anaba, out."

Joshua throws the device into the cargo bay. Alice goes and retrieves it, holds it out for him to take.

"For the others," she says. "When we get closer."

He angrily grabs it out of her hand and replaces it on his utility belt. He sits with his elbows on his knees, his hands over his eyes and breathes heavy and quick. The people that perpetrated the attack on the air ship — Michael, his circle of advisors, the boarding party — should pay for what happened. But not an entire city. Not an entire people.

"I can't stop him," he says, voice hollow. "Any more than I can take on all the rebels myself."

"We have to save Elizabeth."

"And Miranda."

"Sure."

"You need to stay with Meeley."

She grips his hand. "I want to go home."

"There's no going home, Alice."

"If there is, I'll find it with you."

"And if we live? What do we do? Where do we go?"

He can't go back to the agency. That's for certain. If Anaba hasn't sniffed out his treason already, he surely will once he and his task force storm into the city and blast Elizabeth out from under the very thin lid Joshua has kept on her the last nine years. It's not a court martial he fears, or a firing squad; it's not the lies he has told to Anaba, but to Miranda. He fears having to face her, those eyes; and he will have to lie again, and convince her to do the same to save her life. If Miranda learns the truth, it's only his life; if Anaba learns she is an Echo, it's hers. They will do to her as they do all the Echoes they missed the first time; they will strip of her clothes, make her naked as the day she arrived and throw her to the ground before they press a gun to her temple and pull the trigger. Part of him, a very small, dark part of him that he shoves back down in the deep, considers the relief he might find if he were to get to Niurka and discover her already dead.

"You need to live," he says. "And be with people who understand you. You're staying here."

"Mars sounded nice," she says, and the stillborn smile on his face tells her that idea is what it always was: a dream.

"You wouldn't like it anyway. It's cold. Dusty. Like the Gobi, I guess. If you've ever been there."

She smiles. "No."

"Maybe we could go there," he says, indulging himself now. "Some place big. Lonely. Some place I can be just a man, and some place Elizabeth can be... just a woman."

"You care about her. Don't you?"

He shrugs. "Sure."

"I mean you love her. You're in love with her."

"I need to tell them to hurry on," Joshua says, and goes to leave the cargo bay. Alice wraps her arm around his.

"It's ok. It's nothing to be afraid of."

He smiles, embarrassed, like a child unsophisticated in love or sex. "She is... she is incredible to me."

"Well, yeah. She's the queen."

"She's the queen," he says.

"Joshua... you should keep that in mind. I mean... she's someone that... maybe she's not everything she was then, but she's still... she was the center of the world once."

"She doesn't want that life anymore."

"She is who she is."

"Stay here," he says, and leaves the cargo bay. He returns to the flight compartment, where he can just make out the faint silhouette the Niurkan skyline, irregular, splintered and strange; the tallest buildings peak in ovals. He detaches his binoculars from his utility belt and focuses on the tallest building; he follows a long cable tether from its mast to a barrage-balloon, fat and gray like an elephant, swaying in the stiff wind sweeping down off the glacier. Half a dozen of the antique dirigibles hang over the city center, disappearing in and out of the low, persistent cloud cover.

He turns to Meeley. "Drop me five miles outside the city. I'll run the rest of the way."

"I'm picking up a fleet of ships on long range radar."

Joshua nods. "Just set me down. Get out of here."

"How are you going to get out of here, Joshua?"

"Good question."

Meeley looks over at Kitzer, mauling her nails.

"There's a river that runs under Niurka, all the way south down the valley to Bank Head Bay. After we drop you, we'll head there. We'll wait until nightfall."

"Why would you do that?"

"Because I owe Bess everything," Meeley says. "And the way I hear it is that she owes everything to you."

"Thank you."

Meeley only nods. No thanks are necessary; no one can exist in this God-forsaken world without the help of others. There are no Samaritans; only shipmates in survival.

Silence falls over the compartment; the air thickens with the invisible anxiety of waiting. Kitzer drifts out of the compartment, unable to bear it, back to the crew quarters. She finds Alice in hers, sitting on the bunk, weeping.

"The world's gone mad," Kitzer says.

"He's going to get killed."

"We'll wait for him. At Bank Head Bay."

"I always told myself... if I ever had a chance to go find my brother... I'd try. I'd try to save him."

Kitzer sits beside her. "What happened to him?"

"He was in the war. Vietnam. He went missing."

"I'm sorry."

"Thank you."

"My father was Army. That's how he met my Mom."

"Where? You sound–"

"German, yeah. Landstuhl."

"So — you must be — when were you born?"

"'76."

"When did you disappear?"

"'97."

"And none of this — of course not. You know who Elizabeth is, right? She's the Queen of England."

"She looks a bit better than Liz."

"No, like the first one."

"Shit — really?"

"I wonder if I'm still alive in 1997. I'd be — yuck. I'd be older. What's it like? Who's queen now? Diana?"

"Just. You'll see. Or I guess you won't."

"Elizabeth said someone brushed the line. It got all confused somehow."

"It's beyond me, love."

"We need to find out what happened," Alice says. She feels the ship slow, start to lower. "We need to fix it."

Joshua arrives in the doorway. "I'm going."

"You know," Kitzer says, standing, "I'm sore you don't remember me, Joshua."

She pulls the cloud of hair around her head back into a single thrush; he looks on her for a moment, and then it hits him. Kitzer. The first Echo he saved after Miranda. He hid her, lied about her fate to Anaba just like he did Elizabeth and all the others, too many now to count.

A giddy, almost childish smile betrays heavy lines of wisdom saddled beneath her eyes. She's too young to have such old eyes, to have to fight a smile; she loses anyway. It devours her entire face, pale and intent, those eyes too dark by contrast, black like coal.

"We never thought we'd be saving you," she says.

"Who's we?"

"Yours," Kitzer says. "Like me. All yours."

Years of buried memory well up within him. He forgot

them all, purposely, later unconsciously, out of habit. It became as routine as tracking them, killing them, filing the report; he found them, set them up in their new lives, delivered the same exact account of what happened — the details changed slightly to reflect the circumstances — and simply walked on to the next assignment. He never invested anything in them more than the hours or days it took to secure them. They do not exist, as none of the missions he has ever participated in exist; there has never been record of his life - no evidence he exists at all — until now.

"How many?"

"You've saved 47 souls," Kitzer says, her smile spreading to Alice. "47. You inspired us, to take up your cause. Bess — Elizabeth — gave us so much more opportunity."

"This isn't my cause..."

"Joshua," Alice says. "Don't you see? Look at what you've done. The good you've done."

He only sees the faces of those he didn't save. Those he killed. Hundreds more. A thousand maybe, by now. He never counted them either, and as good as he was at forgetting the saved, he was much better at forgetting the dead.

"We've rescued hundreds," Kitzer says. "We track them the same as you. Find them, catch them before the agency does. Most of them are living in Clockwork, in Little Hand."

He is wordless, breathless; he gestures desperately. What does he say. "This isn't something I was trying to do."

"You've done it. And you don't have to do it on your own any more. We've been talking. You can help us."

"I can't..."

"Look at what is going to happen here, Joshua. What the Kuzar did is unforgivable. But so is the apocalypse that Canon is going to rain down on Niurka. It's wrong."

His stoic resolve resurfaces. "You're talking about open

war against the republic. Everything it stands for."

"The murder of Echoes has to stop. With you fighting with us, we have a chance."

"This is our world."

"It's never been your world. Echoes have been coming here since the very beginning. Before there was an agency to 'mitigate' them, and before there was ever a Canon. They came with knowledge, just like your Elizabeth. Where did the ancient Canon get their technology? Who gave it to them?"

"M," he says.

"And who was she?"

Joshua doesn't know what to believe. He's never believed in anything; only followed orders.

"I thought Meeley was the one in charge around here."

"It's her ship," Kitzer says. "Come back with us. Save the lives you can. Save yours."

"I have to go get her."

"Then when you get to Bank Head."

"I won't betray the republic."

"You already have."

"Good luck," he says. He touches Alice's hand, and then leaves the cabin, to descend to what can only be his doom.

XIV

The streets of Niurka smell of fish cooked over open fires, brewing in pits out on the shoveled paths in front of the buildings, the majority of them large, wooden boxes, the bare minimum of human shelter; in neighborhoods where the electricity has failed, the people broke down the houses and burned them for heat. The streets smell of the mammoths that walk them, dragging carts of goods, sometimes small sheds on wheels, all the home some have. They smell of the significant reminders the animals leave behind. Elizabeth steps around the dung piles, small hills reaching up to her waist in some cases and the smell makes her nauseous; she covers her mouth with her hand, stumbles through the muck of mud and shit and water, the streets nothing but paths cleared in the grass-covered plain by growling, earth-quaking diesel graters.

Niurka shares none of the amenities Lenapolis takes for granted. Discarded cans and fish bones from months back poke through the most recent layer of snow, a constant attraction for the stray dogs and wild wolves that roam the impromptu streets, lurk in the same shuttered buildings that Alephmen do. One stands on a corner, its chest compartment open; a young boy holds his hands to the billowing steam. Its guts glow red, like a hot stove burner. The power fails, and the people leave; the Alephmen move in, sharing nothing of the most basic human needs. The machines — they walk like people, or lumber at least, burly and hunched, often dragging their knuckles on the ground — astound Elizabeth.

She stops and looks in wonderment, causing the Alephmen to turn away, lower its head even more. The Alephman drifts toward a family camped on the side of the street. The father shoos him away, and the Alephman falls down in an awkward dance to obey, splattering mud all over his corroded shell.

"They have protected these people for a thousand years," Michael says, standing on the corner with her, "through thick and through thin, and yet they still command no respect."

"They are awkward," Elizabeth says, clutching the heavy shall he provided for her. "And slow."

"Not in a fight. They made comedy of armies and men. Or did, once. A hundred of them destroyed a Canon army of 10,000 men at Jerusalem. This was a long time ago, and you won't read about it in any Canon history book, but it happened. Now they seem antique. Awkward, as you say. But once upon a time, there was nothing like them on earth."

"If there is no record, then how do you know this?"

"Stories remain in the archives, of armies of metal men in the desert. These must be the same."

Michael watches with Elizabeth as the father hurls obscenities after the Alephmen, long after they have gone out of sight. He returns to the ragged tent he shares with his wife, his

three children, and the weak fire he tends in front of it. Someone has to pay for all this; the centuries of war, persecution and
perpetual eviction from one home after another. The Kuzar
take it out on the Alephmen because they embody failure. The
years — and the loss of the knowledge that built them — leave
them slow and decrepit, easy targets for ridicule. At the same
time, their existence suggests a history lost to these people, a
birthright; the sight of them is a daily reminder that once, they
were lords of the earth. Now they eat from tin cans, scraping
them out for every last morsel, huddling in drafty wooden huts
squeaking in the wind.

"What art animates them?" she says, focusing on the
strange glow emanating from within them.

"It is lost to us. Some say it's beyond science. Some think
the inscriptions on the armor — you see it, the odd cuneiform
— are the words of a language so powerful that if spoken it gives
life to the inanimate. This language is lost, as well. These machines are like the fragments of barely remembered dreams.
Only propriety keeps them with us now," Michael says. "A sense
of honor and duty."

"It appears quite one-sided."

"It is," he says, and goes on to elaborate the history — as
he has deduced — of the long suffering Kuzar. As man or nature
has continuously displaced the Kuzar from country to country,
continent to continent, their metal creations — their only true
allies in the world — have followed with them, no more welcome
or comfortable than the Kuzar were in the lands they left behind. The 12 tribes of Israel — as they were know then - built
the Alephmen to defend them and for a time, very early in the
struggle against the invading Canon, the Alephmen did; but
the Canon were persistent. Stubborn. Worst of all, immune to
the powers of the Jewish God.

The Alephmen failed. Canon decimated the 12 tribes. The survivors, the very few survivors, fled into the east. No country wanted to harbor them and their story became one of constant wandering, out of Africa into Europe, where they disappeared from history. However, he says, they did not go extinct as history assumes. The survivors eventually found refuge far in the western wastes of the Asian steppes; the people that lived there, the ancestral race of the Yukalut and other northern tribes, held none of their prejudices others did. On the frontier, prejudice got you killed. You either worked together, or died together. The survivors of the 12 tribes — a single, tattered tribe now — married into the families of this nameless people, bore children, and within a few generations, the Israelites, as such, no longer existed.

"At least that's the story I tell on the radio," he says. "And to anyone that will listen."

Elizabeth, shivering, looks at him warily. "You mean to say these people are the descendants of the Jews?"

"For a thousand years, that meant nothing, not even to them. Some of the stories of Israel remained in their tradition, but they had mutated. Fused with those of the people they melded into. They truly became a people without a home. An identity. Until you. Until your book."

Somehow, she commands the chill spidering over her skin to stop; Elizabeth straightens, because impossibly still.

"Again, you are greatly confused, sir. I do not blame you entirely, for I seem to find myself all too often at the center of great and odd conspiracies. I am not this Elizabeth you seek, nor the author of any such book. At any rate, I do not see how such a document could deliver you to such a notion as this. The Jewish people vanished, as you say. And so did their God. It is quite plain in the history books."

"History is written by the victors."

"Such is their prerogative."

"Why deny it? Only a person of tremendous faith could have written that book. What other purpose did you have if not to bring that faith into this forsaken world?"

"I — I do not presume to impart my faith on that of others," she says. "People may believe as they wish."

"That's not a very Canonical thing to say."

"And that suggests what, sir? I am not Canon? Am I to take it you are not either, given your words? Your actions? Why have you turned your back on your people?"

"These are my people," he says.

"How so?"

He leads her up a small hill, each slick step more treacherous than the last. "They sent me on missions into the north, right from the start. You look the part, they said. And I did. I do. I blended in. I learned the language, the customs. I sabotaged harvests. Power stations. Whenever it seemed they might be taking a little step forward, I was there to make sure the Kuzar were always two steps back."

He smiles, ruefully. "I've killed people. I've killed men. Women. Children. I killed people like you, Elizabeth. People from another world. The world in the Bible. I did it without asking, just like Miranda, and just like Joshua."

"What changed?"

"I met a man... I was up here, spying on this solar generator they were experimenting with, I met a man working on the assembly who told me: 'I know someone who looks just like you.' And he introduced us. Sure enough. Spitting image. I get to know this carbon copy of myself. Adrian. He tells me about his father, his mother, his brothers and sisters. Seven of them. Eight, if you counted the boy the agents took."

"You?"

He nods. "I went back to Lenapolis, to the archives and found the records we're told don't exist. There it was. Not my birth name — I was only "Child #20205" — but there was an address, and a last name. Adrian was my brother. This was my family, living in squalor in Niurka. These were my people."

His breath clouds in the air before him. He rubs his hands together and cups them over his mouth, breathes into them. "You know, I never quite fit in. I did my duty. I was a good soldier. But agents look toward the horizon and see a border. I look toward it and see something beyond."

"So you renounced your service."

"Not at first. I spent a few years researching what was known of the Kuzar in the archives. For the most part, Canon sees no difference between them, and say the Sukaizo, or the Yukalut; they're just remnants. Living fossils they've yet to unearth from their resistance. I started to explore these 'fossils,' and I came upon the Jews. Canon had destroyed all record of them, except for what was in these archives."

The war with Canon, the defense and then the sack of Jerusalem, the destruction of the Temple; the exodus into the east and after, the second-hand stories through the succeeding decades of their migration ever north. Then, a century after they lost Jerusalem, the trail goes cold. The Jews disappear.

"But I found these off-hand references in the lore of eastern Europeans to this itinerant people, these nomads that drifted from place to place. In some places, the local legends have them as ghosts. Goblins. The exaggerations are grotesque, steeped in fear, but in every case all these stories have a root in truth: they pop up, in and out of the centuries, always with some strange language and distant origin. I connected the dots. I could see the progress of the survivors, from Arabia to the Arctic, from Jew to Kuzar."

Michael smiles, his pride in his discovery no less than it was the day he made it. "From that moment on, I knew I couldn't continue to be an agent. Not after I had seen what has been done to my people, time and again. Not after what I had done to them. I resolved myself to not only fighting for their continued survival, but for their heritage as well. Our heritage. My mission here is not one of general or king. I am merely a shepherd, leading his flock home."

Elizabeth finds it odd he needs the book at all; some one of his verve could have written their own.

"Perhaps this is merely what you want to see."

She looks at the people stooped over the pit fires, passing her on the street; none of the faces ensconced in layers of fur and cloth seem to her as a Jew's does. They seem almost Oriental. At least, her conception of an Oriental, gleaned from travelers' accounts in books; she had yet to meet anyone from the Far East when she left her world.

"Their words do not kindle any Hebrew fire. Your own account betrays inconsistencies in what you suppose."

"I had no real proof, to be sure," he says. "Only my instinct. I toiled away up here for years, my beliefs falling on deaf ears. The Kuzar are angry. Bitter. Disaffected. So what if their ancestors were the lost tribes of Israel? They had no history or legacy to embrace but the tattered fragments I found in the archives, and they only reinforced their — not denial, but — rejection of the past. Why go back there? If they took possession of their heritage, they took possession of all the hard facts that came with it. Their ancestors fell from a very high perch. They have been falling ever since. The past is no parachute."

Michael found even in the theistic tradition that survives among the Kuzar — thread bare in the form of the Sefirists

— that they pin their endless suffering, their eternal diaspora on the sin of their forefathers. The first Kuzar inhabited a nebulous garden, and after angering their god, were cast out, forced to wander without a home, forever.

"They didn't trust me, anyhow," he says, "and why should they? I spent most of my time fending off calls for my head. I earned my keep by disrupting Canon plots in the north."

He pauses, his pride falling under a brief cloud of melancholy. "I always respected Joshua. I suspected he and I shared some of the same concerns with our duty, and now I see he did. He protected you, didn't he? Just like the others."

Her denial — ready for lift-off — stalls when faced with the weather of her own mood. She mourns him, the charity he showed and the devotion to it through nine long years when they never laid eyes on each other. No; that's not true. He watched over her, like the guardian angel he was. Miranda inspired sympathy in him; Elizabeth inspired love. He was in love with her. Before Miranda, Joshua had been a ghost, gliding through the world like a cloud of smoke, without form and without feeling. She gave him form. Elizabeth, in her own limited way, gave him expression. The opportunity at least; he never did express his true feelings. He couldn't. They died with him, with all the mysteries of Joshua.

"You have murdered an angel, sir," she says, her voice quivering. "There shall be no mercy for your deeds."

"I ask only for your forgiveness," Michael says. "Much of what I know of forgiveness I learned from you. Your book. It's been circulating in the north for nearly five years now."

"Five years?"

"News spread word of mouth for some time before actual copies became available. As soon one came to me, I knew. I knew this was the key to unlocking the past, and all the Kuzar reservations to it. Here it was in writing, the history we should have had! What shame would there be in this legacy? In your book, the Jews are a proud, resilient people. You present is a past they never had, but could. A future."

"A future?"

"'And then God's temple in Heaven was opened, and the ark of His covenant was seen within.'"

"You speak of Revelation..."

"I have had one, Elizabeth," he says. "And so too have the Kuzar."

They round a corner to an open square. At the east end, the most marvelous, unblemished building in the city: high, sheer walls of bronze or gold reflect the dull sun. Towering pillars engraved with figures from the Bible — Moses, on Mount Sinai, Noah, in the Ark, Jesus, on the cross — mark the only entry into the structure. Michael and Elizabeth pass between them and she sees the outer walls form a barrier around an inner building, equally uniform and precisely square. In the lobby between the outer wall and the inner, people stand, walk and sit, in clusters of twos or threes, all of them engaged in intense discussion, all of them equipped with the same book, jacketed in plain, naked black: a copy of the Bible.

Michael stretches out his hands. "Four cubits square," he says, his voice lower in respect for their surroundings. They astound Elizabeth, and also frighten her. Any fervor of religion apart from her own made her wary, and what she sees inside the temple — he smiles, nods *Yes, this is what I have done* as she looks at him with the same recognition he did once his brother, sensing some unnamed connection — suggests a religion entirely apart from her Christianity. She did not make windows into men's souls; as queen, she left her people free to believe what they wished, so long as it never encroached on her faith,

England's faith, God's faith. She would no more accept the Star of David in Westminster Abbey than she would the papal red, but neither reside here; not quite. The crucifix suffuses a circle of thorns, unbroken.

Elizabeth rubs her neck, suddenly sore. She feels light-headed. Hot. For the last nine years she has lived in a world free of faith, free of all its comforts but also all of its divisions; she thought she was free of the weight of the warring church forever, its zealotry and passion but here it is, in full effect, delivered to this world through her pen.

"You... you have rebuilt the Temple..."

"I have built a temple," he says. "As I saw it in the book. And as the Jewish in your own history did in places other than Jerusalem. Elephantine, if I remember. Israel is not God's only country. Jerusalem is not His only city."

"And the Israelites are not His only people?"

"His chosen people."

She thinks he would like for them to be chosen; appointed with some destiny greater than eternal listlessness, than cultural amnesia. They are not Jews. She's seen it before; how many nations took up the mantle of God. How many men.

"So. It is a launch pad you have built then, for the delivery of Judaism into the unsuspecting world?"

"I built a sanctuary. For my people, for their faith and their history. You planted the seed. Here we nurture it. And I watch it grow, every day, from a tiny sapling to a magnificent tree. Soon these walls will be too close for its branches. It is winter here. It has been for a very long time. But spring is coming. Soon the currents will shift. The air will warm, and the glaciers will retreat. Dead rivers will flow again. There will be a flood like onto Noah, so much ice will melt, and a garden shall grow in Eden again."

She thinks she understands; the book, this temple, are not just catalysts for the rejuvenation of the Jewish people. Michael wants more than just freedom and peace for them.

"The Gibraltar Dam made a desert of the Mediterranean," she says. "And a wasteland of the fertile crescent."

"It also cut off the flow of warm water into the Ontarian, which brought the ice down from the north."

"If this enterprise had such disastrous consequences, why persist in it? Why do the Canon not remove the dam?"

"If the dam weren't there, the north would warm. The desert would bloom again. The people would come back. The people they spent so much blood and treasure on removing. The dam is a wall. It keeps us out. Out of the east, and in the little box they have us in here in the north. Why would they take it down? So what if the world is colder, drier than it could be? They shield themselves in technology, the same technology that allowed them to alter the face of the earth."

"Besides," he says, as if it were nothing, "they seem to like cold and dry. Look at all of them living on Mars. Well. They can have Mars. We'll have what's ours."

Elizabeth steps away from the wall, from Michael. He speaks like the most fevered believers of either tradition — Protestant or Catholic — in England, who saw every assault on the existence of the other as a biblical crusade, a holy cataclysm like the one prescribed in Revelation. He speaks like the men that often wrote to her in the days her sister was still queen, men that suggested an end to the Catholic winter in England. They wrote in code, to conceal their plans for rebellion, to protect her from complicity if their gambit failed — which it did — and Elizabeth learned and mastered the art of saying everything and nothing at the same time.

"You speak of forgiveness, my lord. Of regret for actions

you have taken that have resulted in the deaths of innocents, but I do not hear in your words now those of the Messiah. I hear anger. I hear entitlement."

"Did he not say the meek shall inherit the earth?"

"And they shall," she says. "Yet one does not inherit through violence. Or bloodshed. I do not find your misgivings over the attack on the air ship sincere, not when you clearly design to perform even greater calamities upon the Canon people. How do you suppose to grow your garden?"

"With God's will."

"Indeed. Nor do I find sincere your intentions towards these Kuzar. You ask for my blessing? I shall not bless murder. No matter the grievances of the past, they are no cause for more in the future. If it is freedom for you and your people that you seek, then I wish you success. I will not, however, be any party to any vendetta."

"You misunderstand me, Elizabeth."

"You misunderstand a great deal, sir, as I am forced to remind you *ad nauseam*. I am not she that you seek."

He smiles; that's all her denials are now. Humorous. "I don't ask for your blessing for us to fight for our rights. We need no such endorsement, from anyone. I only ask, as I said before, that you tell the truth. Many still have doubts. Many more have questions. It's more than a dam I intend to bring down. It's a wall of lies going back to the foundation of Canon, to the very beginning of the world. And to the end of yours. Only you can explain to my people why what is written is true. Where it came from."

"You do very well without me so far, sir."

"People need *you*, Elizabeth. You are the prophet. The apostle. A living genizah. You have brought the truth of the Jews to us. The truth of the other world. Our crusade has its voice. Now it needs its face. Without you, in the flesh and blood, no one will ever believe that there existed a history in which Canon didn't exist, but Israel did."

"I will not help you."

"You can deny me, but you cannot deny your people."

"These are not my people."

"Then tell them. Dispel their foolishness."

He gestures for her to follow him, into the inner chamber. She reluctantly follows; where else will she go? She doesn't see how this will end. She never sees the ends.

They enter the inner temple. The mute sun shines like an old, faded light bulb through an ocular window above. The light glances off golden pillars that form yet another chamber within in the inner temple, populated with men and women both. They kneel or sit on cushions arranged in concentric squares around a majestic altar, marked with the starred cross, quietly speaking or studying copies of the Bible. Tapestries of major scenes from the Testaments adorn the walls, as do bizarre representations of a boy called 'King Edward the Sixt,' holding the original text of the Book in his hands. He sits in the lap of his sister — Elizabeth — the 'quene highnes', who wears a halo for a crown and in her royal blue habits, flowing off her rivers down a mountainside into the green, forested world that resides below them (the two of them occupying the sky, like some ancient constellation), she seems more like Mary mother of Jesus than Queen of England.

Michael strides to the altar, ascends the pedestal-like podium beside it and immediately commands the attention of those gathered around it. Sensing disaster, Elizabeth rubs her fingers deep into the skin of her neck; rubs it raw.

"Friends. Brothers and sisters, at long last our day has come. I know many of you have questions. Many of you have doubts. I promised one day I could give you the answer, and with thanks to God, I can. I give you the answer."

He gestures to Elizabeth, shrinking in the shadows cast by the pillars. All the people turn to look at her.

"I give you Elizabeth," he says. "Queen and Supreme Head of the Church of England. England a nation, like Israel, dashed from the world by the machinations of the Canon. Elizabeth, prophet. The voice of Almighty God in our world."

XV

She is led down stairs under the building into its cellar, hollowed from the cold earth. A lantern throws dirty light on old, rusted machinery, engines of things the ice long ago made lame. Some hay in the corner. It smells like a barn. Like they kept horses down here, or dogs; during her childhood, at the Long House, Miranda always wanted a pet. She would bring in rabbits or birds she found out on the sidewalk and keep them until they died, or the Headmaster took them away. Nothing belongs to you, she said. Not even your service. The two Kuzar lead her to the corner. To the hay.

They strip her. In the dull light, the bruises that map her pale body are shadows on ice. It feels like another body. Like these skinny arms and legs, those hinting breasts, belong to someone else. She is naked, like the Echoes that come here from the world that vanished; like the Echo she is. He should have killed me. Why didn't he kill me. The men argue her death in the present. Gun or knife. The heavier man lobbies for slitting her throat. He wants to watch her die. To see the knowledge of her death in her eyes. The other, thin as the straws of hay littering the earthen floor of the cellar, wants to shoot her and be done with it, same as they do any other Eye they find hiding among their own here in the north. They're wasting time. History unfolds upstairs.

The man with the knife, with scars Miranda can see and scars she can't, imagines the blood hanging off her pointed nipples. Her hand slopping about the cut, fingering her jugular. He imagines her expression — desperate, certain - as she falls to her knees in the scarlet hay. A Canon bomb killed his baby brother. Left nothing but teeth. Like fragments of sea shells in beach sand. Broken and pointless for souvenirs. A bullet would be too good for this bitch, this child butcher. He will make her suffer. She will be as his existence every moment of every day since the day his brother evaporated in Canon fire. She will be suffering.

Her eyes first. Then, maybe the throat. The Eye should go blind; then she will see. She will see her death.

"Do you know his name?" he says.

Miranda knows nothing now. She never did. She believed — she believed nothing; she only knew what he told her. He named her. He chose her from the others. The world is cold and the only warmth Canon. She saved the world, every Echo she silenced. Every rebel she killed. The both of them stones, solid, indurate, in the invisible wall between order and chaos. Who she was, who she may have been, it didn't matter; the life she never knew was the life she never knew. Not even a star in her sky; her only constellation Joshua.

"I said do you know his name?"

"I know my name..."

"What do you say?"

"I know…"

"You will listen to me," he says.

"Just get it over with…"

"You will know his name. You say it before I empty your throat. Your last word will be the name of my brother."

"Then you better spit it out, because otherwise I'm going to die of boredom."

He rushes toward her. He yanks her head back by her hair and the jagged edge of the knife bites her neck.

"Yamit! His name was Yamit! You will say it!"

"Fuck you."

"Say it!" The knife enters her skin. "Say his name!"

Joshua. Say it. Let it be the last words on your lips; the only word of any value to you.

"Kill me," Miranda says.

"You want to die? You want to die, I will cut you!"

"Just do it."

"Yamit!"

"Do it."

The stairs rattle with quick feet. The thin man holds up his hand, and turns around. Another of Michael's guards blitzes down into the basement, almost tripping in a dip in the uneven floor. He grabs the thin man, kisses his cheeks.

"She is found!"

"Who?"

"Elizabeth. In the temple. It is she. Come!"

"She said she wasn't," the thin man says but the new man will hear none of it. Michael announced her in the temple. There can be no doubt. "What did she say?"

"Come! Come, both of you!"

"The girl," the heavy man says.

"We'll come back," the thin man says, and rests her from his partner. He shackles her to a rusted chain staked in the floor. "Let her think about how we will kill her."

"But…"

"She is found!" the new man says, and kisses the heavy man's cheeks. "We are found, brother. Come."

"She has to pay!"

"Leave death. Leave Canon. We are found. It is a new country we are in. A new world. Thank God. Thank God."

The new man praises God all the way up the stairs. The heavy man — heavier still — sheathes his knife. Later then. He crashes his fist in Miranda's temple. He buries his boot into her stomach. She couldn't cry if she wanted to.

"Thank God," he says, and follows the others out of the dark cellar into the wavering light from above.

Miranda shrinks in the cold dirt. In the needling hay. *Come back. I just want to die. Come back.*

The stairs creak again. This time, it's with less speed and enthusiasm. Miranda looks toward the doorway, sees only a silhouette in the wan light from the lantern.

"Who's there?"

A girl — her age, maybe a little older — steps into the light. White powder masks her face, round, full as her lips, painted bright red. She is wrapped head to toe in cloth frayed such that the ends seem like yards and yards of blood wet veins, splayed and free. The girl comes to Miranda, and kneels beside her. She holds her hands above Miranda, to the two centers of her soul, and she prays.

"What are you doing?"

"You are as suffering," the girl says.

"You're a Sefirist," Miranda says. Countless missions to the north and until now, they have been only a story.

"You are a spy."

"Get away from me."

The Sefirist girl puts her hand on Miranda's bruised, bloody temple. Miranda flinches.

"I said get away from me!"

"You are pain," the girl says. "You are agony."

"Get away…"

"You are hurt. I am hurt with you. We are as suffering. We are as existence. And so we are at peace."

"What?"

"Peace," the girl whispers. She puts her red lips — a ghost of a kiss — to Miranda's wound. "You are peace."

"Why are you doing this…"

"Those men. They suffer. But they are not at peace."

"Then go help them."

"They will not hear their own voices any more. My people… you make us suffer. Again and again."

"Then why don't you kill me. Kill me."

"Why do you want to die?"

"He lied to me," Miranda says, and to speak it is to know it, through and through. "He lied to me…"

"About what?"

"Everything."

"We can never know the truth," the girl says. "Only existence. We must accept our lives as they are, or else we will never know our suffering. If that's truth, then… my *catmad* says it's the only truth there is. I don't know."

"I'm an Echo."

"What is that?"

"I come from somewhere else. Like Elizabeth."

"You are a prophet?"

"I don't know… I don't know who I am. I came as a baby.

He found me, and... he should have killed me."

"Why didn't he?"

"I don't know."

The girl smiles. "He must understand."

"Understand what?"

"Suffering," she says.

"What is this bullshit? You're crazy."

"Let us be friends in madness. I am Alia. I am a fourth level Sefiria."

"Is that like... why don't we ever see you people?"

"We contemplate," Alia says. "Existence cannot be seen, or heard. It must be known."

"How can you know something without seeing it?"

"Eyes deceive."

"They do," Miranda says. She starts to shiver. Alia removes her frayed shall and places it over Miranda.

"Why are you helping me?"

"Am I?"

"Won't they get mad if they see you with me?"

"They will not see me. We are not seen. They have been blinded, by this Elizabeth prophet. By this Michael. We suffer, and rather than know it, he wants us to forget it. To imagine we are some other people, in some other time."

"I thought you all were believers or whatever."

"Belief is an exercise in weakness. You must know."

"Miranda. That's my name."

Alia smiles. "Miranda. I am very welcome to know you."

"How can you? Know me?"

Alia places her hands on Miranda's head and heart, the two centers of her soul. "I know. You are lost. Confused. You are young. And yet older than you know."

"Don't."

Alia grimaces. "You have made others suffer."

"I'm an agent. I protect Canon."

"Why?"

"What do you mean, why?"

"Why?"

"Because I have to."

"Why?"

"Because the Echoes will take over if I don't! All of you people will! We'll lose everything."

"Why?"

"Do you want Echoes to take our world away from us?"

"You are the first Echo I have met. If they are all as you are, then I do not fear them."

"You should be afraid of me. If I wasn't chained up..."

"If I unchained you, what would you do?"

Miranda explodes out of her sorrow. Alia falls backwards into the dirt as Miranda forces the chain connecting her shackles into Alia's throat. Miranda sees the same question in Alia's eyes. *Why.* There is no fear in them; no hope, either. Only her peace. This is suffering. This is existence, she knows. Why. What's the point of anything, now. Her anger evaporates. The chain relaxes. Miranda collapses against the girl she just tried to kill, and disintegrates into sobs. Why, she doesn't know; the reason for anything is gone. She is only this emptiness, this cavity left in wake of the lie she has lived her entire life.

Alia puts her arms around Miranda. "Now you know why."

"Please..."

"You have to decide. How you will live your life."

"They're going to come back and kill me."

"Then you have to ask yourself if you will die as a soldier, or as an Echo."

"Why did you come down here? How did you find me?"

"I heard you," Alia says. "I heard your voice from upstairs. This is one of our studies... he comes in here because no one else will. Because we will not bother him."

"He's no better than I am."

"And no better than me."

"He's going to get all of you killed, you know," Miranda says. "You know what he did? He blew up an air ship."

"He is who he is. And if we are to die, then we will die as we are."

"You're not afraid."

"No."

"How old are you?"

"Fifteen."

"I'm thirteen."

"I know."

"Is there anything you don't know?"

"I don't know how you have such strength in your little arms."

Miranda realizes the death grip she has on Alia, and instantly releases her. She looks down, into those eyes, into the bruise she left across this girl's throat. How many girls did she kill. Echoes. Kuzar. She shot them without a thought. Still it doesn't seem wrong to Miranda, though the idea that it could be is new, foreign and sudden, like Alia.

"I don't know who I'm going to die as..."

"You must find yourself."

"In five minutes?"

"In your life. However long it must be."

"I'm an Echo..."

"An Echo is a passenger. You have only been delivered to me. What has been delivered is still a mystery."

"I just wish he had killed me..."

"Why?"

"No more... no more why," Miranda says, and leaves Alia's embrace, though she wonders why almost immediately.

"You may not have the time to delay."

"You don't care? You don't care they're going to come back down here and cut my throat?"

"You have chosen this."

"How? I didn't choose anything - I didn't choose to come here! I didn't choose to be an agent, he made me!"

"Did he make you pull the trigger?"

He was always telling her to — Joshua always seemed so flustered with her. *I don't want you to* — what? He should have killed her. If he saving her life meant turning her into what he was, what obviously now he hated so much, then she believes it with all of her gutted heart, he should have killed her. She will let the men come down and end her life. It is not a life she knows, and never did. She never can.

"I hope he's dead," Miranda says.

"Why?"

"Because if I ever see him again, I'll kill him."

"This is who you are?"

The stairs shudder again. The men come back, heavy and new. She is found.

XVI

They surround her. They stare. Some drop to their knees. Elizabeth finds every exit blocked. No way out. She retreats to the altar, the island of the podium; Michael descends from it into the crowd, leaves her alone above them.

"Tell them Elizabeth," he says. "Tell them the truth."

"I am... I am not who you seek."

Michael kneels on the floor below her. Gradually, the gathered follow suit. Her chest heaves with stillborn breath.

"I lead us now in our Morning prayer," Michael says. "Our Father, which art in Heaven, hallowed be thy name. Thy kingdom come. Thy will be done on earth as it is in Heaven. Give us this our daily bread. And forgive us our trespasses, as we forgive those who trespass against us."

He looks up at her, pleadingly. "And lead us not into temptation, but deliver us from evil. Amen."

The gathered respond, "Amen."

"O Lord, open thou our lips," Michael says, and as one they answer "And our mouth shall show forth thy praise."

"Stop," Elizabeth says.

"O God, make speed to save us."

The people say, "Lord make haste to help us."

"Glory be to the Father, and to the Son, and to her Highness Queen that delivered his Word to us here."

"Lord protect our Highness Queen Elizabeth."

"Please stop..."

Michael rises. "God sent you to us. To give His word and His wisdom to this heathen world. You are Moses. You are Christ. You are Elizabeth, Supreme Head of the Church and voice of God on Earth. And we are your faithful subjects."

"Jews do not accept Christ as the messiah."

"We believe in his resurrection, as we do the resurrection of our race. The end of the Canon world is nigh, and the new world of the Father is upon us."

Her hands tremble. They feel clammy against her skin, hot, damp. She rubs her neck. It feels like an apple there.

"I... I will not help you. I cannot."

Michael crosses his arms. What does she want? He's put her on a pedestal higher even than the one she was accustomed to, and still she refuses. "I don't understand why."

"You cannot possibly understand."

"You can deny us... but you cannot deny God."

Michael ascends to the altar. He carefully removes the white cloth draped over the top of it. Slowly, to the rapt attention of the men and women in the midst of the most spectacular evening prayer they have ever known, he opens the lid. The irises of his eyes collapse in the bath of golden light that shines from within to tiny, dark cores.

"You deny your faith. You fear its consequences. But you cannot deny who you are Elizabeth, or what you have done. And you cannot deny the truth of what brought you here."

"No one knows the truth."

Michael hesitates as he holds the lid up and peers down into the container of the altar. "For the longest time, we thought it was only people that came over from your world. You came naked, after all. Devoid of clothes, watches, jewelry. We thought no objects came over at all."

He passes the lid off to the two men directly before it and reaches down inside. "And then in the archives, lumped in with all the other classified material on the Echoes, I found references to archeological papers and journals, some going back centuries. All of these papers concerned the same theme. Someone discovers a strange object, buried in the earth. They find them all over the world, and all of them found at the same geological level, a time dating back to thousands of years ago. Only these objects are made with technology available only for the last few millennia — and in your history, for only a little over one hundred years."

Michael takes a small object, wrapped in white linen, out of the altar. He holds it like a newborn baby in his hands.

"And each one had the same exact radiation signature as the other, a signature found in nowhere else on earth. As a matter of fact, the only other place it has ever been found is in the blood of people just like you, Elizabeth."

He unwraps the cloth. One fold. Two. He peels the last fold away and the object is naked before them. As best she can tell, it is a piece — a fragment — of metal. Heat warped it; smoothed and melted it around its edges. Time eroded much of its detail. She touches the strange scabs where two different sections of metal meet, and fire melded them.

"This is a piece of steel. Given how much has been re-covered, I suspect it is from a building. A tower. And given that no Echo has ever been recovered beyond the early 21st century, it stands to reason that's when this building stood, and when this calamity happened," Michael says.

"I do not understand..."

"Every trace of these objects has been expunged from the public record, but I found this piece in the collection of a professor retired from Anuja University. Its mystery possessed him, and knowing already the agency's campaign to suppress knowledge of other pieces like it, he kept its discovery to himself. He kept digging. He found pieces just like it, from the same steel, the same era, all over the world. This building—this tower—was the epicenter of what happened. And when it fell—in the 21st century—it did not just fall to earth. It fell through time. The debris scattered across thousands of years. The earth shook and the shockwaves rippled throughout the decades and centuries after, scattering everything—everyone—throughout them."

Michael lowers the piece into her hands. Elizabeth holds it, as uncomfortably as she would a child, anathema to her, and struggles to understand its meaning. She palms the fragment in her hand, tries to picture the puzzle it belonged to, imagines something like the skyscrapers in Lenapolis and then some-thing he said—scattering—trips a wire in her mind. A tower once fell to earth before.

"And the whole earth was of one language and one speech..."

Michael nods in understanding.

"Not Babylon," she says. "Babel..."

Of course; what other explanation could there be for the dashing of man through the many ages of history than the hand of God? Man angered God somehow, far in her future; their reach exceeded their grasp as it did in Babel long ago and He did more than confuse their tongues. He unwrote all their progress and achievement through the centuries and millennia before, scattered their greatest minds and thinkers to the ends of time. This tower symbolized the final affront to Him, somehow; perhaps it was a temple not to Him but to science. Technology. The same kind of extraordinary structures that populate Lenapolis and hundreds of cities like it by the dozens, cities united under one banner, one creed.

One language.

"Don't you see, Elizabeth? Canon is Babel. As your world was at its end. It is as it was before."

"You reach, sir..."

"We anger God in our idolatry. Our worship of our own power and skill. As God Almighty confused the tongues of Babel, and scattered the people to the ends of the earth, as He destroyed the Tower and scattered your people through time, He sent you to us. The new heathens. He sent you with the Word and language of God to confuse our own. To split us at our seams, and make many nations of one."

"Amen," some of the people in the temple say, their tongues not confused or stilled with what they have heard.

"This is God's will," Michael says, and the expression on his face is one of satisfaction, of earned relief; he has her. He's made his case. She can't deny him - her destiny - now.

"No," she says.

Dead silence. "What?"

"You cannot claim to know the will or mind of God," she says, and hands the fragment back to Michael. "It is the hubris of those who claim His agency as theirs that angers him, not the ignorance of others. Men have divided the earth, scattered its people from time immemorial, and all in the name of God. I will not be party to the splintering of souls. Families or nations. God is to be found. Not delivered."

"This world must be saved..."

"If God did as you say... if He caused this world to emerge from the ruins of ours, then Canon is His will."

"And so is your arrival."

"That I cannot argue."

"Then you agree. He sent you to us."

"I wrote the book," she says meekly, and gasps erupt at her admission. She flinches, not realizing what she said.

"There," he says. "That wasn't so hard, was it? I told you. Friends, I told you. We are all Elizabeth."

A woman next to Elizabeth falls to her knees, kisses her feet. They paw her. They pray, they weep in relief.

"We are Elizabeth," they say. "We are Elizabeth."

A man in the back launches to his feet. "Praise God! She is found!" He runs from the temple. "She is found!"

His voice becomes many outside. Elizabeth staggers to the altar. "I never should have written it..."

Michael stares in open wonder. "Why?"

"What have I done... God forgive me. I have committed greater sin than the Babelites. Lord, make me a pillar of salt, what have I done? I have spoiled Eden. I am as Eve."

"Elizabeth... you do not spoil this world with your actions or presence. God came here long before you."

He unfolds the cloth further. "There was something else the professor found. Something more extraordinary."

Tucked inside the cloth is a tiny crucifix, perhaps part of a rosary once, faded and worn with time.

"Take it, Elizabeth. Look on the back."

She hesitates. Michael strains to understand her, the

terrible conflict within her, so apparent on her face. She takes the crucifix, turns it over and sees written on the spine *Blessed By His Holiness, PJP II, D.M., IA, 10/4/79.*

She shakes her head, heavy and swimming now with a nauseous headache. "I do not understand…"

"Our destiny has been written from the beginning of our time, and the end of yours. You cannot deny this."

The commotion outside builds to a fever pitch. Throngs of people flood into the temple. Michael's guards push them back. Michael stands at the altar, and raises his hands.

"She will see you. You have been patient so long my brothers and sisters… what is one more moment?"

He takes Elizabeth by the arm. "Come."

"No, please…"

She is borne along, by the current she cannot see and cannot fight. It delivers her to the steps of the temple, and to the forefront of a crowd gathering mass by the second.

The crowd hushes. Michael kneels first, and then like a wave, the people drop to their knees, their lips quivering with her name, they kneel in mud and in ice. Not all of them do; many people remain standing, most of them women, draped in layers and layers of frayed red cloth.

A man stands on the steps. "Why do you not kneel?"

The women, their faces painted chalk white, their lips blood red, say nothing. They make no move.

"Who are they?" Elizabeth says to Michael.

"Sefirists," he says, and rises. "Sisters - the prophet Elizabeth stands before you. She brings revelation of the true history and faith of our great people."

One of the Sefirists steps forward. "She brings lies," the woman says, setting off a concussion of gasps and boos.

"She brings a false God from the other world!"

"You deny her, and you deny God!"

"God is the truth of existence. God is ice and dust and sorrow. There can be no denial of what you are."

"Our God is more than what can be seen or conjured in dust," the man on the steps says. "And so are we!"

"The Elizabeth God is a hoax. A lie meant to deceive you of yourselves."

"This is who we are! This is what we have lost!"

"We are as existence," the Sefirist says.

"And now this is yours! Kneel!"

The mob clamors for the Sefirists to go to their knees. Words and then spit and then rocks exchange between the Sefirists and the crowd. The women in red — not all of it matching now - do not go to their knees. Elizabeth does.

I am everything I resisted.

"Please... stop..."

Anger — so long frozen beneath defeat and drift — washes over the Elizabethan Kuzar in a tidal wave, melting in the runaway warmth of their rediscovered legacy.

"I command you..."

"Kill them! Stone them like the Eye!"

The words of the man on the steps, and that phrase — 'Eye' — plants a fear deep in Elizabeth's heart, one confirmed in the hapless guilt that emaciates Michael's expression.

"What have you done with her?"

"I have shown her the truth."

There is no way down now. Elizabeth runs back through the temple, out the rear gate. She staggers down one side-street after another, some Kuzar falling to their knees in the slop before her, some just staring. In the gray fleck, a flare of rust; Elizabeth follows after it, manic inside a throng of men and women. They lug her like a sack of pennies through the muddy street. Miranda's gaze shifts from one person to the next, to their hands, full of rocks big as apples; there's so many of them. They drool, they weep with their ancient anger. The steel in her eyes melts. Elizabeth looks at Miranda and for the first time since she has known her, she sees a little girl.

"Release her," Elizabeth says.

"She is a murderer," the heavy man says.

"I command you to release her at once."

"Why?"

"This is not Christian."

"It is Kuzar."

"Release her," Elizabeth says.

"Our children starve because of them!"

"Do not question me."

"Maybe she is one of them, too," another man says. "Maybe she is a spy! She's a fake!"

"No," Elizabeth says and the fire of the crowd finds new oxygen. Half the men dragging Miranda along avow Elizabeth's legitimacy; the others insist on her being a Canon plant.

There are hours, and days even, ahead of protestation and violence among the Kuzar. This is their moment, of decision, of acceptance or denial but yet like every other moment in their unfortunate history, they are not allowed to have it.

Thunder rumbles through the streets, rattling the loose windows of the decrepit buildings in their frames. The buildings themselves tremble, and in the distance, Elizabeth hears the crunch of wood and the crash of glass; screams explode first, and then missiles, over their heads. Shrapnel sprays the streets of Niurka. Miranda's captors spit clouds of red and crumple. Elizabeth dives for cover in a small alley between two buildings; Miranda, abandoned, stands in the rain. She looks up, into the darkness falling across her.

Only the conning tower of the Ice Dragon is visible as it rolls through Niurka, and right through entire neighborhoods; it is a fin, knifing the surface of homes and buildings and as the nose of the tank-sub appears in an intersection several blocks away, it looks like a Great White shark, painted up with demonic eyes and teeth. Sinewy arms sweep back off the port and starboard sides of the main fuselage, fitted with massive tank treads that now propel the craft through the city as they traditionally do unbreakable sheets of ice. Machine guns rain fire from glass bubbles all over the caboose.

The joy Miranda might have felt once — the relief — at this turn of events never manifests. She feels nothing.

"Miranda, you must take cover!"

She barely acknowledges the bullets landing in the mud around her. The men didn't see Alia. Invisible, like she is now. A phantom nothing.

"Miranda!"

Michael arrives in the alley. His men sweep up Miranda as he grabs Elizabeth by the arm and runs back out into the escalating hell — Canon soldiers slide down from the tank-sub on rappel lines — across the square to the building that for three years now has served as his headquarters. Agents spray machine gun fire at anything that moves. Flak explodes in tiny black puffs against the hull of the tank-sub; a shell ricochets off its thick armor and skids across the square into a building adjacent to Michael's burning headquarters. The entire structure disappears in flame and under the cover of the acrid black smoke that rolls across the square, Michael and his men scramble out of the kill zone down a side street.

The narrow street funnels the sound of battle to a pitched jumble of echoing gunfire and layered screams. People empty out of their homes, join the growing entourage accompanying Michael as he runs down a narrow alley between two old buildings, to a little shop tucked in the bottom of another, closed in by the other; a bell rings as he throws open the front door. Clouds of dust rise from the floor as the people charge across it. An old cash register sits on the front counter, an empty case with all the glass busted out.

Michael continues on behind it, through a door to the back room. The place smells old, musty; water stains the ceiling above, cracked and splintered from the back all the way out to the front. They run through the store room, down a steep flight of concrete stairs into the basement.

Michael rips away a dusty scrap of carpet sitting out in the middle of the concrete floor, revealing a cellar door. Another man pulls it open and Elizabeth is off her feet in the strong arms of Michael's soldiers, down the stairs into the darker, colder deep without her feet ever touching the ground. Dim gas lanterns provide the only light. Silt and lime stain the walls, bulged in their middles. A reedy, thin stream runs down the center of the tunnel. She holds her hand to her mouth, but can't keep it in; this sewer stinks worse than the ones back in London. Above, the earth groans.

"The voice of thy thunder was in the heaven: the lightnings lightened the world: the earth trembled and shook..."

"Go back," Michael says to one of his men. "Lead as many down to the catacombs as you can."

"The river?" his man asks.

Michael nods, wipes the sweat, the dirt and the blood from his face. The children they collected on their way down the street tremble with sobs. Where are their parents?

"We'll get as many on the boats as we can, and..."

"Bank Head Bay. We're just going to run?"

"Niurka will not be Jerusalem. Go, my friend. I'm going to the bunker."

"Now?"

"I'm going to put a call out to all Kuzar, everywhere. They have their voice now... and now they must speak."

The sight of his prophet, his redeemer, on her knees begging him, confuses him, but doesn't deter him.

"Please... you cannot let our sin shadow the world."

"I lift shadows," he says, and runs.

XVII

The Sally Gap hovers mere feet off the valley floor, its twin propulsors stirring up a whirlwind of dirt and snow. Joshua leaps down from the gondola, and holds the hood of his parka tight against his head as the maelstrom swirls around him. The ship rises back into the air; the distant thunder of exploding bombs punches through the din of the air ship. The cyclone dissipates and Joshua sees in the distance that Hell has come to Niurka; he sees that he is not alone.

"Alice!"

"I'm sorry," she says, wiping dust from her eyes.

"What are you doing?" He looks back toward the ship, already too far gone. "What did you do?"

"I'm going to find my brother."

"Alice…"

"We're going to go home."

"We're not going to make it out of this."

"You will see us out. I know you will."

Kuzar flee past them now, away toward the mountains. Diesel trucks rumble past them, their carriages crammed full of people, drowning out the sobs and wails of those on foot. A man begs and pleads for Joshua to turn back; he cries, his hands held out as if for mercy, and asks why. He looks to Joshua for the answer, even as others drag him on.

I caused this. My foolishness. My weakness.

Bomb blasts flash like lightning in the distance. Tracer fire from ground based artillery bounce off the trio of Ice Dragons rolling through the houses, all of them the same triangular shape, different only in their color, blue, yellow, red, green; Alice thinks they all look like Monopoly houses. The few lights that shine in the larger buildings, all of them dull from run-down electric generators, twinkle in the haze of smoke rising from fires all over Niurka. The eastern city burns out of control. Joshua eyes his watch. 0814.

"We're too late..."

"We have to try," Alice says.

Joshua grabs Alice by the hand and runs. The top layer of snow grinds under her feet and she thinks it sounds like someone eating Cap' N Crunch. She's starving; she only nibbled at the food on the ship, cold and strange. Her mouth waters for real food. All she thinks about are fat, greasy hamburgers. French fries light as air. Those little candy-covered chocolate eggs they have at Easter. Easter dinner. The giant ham and turkey her mother made, always too much for them to eat it all and the dog groaned with stomach pains for the week after. She pictures herself at the dinner table with her mother, her father and Danny, gorging on apple pie — warm apple pie — and she sees Joshua there, too. He seeps into her all her fantasies of home now and she wishes it could be real, that she could take him back to Iowa, out of this place that has left him like everything else here, hard and cold.

She falls farther and farther behind. He doesn't stop to let her catch up; he can't. He can't let the weight in his own legs, the hunger in his own belly slow him up. Miranda needs him. Elizabeth does too, but he suspects — hopes — she has less to fear from the rebels than Miranda does. He keeps his tracker out in front of him like a compass. Her homing signal radiates from the center of town; he switches over to a virtual map of the city, a panorama of satellite photos. From space, Niurka looks like a pile of rocks strewn on the glacial plain, as if some asteroid fell to earth and instead of plowing a crater into the ground, simply crumbled to dust.

The Canon strike force makes even less of it now. Joshua and Alice enter the outskirts of Niurka. The city is madness. A great mammoth charges down the street, it's back on fire; the smell of burning hair and flesh fills the air, heavy already with screams and gunfire. They run past civilians confused for where to go; Canon agents fill the streets. Joshua runs right past them. They shoot at everything. He doesn't stop to declare himself. He doesn't shoot back. He just runs, following Miranda's homing beacon down the back allies and side streets of the dying city.

He crashes through the throng of civilians manic in the street; agents arrive shooting and the people disappear screaming into their houses. The agents go in, house by house, room by room. An old man too frail to walk remains on his front steps. He clasps his hands together, begs the soldier approaching him for mercy, for reason. The agent pulls the old man's hands down and shoots him in the face.

"Joshua," Alice says, choking.

"Move," he says.

"Wait up."

"Move!"

His feet never stop but his eyes linger on a deflated barrage balloon, fallen over the ruins of a burned out building. Support beams curl out of the piled stone like rigored fingers, forming tent poles here and there. Fires glow softly inside, like the sun through the skin of your hand; the fluttering walls of the impromptu homes move with shadows, until those inside dowse the fires with water, in hopes the draped nylon curtains will conceal them.

Agents with blowtorches put flame to them. Others shoot the people running out. The screams end abruptly, like the screech of bottle rockets right before they explode.

A missile flies over his head; he falls flat to the ground. It explodes in the center of the agents and a single Alephman, this one a walking tank, shuffles down the snow-covered street toward them. More agents arrive and experience the same fate as their forbearers a millennium ago in ancient deserts; Joshua, caught in the crossfire with Alice, crawls to what safety there is behind a battered, parked diesel jeep.

Bullets carom off the jeep. Alice covers her head with her arms and screams for them to stop. Joshua crawls under the vehicle, forcing Alice to follow suit; he watches the Alephman walk headlong into the blistering pelt of bullets hurled at him, returning fire with a battery of rockets fixed to his shoulder. One of the rockets strikes an agent square in the head and the explosion nearly flips the jeep over; Alice screams and screams and he covers her with his body, waits for the slight pressure of the bullet entering his body and then the bliss of nothing, no pain, just instant release.

It doesn't come. The Alephman decimates the agents. The few surviving call in for support, and then retreat; knowing what's coming next, Joshua scrambles out from under the jeep. He drags Alice up by her wrists, races across the street —

the Alephman fires a few wild shots at them — and puts as much distance as he can between them and it before the tank-sub delivers oblivion from its forward cannons.

The heat from the explosion ignites every wood shack in the eastern city; the shockwave knocks them all over. It shatters windows, and lifts the jeep they hid under into the air; the blast flings it with gale-force over the heads, into the upper level of an apartment building blocks away. It sweeps Joshua and Alice off their feet, rips them from each other and when he comes down, he comes down alone, in darkness. A cloud of gray dust rolls over the city, so thick he chokes on it. He covers his mouth, crawls on his knees under the dust-cover. It fills his mouth; it's like he's swallowed a carpet bag. He can't see anything; someone stabbed out the sun, the moon, all the stars.

The sounds of war fade, replaced by a high-pitched ringing; Joshua rubs his ears, taps the butt of his palms against them to get them back going. His head screams with pain. *Concussion. I have a concussion. You can't have a concussion. Alice.* "Alice," he says, and can't hear himself.

"Alice!"

He moves clumsily — dizzily — on his hands and knees toward her. He keeps calling out her name, but she doesn't answer; he doesn't know if he could hear her if she did. He stops, coughs the dust out of his mouth, gags on it. He starts to move again, head down, and stumbles over her.

She lies there, half on the curb, half in the street. Someone trips over her — a woman — she gets up and keeps running, disappears into the dust. Joshua grabs hold of Alice's parka, shakes her hard. *Wake up,* he says. Blood streams out her nose, her ears; dust and dirt mix with it, turn it to clay. He checks her for wounds. None. Checks her pulse. Weak. He pats her face gently, afraid to do anything more, and his hearing returns just in time for him to hear the sound of his own voice, breaking, broken, calling her name.

"Alice... Alice, I'll have to leave you."

Her eyes flutter open. "What time is it?"

"C'mon," he says, pulling her up. "We have to go."

"Did we miss the bus?"

"We have to go."

He drags her through the stubborn cloud, and *We're already there,* she thinks; Mars. *I'm lost, in a dust storm.* She digs a hole in the ground to escape the wind, and hits a hidden aquifer. The water bubbles up from beneath the surface, curdles like blood and then flows, lumpy, across the red dust until it freezes solid. She scoops it up with her hand. It tastes like pennies. Like blood.

Joshua trips over a body, and they both fall down. She's not on Mars. She's not digging for cover. The cloud begins to dissipate, finally. Niurka, still. Hell, still.

"Joshua. I think I'm concussed."

"You're what?"

"I really need to lie down."

"A little farther," he says. "Just a little farther then we can sit down, ok? For a minute."

He checks the tracker again, regains his direction; he heads up a northbound street, toward the center, though Miranda now seems to be moving south. In a few blocks, they might run into each other. At least she's still moving.

Gunfire, ahead; Joshua ducks behind a burning car. The dust clears a little, and he sees a lone agent in the center of the intersection with a rifle, glibly shooting anyone that emerges from any building on either street. Joshua watches him calmly reload as Kuzar use the lull to run. They only get ten or twenty feet before he finishes reloading.

"Let's go back the other way," Alice says.

"We're going this way."

Joshua fires a shot at him, to ward him off. It only emboldens him. The agent walks casually toward the car, shooting as he comes. Joshua huddles in the small area of protection he has, waits for him to empty the clip. As soon as he does, Joshua launches out from behind the car.

"Why didn't you shout the safe word—"

The bullet sweeps through the agent's throat. It takes almost a minute for him to die.

Joshua grabs the rifle off of him. He passes the handgun to Alice. "You know how to use it, right?"

She shakes so bad, he can't tell is she's nodding yes or shaking her head no. "He's one of yours..."

"Do you know how to use a gun?"

Alice doesn't know what to think; only adrenaline pilots her now, that and a serious desire to live.

"I've seen you do it enough."

"C'mon."

They continue on, their advance through the city like a game of hide and seek. Fewer and fewer Kuzar pass them in the streets; more and more Agents roam them, in packs like wolves. Joshua follows Miranda's beacon on a labyrinthine course toward the city center. She continues to move south, toward him, and he slows up, expecting to run headlong into Michael and his men any moment. She passes right by him.

The street is empty. He watches as the blip representing Miranda carries on past him, down the street.

"Below... they're below..."

Sewers. Michael's taking her through the sewers. Joshua leaves the street, heads down an alley between smoldering homes. He falls to his knees at the first manhole he finds, pries at it with the butt of the rifle. He strains to lift it open. Alice, waiting, gestures halfheartedly up at the shimmering northern lights arcing across the speckled sky. The aurora fluctuate wildly in color, going back and forth from blue to green to red, and then an odd, metallic yellow.

"Is it happening again?"

"What is?"

"It's just aurora..."

"Help me," he says, and she squeezes her fingers into the gap and with the two of them, the manhole cover comes off. It wobbles on the cement, faster and faster until it comes to a sudden stop and he vaults down the bars into the sewer, darker, colder than even above. She eases down after him, woozy, legs like jelly; she drifts against him, against the curving wall of the sewer and he props her up as he gets his bearing once again. "This way. She's this way."

Ducking under the low ceiling, they rush down the sewer tunnel south, after Miranda. Voices echo back to them, voices charged with fear and a visceral knowledge of the amount of time left in one's own life. Joshua follows them as much as her homing beacon, his legs finding new strength.

"Wait," Alice says, trailing behind again.

Alice reaches for his hand. Her fingers just brush his; he reaches back for her, and finds only air.

The sewer opens deeper into the earth, through flesh to bone. Its fluids and bile seep out from the walls, drip from between the seams of the stones that hold the arched tunnel up only a few feet over their heads. The things the world keeps. The things it hides; the wet, clumped trash lining the edges; the piss and the shit, the rats, the toes they nibble at, of dead men with nowhere else to go, pearl white bone sticking out skin bruise yellow as the illuminated sky somewhere far above. The only clean thing here. Everything is dirty. Everything is a city, sitting over the piss pot every single one of them has below, like a bird over an egg.

The world is exactly as Michael described it; a lie. Miranda sees that now. Everything a veneer; everything a mask to hide the truth. But there is no truth. Her few years in the Long House taught her that. Truth and reality are only what the agency says they are. If a horrific civil war destroys Niurka — no doubt the party line on the murder raging above — then a civil war destroyed Niurka. Here, in the world after the world of Elizabeth, of Alice, truth does not come handed down in books, or in wisdom passed from generation to generation. It doesn't exist. Only facts do, prefab, evolving, mutating; the circumstances and details are malleable, contextual. Truth is trivial. Origin is trivial.

The tunnel branches out. They leave the sewer, and now walk in the natural catacombs beneath Niurka, carved out by glacial runoff filing through rock and earth for the last few hundred years, as the climate has generally warmed a little throughout the world. The architecture that supports the arches and winnowed pillars of the underworld — all of it vulnerable, temporary — is positively gothic. The myriad pathways of the catacombs often terminate in dead ends, majestic vaults buttressed with clustered columns of steel, stone or wood; they seem to Miranda like tombs. She never thought about death before today. She thought, in the way young people often do, she'd live to some unimaginable age; she and Joshua both. Partners, always. Nothing would ever separate them, despite Joshua's frequent warnings otherwise.

Just on the way to Lenapolis, the way to find Alice and the beginning of this whole mess, he told her: *It won't always be this way.* They were talking about the book, the Samaire book they

found in the bazaar. She complained about the discrepancy between her Samaire and the older one.

"Samaire should never change."

"Everything does," he said. "It's just how things go."

"I like things the way they are."

"You do now. Pretty soon you'll get tired of the way I
crack my fingers. You'll want to grow up, become an agent.
Have a partner of your own. It's all you'll want."

"But I want to stay with you. Forever."

"We can't."

"But I won't want to be with someone else."

"You'll get bored of me," he said, his eyes closed, trying
to get some rest. He was always so tired.

"I won't," she said, like a child, pleading meekly with a
parent. *I'll be good. I'll be quiet.*

"Do you want to have another partner? A different one?"

He didn't answer. She thought maybe he fell asleep, but
he never slept. Sometimes she woke up in the middle of the
night, wherever in the world they happened to be, and he'd be
sitting beside her, watching her sleep. She never told him, but
that was the only thing that let her go back, that cured her fear
of the nightmares and anxieties that every mission came with:
his constant vigil over her, her doubtless safety.

Elizabeth walks beside Miranda, watches with each passing moment as the mask comes undone. She is a ball of string,
with no center; without Joshua, the identity he gave her, that
she clung to, she is nothing but scraps of material. Agent. Echo.
Girl. Soldier. She makes a hideous pastiche. Elizabeth knows
the feeling: all her life, she has been a stone, skipping across
water, evading destiny and gravity but now — now she sinks. Water rushes up around her, fills her lungs and her ears and her
nose and she's drowning.

"Chin up, girl," Elizabeth whispers to her. "Never let them see you weak. Strength and poise, always."

"He was helping you..."

"He hid the truth from you, only to ensure your innocence, if ever he were discovered."

"Why? Why did he stay with the agency if he..?"

"One often learns that the best course for change is one laid from within," she says, raising her voice a little so that Michael hears. "Not without. One cannot accomplish such change with naked aggression. We arrive in this world naked, but as we clothe ourselves to protect our bodies from the elements, we must clothe our intentions from the weather of politics. Religion. Family. Do you understand?"

Miranda shakes her head, despairingly. Elizabeth puts her hand on her shoulder.

"We must shield our true thoughts and feelings within our heart. We must make a fortress of our hearts, Miranda. A castle keep. It is only there from which we can protect that which is most sacred to us, and only from there that we may act, from a position of power, when the time is right. Do not despair. You will understand this, I have no doubt."

"I did what I had to," Michael says from the front of the pack, his voice frayed; unsteady. "To hide is cowardice."

"And yet," Elizabeth says, "we descend."

The tunnel slopes ever downward, deeper and deeper into the earth, a gradual but certain descent into hell and hell isn't hot like myth has it; the absence of God is the absence of His light and warmth. Everyone here says when 'Hell freezes over,' but hell is frozen. It is a glacial wasteland, worse even than the Arctic, worse even than far flung Pluto Alice spoke of that at least has a dawn, modest as it is.

They reach at last the river, and the quay the Kuzar built

there. Several motor boats line the concrete shore, already filling with refugees from above.

"All of you, get aboard," Michael says to the entourage he collected on the way down. "Get to safety."

"What about you?" a woman says.

"I must not let this happen to our brothers and sisters elsewhere in the world. And I must not let this go unanswered. Go on. I will be right behind you, I promise."

The woman hesitates, as many of them do. "Go."

Michael walks away from the shore, to the protests and cries of those in the boats. His two most loyal bodyguards accompany him back up into the tunnel, and so do Elizabeth and Miranda, though not by choice; the guards shove them along, down another tunnel that curls to an end in a small bunker. Michael opens the door, revealing a condensed office; a desk beset with a large transistor radio, a chair, and a cot, for the long nights he spent down here, sharing the truth.

Michael sits down switches on the microphone. He pauses. This is it; no turning back.

Michael tunes to an old Division I frequency. "Red Light to The Fly, over."

Static crackles over the line. "Michael? Is that you? Bit hard to hear with all the shooting and what have you in the background. It's been a while. Ten years?"

"Something like that."

"I bet you've gone all gray by now," Anaba says.

"More or less."

"Where are you, Mike? Wouldn't be down in those tunnels under the city, would you? You calling me from that same box you broadcast your Christ mumbo-jumbo from you, would you?"

"I am."

"How about that. The voice of God, as I live and breathe.

Just call to say hi, or what?"

"I call to ask you — to beg you — to call off this bloodshed. This is wholesale slaughter, Anaba."

"Something like that."

"There is no cause for it."

"Ah, but there is. About ten thousand itty bitty ones floating on the surface of the Ontarian Ocean."

"That is my responsibility, not my people's."

"So goes your nation, Mike."

"End this madness. Now."

"Or what?"

Michael leans over the desk. He looks at his guards, ready to die for him, but not ready to see their people broken like this. He promised them revolution. Revelation.

"It's like you were asking for this. Fuck's sake, Mike. What did you think I was going to do?"

"Anaba," he says.

"Yes?"

"Call off the attack."

"Or what?"

"Call it off, or I put the word out to all Kuzar in the world. To rise up, wherever they are. To fight."

"Go, on. Get them all killed."

Michael looks to Elizabeth as he speaks. She closes her eyes, shakes her head.

"We've been preparing for years. We are armed. Not just with weapons. With faith. With destiny."

"Yeah, yeah."

"You can't stop them all."

"So why are you still talking to me?"

"The world will know. Not just Kuzar. The whole world, Anaba. They'll know what you've done here. All your lies will come crashing down like a house of cards."

"Who you trying to convince?"

"I have Miranda here."

"Oh, I know. Don't know why you went to the bother, really. Maybe you thought you'd be here, now. Bargaining."

"End the attack now, and I return her safely."

"Miranda is a soldier," Anaba says, annoyance creeping into his glib tone. "You remember what is to be a soldier, don't you? Mike? Huh? She knows the score. She swore an oath. And if I tell her to lay down her life for her country, then she'll do so without blinking an eye. I've already lost good soldiers today. It won't break my back to lose another."

"It's nothing to you, then. Losing Miranda. Joshua."

"I haven't lost Joshua."

"What?" Miranda utters.

"Matter of fact," Anaba says, "I figure he's going to beat me to the punch. You're begging the wrong man, Mike."

"He lives?" Elizabeth says. "Speak the truth."

"Who's that?"

Michael glances toward the door. Joshua will arrive any moment. There's a homing beacon on the girl somewhere. He didn't bother to search her. There was no possibility that Joshua survived; what faith is his that he gave up so easily? He took himself so seriously, his role as messiah; his great plan for the revelation and rejuvenation of his people. He never saw their doubt. It was a given the Sefirists would accept Elizabeth, her book; it was a given that Joshua, clearly now more cunning and tenacious than he, was dead.

"Mike? You there, man? I said who's that?"

"Elizabeth." Silence. "Ask me. How I found her."

A long pause. "She was on the *Liza Blay*?"

"How did she get there, do you think?"

"Do not do this," Elizabeth says.

"Joshua was one of your best agents, Anaba. The best, perhaps. And he's been lying to your face for nearly fifteen years now. Hiding his treason right under your nose."

"What the fuck are you on about?"

"You think it's just me, Anaba? There's more of us. Dozens more. You walk among shadows. One day — one day, so help me God, you will walk in darkness. Alone."

"What the fuck are you on about, Michael!"

"God be with you," Michael says, and spins the dial. He resets the frequency. "My dear friends..."

"Do not do this," Elizabeth says.

"To all that can hear my voice. This is the last time you may ever hear it. Right now, as I speak, Canon agents are bombing Niurka. They are slaughtering men, women and children like animals. They kill us to the last. And they want me to tell you. They want me to incite you to arms, so they can kill you, too. Christ said... Christ said to turn the other cheek. To forgive those who trespass against us. I cannot forgive. Not what I have seen. God help me, I can't but if you can, do so. Go with God. Go with Elizabeth, our Queen Highness, who delivered His word to us and now-"

She lunges for the microphone. The guards pull her back away from him. "Michael. Do not compound your sin."

He should listen to her. He should do what his people have always done in this world: live to fight another day. Life, in any measure, is life. The world constantly tries to leave his people for dead in the desert, in the arctic, in the limbo the rest of the world forces them to inhabit but they live today, a thousand years after they first disappeared into the ether of history, and may exist for another thousand if he leaves his finger off the trigger of the microphone. But what kind of life; will the future ever be different than the past?

"See now who we are," he says. "We are all-"

His guards spin around, reacting to the commotion outside the room. They shout, "Mir! Mir!" and drop their guns. Michael looks on, unmoved, as Joshua rushes into the room.

He sees it in her face, even beneath the blood and dirt, he sees the fracture. Miranda, shattered.

"Buddy..."

She just stares at him.

"What did they do to you?"

Miranda looks back at Michael. There aren't words. Joshua draws his pistol.

"What did you do? What have you done, Michael?"

Michael lets go of the microphone. There aren't words. He looks at Elizabeth, the sum of all his hopes. The sum of all his failures. She denied him before. He gave her a choice then. He forsakes the microphone for the pistol, holstered on his thigh. He press it against his temple.

"They are here for me," Michael says. "Now my voice is yours. My people. O my people. I will open your graves of exile and cause you to rise again. Then... and then, I will bring you back to the land of Israel."

He pulls the trigger, and those listening in the north, around the world, only hear the shot. Elizabeth hears the sound of damnation; Michael leaves the world a martyr, and her the custodian of a legacy she had thought — hoped — forgotten.

XVIII

He asked Michael once, *Why did you name me Joshua?*

We took you, Michael said. *We stripped you of your parents, your history and your legacy. I won't just give you any name. Joshua is a strong name, a proud name, an old name.*

But I don't know what it means, Joshua said.

Salvation, Michael told him. *It means salvation.*

The earth trembles above. The lights flicker inside the bunker, and the ceiling coughs dust. No one speaks. The world is upside down. The man who was a father to Joshua, a brother, a comrade, an enemy, lies dead at his own hand and for the rest of his life, Joshua — ignorant of the art behind today - will wonder if he delivered Michael to it.

Joshua, one arm still around Miranda, reaches for Elizabeth. "Are you ok?"

Elizabeth looks at him in mute shock. "Joshua."

Alice squeezes into the room behind him, half

a smile on her face at the sight of Elizabeth, half a frown at the sight of Michael, bleeding all over the floor. Anaba's voice crackles out of the radio. Michael, he says. Michael.

"We're getting out of here," Joshua says.

"Where?" Elizabeth says, dazed. "The world is spoiled. We see our shame, and we are cast out from the Garden."

Joshua looks down at Miranda, his shame written vividly on his face. He takes her face in his hands, kneels down to be eye to eye with her, but she isn't a little girl anymore. She looks down on him now. The lies he told. The blood he shed, all to protect her, to make her indistinguishable from any other child in Canon and all he has done has make her indistinguishable from any other agent. He made a monster of her. He taught her, fed her, clothed her, raised her like his own child but she was a wild thing, brought in from the cold. Wild animals do not make for pets; they do not keep to cages.

"Miranda..."

"Is it true?" she says.

"Yes..."

She slaps him across the face. He lets the sting sink in. The shame and humiliation.

"You were just a few days old... Miranda, you were just a baby, with your entire life in front of you. This is your life. This is where you belong. Right here, with me."

Her eyes drift past him, focus on some distant point. "They'll take me away from you..."

"I won't let them."

"They'll kill me."

"I'll protect you."

"What's going to happen to us?"

"We're going away," he says. "Some place far away. All of us. Somewhere safe."

Miranda looks to Elizabeth. Alice. The very people she has spent her entire brief life seeking; destroying.

"You knew all along she was Elizabeth."

"I'll explain later."

"The Kuzar think she's some kind of prophet. They want to destroy the Gibraltar dam. They want to destroy Canon."

"We need to go. I'll explain." He stands up, her hand firmly in his, and turns to walk out of the room.

Her hand slips from his. "We can't let them."

"Miranda."

"You're helping them. By helping her."

"I said I'll explain."

Miranda grabs the gun from Michael's hand. She points it at Joshua. "You can explain now."

"I knew it," Alice says frightfully, but Joshua signals to her to be calm. He lays his pistol down on the floor.

"Anaba's men are coming."

"You're a traitor."

"This isn't you," Joshua says. "Buddy, I never wanted for you to — I wanted you to live. This isn't you."

"I'm what you made me."

"And what Michael made me. But I made a choice. Like he did. To be something else. You think you're defending the truth. It's all you know. You're a good soldier, buddy. Honest. Loyal. But Canon isn't the truth. I've known that for a long time, I just never... I just never could bring myself to say it. I lied to you. I did. But I'm telling the truth now. Someone has to tell the truth."

He raises his hands. Sinks to his knees. "But do what you think is right, buddy. You decide this time."

Alice looks on in horror as Miranda steps forward, the barrel inching toward Joshua's face, still warm from the shot

Michael put into his head. Elizabeth, lost in thought, in despair, realizes late what is happening; she gently puts her hand on Miranda's shoulder.

"Our hearts," she says. "A castle keep."

The gun trembles in Miranda's hand. There is no truth. Origin is trivial. She is her own beginning. The world spins out of her, not underneath her. The world as it was before Miranda, a world without monsters, no longer exists.

The gun droops. Elizabeth cautiously takes it from her. Miranda collapses under the weight of what has happened to her today; Joshua catches her, as he has always done.

"It'll be ok," he says. "I promise."

"Don't ever leave me."

"Never. C'mon. Let's get the hell out of here."

He looks back one last time at Michael as he leaves, sees the fragment lying on the desk. "What's that?"

"It is nothing," Elizabeth quickly says.

"There was a tower," Miranda says, wiping her eyes. "In their — in my — there was a tower. Like in Samaire."

Joshua drifts back to the desk. He takes the fragment into his hand. "Only people come over."

"Pieces of this did, too. They're everywhere, all over the world. That's what he said."

"A tower?"

"There was something else, too. Some other piece-"

"It is nothing," Elizabeth says, but he finds the crucifix in the cloth before she can pocket it.

"What is it?" Alice says.

The radio crackles with static. "Michael?" Anaba shouts. "Michael, if you're still there, answer me!"

"They knew about this?" Joshua says.

"He said they did."

"Joshua!" Elizabeth exclaims. "Anaba said his men would be here for Michael at any minute."

The flipside of there being no truth: there's no reason either. He believed that wholeheartedly. There was no grand plan; no greater destiny for him, or anyone. People lived, people died, they were selected to be agents or doctors or teachers and they did what they were chosen to do. Fate never intervened, steered its own course in his life. Not until Miranda. Not until Elizabeth and her book, a drop of ink in a cup of water; he clutches the heavy fragment in his hand, Miranda's tears hot against his neck and it's perfectly clear now: fate has always acted in his life, in the life of every soul on earth. Every arrival of an Echo from the very first to Alice has been a nudge - sometimes gentle, sometimes not — toward some larger purpose. There has to be a reason for why their world disappeared, and why they arrive here in his, one by one, refugees out of the fog. There must be.

He sets Miranda down. "Go with them to the boat."

"What about you?"

"I just need to do something first."

"I'm staying with you," she says.

Joshua caresses Miranda's cheek, and relinquishes her into the cautious embrace of Alice.

"I know you want to stay. But please do this for me. Nothing matters but you. Please, go."

"You're going to say something on the radio?"

He looks at Elizabeth. "We are, yeah."

"Joshua?"

"People have to know."

Elizabeth rubs violently at her neck. She puddles against the wall, Michael's gun still in her hand.

Miranda doesn't want to leave him, she's just got him

back; he feels so heavy now, the fatigue in him dead and making him hunch, slouch. He looks so old. Scared. She's never seen him scared before. She thinks she should stay. She thinks she should run; she doesn't know what to think or feel and so she obeys. Not before collecting the Samaire book; she needs that. Wavering like she just woke up, she follows Alice out of the room. Miranda looks back, unsure. Joshua weeps. It is the only time in her life she sees him cry.

"We'll wait," Alice tells him.

"Five minutes. Then go."

"I'm finding a way home. With you."

Elizabeth, stranded between them, holds her neck like someone slashed her throat; both of them are mad. Both of them as desperate to undo her, this world, as Michael was.

"Go."

"Michael!" Anaba shouts. "Answer me, you fuck!"

Go, Joshua says, with his eyes, and reluctantly, Alice does. Joshua picks up the microphone.

"Anaba."

"Joshua? Joshua, fuck's sake it's about time. Tell me you killed that piece of shit traitor."

"He killed himself."

"Coward. Knew it."

"Did you know I'm a traitor, Anaba?"

"He mentioned something about that, yeah."

Elizabeth shakes her head in open disbelief of what is happening. "Forgive us, Lord, we know not what we do…"

"You knew that, though," Joshua says.

"Had my suspicions."

"I'm going to do something really stupid in a minute. I just thought I'd give you a heads-up."

"Kind of you," Anaba says. "Care to give me a hint?"

"I'm going to tell the world about Elizabeth."

Anaba evens his tone. "That's a mistake, Joshua."

"Why?"

"This is our world, not theirs."

"How can you be sure?"

"You're fucking kidding me. You have got to be fucking kidding me! I never thought you'd fall for this religious bullshit. You were my best man! But you fell harder than he did. You helped her, didn't you? Elizabeth?"

"I did."

"Damn it... so what? You believe in God now, Joshua?"

"I believe in Miranda. Someone or something sent her to me. So I would protect her. And that's what I'm doing."

"What does Miranda have to do with anything?"

"Everything."

Joshua looks to Elizabeth. She is pale, damp with sweat. He holds the microphone out for her. "Here."

"What shall I do with that?"

"Tell them."

"Tell them what, Joshua?"

"The truth," he says.

"Anaba is coming. Right now, do you not hear them?"

"Yes, I do."

"If we do not leave, he will kill us here."

"Yes, he will."

Joshua is becoming too much like her; he tries to have it both ways. Elizabeth fears he means to betray his people and see his justice all in the same maddening act.

"Joshua, you have gone mad," Elizabeth says.

"You have," he says, and opens his hand. "Look at this. This is proof. What other possible reason can there be for you coming here and writing that book but for you to deliver this message to us? About your world. About God."

"God exiled us here..."

"The exiles have a promised land. Right? Isn't that what the whole book is about? We don't belong here. We can't ever get back to where we belong if we don't know the truth."

"There is no way back..."

"There's always a way back. You can lead us there. You led us this far. See what we've discovered already?"

"We have only discovered the madness of the world I left behind. I will not lend my name to such disaster. Look at all my work has wrought. This is... this is an abomination. Listen to me. I beg you, listen; do not do this."

"You're here for a reason, Elizabeth. They sent me after you, I protected you for a reason..."

"My guardian angel... you're my angel..."

He reaches for her, kisses her. How to say it. "You woke the life asleep in me."

"Joshua... why do you abandon me now?"

"I'm not abandoning you! I came back for you."

"You do this for Miranda."

"I'm doing this to protect you! Both of you! If we just leave, no place on earth will be safe for us. Just like it is now for the Kuzar. They deserve their legacy. We all do. We need them to rise up. To stand with their queen."

Elizabeth takes a step back. "It is as you said. I am not a queen any longer. I will not go back."

"I said we are who we are."

He wants to free himself, the world, of tyranny. To return exiles to the land they were stolen from, but here they have found Eden. He can't understand; he's never known any different. They dwell in the garden of the Lord and they do not know guilt, sin, hunger or death. That these things do exist here makes no difference; they do not know them.

"You cannot do this. You will discredit the entire history of this world. Of its people."

"You sound just like Anaba..."

"He understands. There must be order."

"It's a lie."

"Lies shelter us," she says. "They warm and feed us. And sometimes they grant us the freedom to live, even if in ignorance. You cannot do this. You cannot destroy paradise."

"This paradise is sham. Just like you. This isn't about God. It's about saving your own ass, like always."

"You will address me with respect."

"Speak to them. Let them hear your voice."

"I will not."

"You must!"

Elizabeth's eyes narrow. She straightens, like an iron reed. "Must is not a word used to princes, sir."

"You're turning your back on your own faith."

"I was the voice of God in my world. And so am I here. If I choose not to speak, you will abide the silence."

"You can't be God and be silent."

"You simply do not understand God, Joshua."

"Fine."

Elizabeth stares at him, disbelieving, as he sits at the desk. Her stomach heaves like a ship in a stormy sea. He is betraying her. Himself. What more evidence does she require of the book's — of her — influence here in this world; it is contagious, 100% lethal to the touch and must be contained.

"Joshua," Elizabeth says.

"Hello? I guess I just start talking."

"Step away from the radio."

"If you can hear me, my name is Joshua. I am — I was —

an agent of Canon. I served with Michael for a long time. I have something I have to tell you. Something very important."

"Joshua, I command you to stop."

He pauses. He hears the fear in her voice. The resolve. He hears the gun, rattling in her hand.

"Let the word go out. I know who we are. We are all–"

It's the same sound, the gun firing, the microphone tumbling out of his hand, onto the floor.

XIX

She stands there, an infinite minute, the gun pointed at the space Joshua's body occupied. Elizabeth is aware only on the stifling presence of absence, the negative space Joshua leaves behind. Everything is inside out. Blood, brains, thoughts, all outside their heads; everyone is out of their minds. Elizabeth puts the gun to her temple. She presses it into her skin but the nozzle burns and she rips it away. The gun drops from her hand. She folds in two, vomits what little she has in her stomach. Her knees buckle and she huddles on the concrete beside him. She clutches his dangling hand in hers, holds it to her cheek. She saved paradise — maybe she did — but not for herself. She utters a moan so deep, so large, it has no sound. He was right. Of course he was right; she did what she had to, to survive. *Life will not make of me a Catholic. A wife. A mother. I shall be my own providence. I shall outlive my destiny. I did what I had to.*

She murdered an angel. Did God mourn Lucifer, after He cast him out of Heaven? Did God ever regret or reconsider His actions? No. God acted, in His divine wisdom; God did what He did, to preserve Heaven. *I am like unto God. I am not God. I am Lucifer, turning up my nose at the divine plan.* Alice thought her Europa; she is Io, caught in a tug of war between her siblings, tortured by the gravity of the Lord.

I am what I am.

"Joshua..." She kisses his hand. "Beautiful Joshua..."

The room shakes with a terrible explosion on the street above. Water drips from the cracks in the concrete, widening with each blast. Gunfire echoes in the tunnels beyond. Voices. Screams. Joshua stares at her, in shock. A thick channel of red trails down his nose, like melting candle wax. It drips down his chin, into his open palm, onto the tiny crucifix. Elizabeth takes it from his hand, smearing it with blood. The blood is warm, heavy; growing. Did he understand? Did he ever truly understand what he had become part of? There are always victims. Always innocent blood shed. That is life. Blood is the river by which man sails to his destiny. The river. The boats. They're coming.

Elizabeth holds his hand in hers as she gets up, clings to it until the distance between them is too much. It falls back to his side, where it swings for a moment, like the pendulum of a clock. She does not look back. Queen Elizabeth of England never looks back. The past cannot be cured.

She walks out of the room, into the corridor, half expecting Miranda to meet her there. She thought maybe the girl would change her mind, come running back. Circumstances disappoint Elizabeth again. The sound of shooting builds in intensity and she picks up her pace, guided only by what has always guided her, a pure instinct for survival. Doubt creeps into her thoughts now; where will she go? Who will look out for her? She is alone. Utterly, irrevocably alone. She has even turned her back on God. She thinks her uncertainty a kind of vanity; there's only one place for such people to go.

She emerges back onto the quay. Only one boat remains; dozens of Kuzar push others into the cold river to get at the few remaining seats. The cacophony of machine gun fire reverbs violently through the tunnels, building exponentially as Agents rush down the main tunnel, shooting wildly.

Screams erupt like bombs. People fall. The last boat pulls away from the dock. A man on the deck trades shots with the agents, dozens of them. He sees Elizabeth alone, still with fear amid the bodies between them; he recognizes her from the temple, Her Highness Queen, the prophet Elizabeth.

"My lady!" he shouts. "Here! Hurry!"

Elizabeth hesitates. She wants nothing to do with these people, their war and their grafting of her faith onto their cause — but it's the only choice. Elizabeth chooses. Steps over the bodies twisted and piled on the stones. Bullets fly through the air all around her. She leaps at the retreating boat; she barely grabs hold of the safety rail and clings to it for dear life as the boat motors away down the skinny river. It passes under an archway into a tunnel on its long journey south toward Bank Head, and the man on the deck pulls her up out of the freezing cold water into the boat.

The sound of gunfire recedes. She trembles with an unshakeable chill; it shivers through her body, through her soul. The nauseous, toxic fear she felt on her way down the Thames to the Tower, on her way into Lenapolis for the first time on the air ship, wells up in her stomach. She faces another life, again. How many does she have? *Please God, let it not be too many; let me not be thy wandering Jew.*

She rolls over on her knees. The refugees of Niurka, cold and bloody, huddle together on the aft deck under the flickering, toxic green light of the lights illuminating the tunnel from above. So many faces; a mish-mash of families and neighborhoods, fractured and destroyed, none complete. The oldest remember the last time they fled a city ahead of guns and knives. They remember the stories of their parents, and their parents, the history of the Kuzar a long, nomadic tale of expulsion from one sanctuary to the other. Cursed, some say on the deck, to forever walk the earth, never to know peace or comfort. But this diaspora is different than the others; they do possess a comfort now they never had before.

One by one they unknot from each other, clear a path to the only seat on the deck; they come to their knees and clasp their hands in prayer. They murmur the words Michael taught them, delivered over the radio from beneath the earth, delivered out of the past from the woman before them now. *The Lord is my light and my salvation, whom should I fear? The Lord is my life's refuge, of whom should I be afraid?*

"God bless our Queen Elizabeth," the man that helped her onto the boat says. "God protect and defend her. God give her wisdom and strength to guide us in our exile."

He helps her again, this time to her feet and to the chair. Numbly, she falls into it. She looks down on her subjects, all of them desperate for a word, a mere gesture of encouragement from her. Of affirmation. The boat passes under the last of the jade lights fixed to the tunnel ceiling above, and Elizabeth disappears into total darkness.

The tunnel splits in two; Miranda looks back, afraid. Where are they going? What is going to happen? Nothing makes sense now; her entire life from before she could remember has been one carefully scripted step after another. Pre-education at The Long House. Field training. Initiate testing. Assignment. Graduation. The taking of her own student — unless she stayed with Joshua, equal partners like she had hoped to. Years of anonymous, unheralded service in places no one has ever heard of. Death, either from duty or old age. The entire skeleton she built her life on has collapsed, and she is a mass of skin and tissue, unrecognizable.

The boat slows. Alice cuts the engine, uses the butt of her machine gun to steer the boat around a fat boulder poking up through the surface of the black water like a snaggletooth. More rocks complicate the passage, and they drift with no power for nearly ten minutes with Alice working the gun like an oar. Alice offers some sweet bread Kitzer had made, wrapped up in tin foil. Miranda declines it at first, but then her hunger arrives in one undeniable moment and she eats her portion so fast she coughs for minutes after.

"More?" Alice says, sitting across from her.

Miranda shakes her head. "Save some for Joshua."

Alice folds up the foil. "We waited long as we could."

"He'll find me. Like he did before."

Miranda recognizes now that face adults make when confronted with a child's childish notions; Alice's face is suffused with pity for her, and grief for her own lost hopes. Miranda recognizes too for the first time how childish her belief he will return is. Either the agents that stormed the quay found him on the radio and killed him, or they arrested him, and Anaba will make an example of him to all the men and women in the ranks that ever doubt or question their orders. And he knew. He knew that he wouldn't escape, but it didn't matter. He told her: you are all that matters.

"Turns out I have you to thank," Alice says.

"For what?"

"My life. We all have you to thank for our lives. Elizabeth, Meeley... so many others. So thank you, Miranda."

It's nothing she can appreciate now; someday. When she feels the weight finally of the lives she has saved, and of those she has taken she will, as he did at the end.

"I shot you."

"Don't remind me."

"I was just... doing my job."

"Is that the Miranda version of I'm sorry?"

The boat scrapes up against another large rock. Miranda leans forward, careful not to hit her head on it; she turns around and reaches out to touch its cold smoothness as it passes. The glacier collected this somewhere along its endless journey of advancement and retreat over the centuries, and with this last cycle of melting, the river carried it free until it lodged in the narrow throat under Niurka. Dozens of grooves line its skin, some wide enough to fit her finger in. She imagines the rock is tens, hundreds of thousands of years old. Millions. It began life in a world far different than this one, and it will end, somehow, someway, in one far more different yet. But until then, it survives. Endures. The face of it changes, eroded from time and circumstance, but the inside remains immutable; constant. Unweathering.

"It's cold," Miranda says.

Alice — shivering, not entirely from the cold — moves to the other side of the boat, beside Miranda.

"What are you doing?"

Alice places her arm around Miranda. "Sometimes, when I was really little, I'd go into my brother's room and climb into his bed. It's an old house. Drafty as hell."

"You said he was in the Army."

"Yeah. He liked comic books. Like you."

"Was he older?"

"Almost ten years."

"Was he strong?"

"The strongest."

"He'll come back."

"Shh," Alice says, squeezing tighter.

"I was just doing my job."

"I forgive you."

"What does that mean?"

Alice closes her arms around Miranda. "It means... someday, you're going to be really hard on yourself. But you didn't have a choice before. You do now. You can be who you want to be. It's never too late. It's never too late."

Rocks scrape across the bottom of the boat. Miranda thinks they'll have to get out and walk if it keeps on like this but then they pass the last of the big rocks; the journey becomes much more smooth and the motor revs to life again.

"I wonder how far it goes," Alice says.

Miranda leans back in the boat, takes the Samaire book from her coat pocket. Her face stings with tears freezing to her skin, tears at the memory of Joshua buying the book for her, webbed to every other memory of him and the fear of being without him affords little room for her grief. It will have to wait its turn, a few more days, a week until she's settled into the routine of her new life and there's no doubt; then her hurt and sorrow, depths unknown, will have center stage. She flips on her tiny flashlight and opens the cover. She flips through the pages, to the stories she hasn't read yet. She skips a few, to get to the origin story Michael told her about in Niurka, that she didn't see the point in reading before. This time she reads the story of lost islands and fallen towers with desperate intent, to cling to something comfortable, familiar; of course it's not entirely familiar.

The world is changed; the details slightly different. The plot takes another path. This time, she accepts it; she has no choice. It doesn't matter now if she is the lost daughter of a brilliant scientist, or the bastard of some unspeakable union; shipwrecked orphan, or half-breed freak. Agent or Echo. She is whatever her life demands.

The hours pass like minutes. Soft blue light slowly drowns out the flashlight. She crawls to the prow, fingers trailing against the wet stone above, as the river delivers her into Bank Head Bay, into the fog of morning.

Acknowledgements

Endless thanks to my family and friends for their support and faith — my mother Pam, my aunt Kandi, uncle John and my cousins; my brother Aaron, my step-father Mark, my aunt Charlene, my uncle Jon; Amy and Conan Doherty, Lisa and Matt Hanneman, Mike and Rebecca Nielsen, Sugu Althomsans and Ekaterina Sedia, Alan Hebel and Ian Shimkoviak; and to my teachers who guided me along the way: Ron Roberson, Daniel Dahlquist, Molly McNett, and Martin Roper. Two books were very helpful in my research of Elizabeth: *Elizabeth: The Struggle For The Throne* by David Starkey, and *The Life of Elizabeth I* by Alison Weir.

www.ingramcontent.com/pod-product-compliance
Lightning Source LLC
Chambersburg PA
CBHW070810180626
46818CB00001B/202